The Rules of the Rink

THE SKATERS OF SEQUOIA VALLEY
BOOK ONE

TOMI TABB

Frankie and Charlie's World

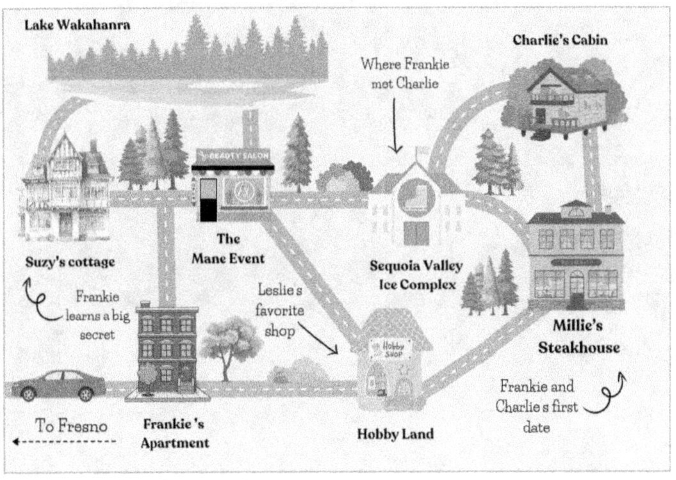

Prologue

Standing in the tunnel, I watch as the houselights dim, and a hush comes over the audience. A prerecorded voice reminds everyone that flash photography and video recording are strictly prohibited.

The opening beats of the princess melody play. I pat the wig on my head one final time to make sure it's secured over my own hair. All my bobby pins are still in place. The last thing I need is a wardrobe malfunction. Especially in the middle of a jump. I can just imagine the horror if my wig went flying out into the audience and landed on a kid. I shake with laughter at the image.

One of the wine-red backstage curtains begins to rise. I force myself to focus. I have sixty seconds before my big entrance. I close my eyes and visualize my opening footwork sequence as my body sways side to side, reviewing the familiar choreography.

"Francesca," one of the backstage workers calls. "Thirty seconds 'til go time."

My eyes open. Even after being with Dreams on Ice for five years, I still can't get some of the non-skaters to call me by my preferred name, Frankie. It's so much less of a mouthful than Francesca. Oh well. I have to pick and choose my battles.

Ahead of me, the ensemble skaters high-five one another and enter the darkened arena. The houselights begin to come back on in time with the music, illuminating the costumes of my fellow skaters, who are dressed as French villagers. I hear the excited laughter and muffled voices of kids as they recognize the music.

"And you're on!" the stage tech says.

Taking a deep breath, I tap the wall for luck and glide out of the tunnel onto the center of the ice. A spotlight turns to me as I plaster a big smile onto my face. Picking up some speed around the perimeter of the makeshift French village, I lift my leg into a spiral and try to make eye contact with as many audience members as I can. It's dark, but I can just make out their silhouettes waving to me. That's one of the keys to success in show skating—big movements.

"It's Beauty!" someone shouts.

"Hi, Princess," another voice yells.

My smile grows even larger. I don't have to see the kids up close to know their eyes are tracking my every movement. Or that they'll be talking about today with their friends at school in the days to come. This is why I do what I do. I may not be a real princess, but for at least the next two hours, I can make the kids' fantasies come to life. When it comes to an end in a few weeks, I'm going to miss it all so much.

"Bonjour. Bonjour . . ." the music plays.

Coming to a stop, I breathe shallowly and pick up a basket laden with fake books. Around me, members of the cast pretend to sing the lyrics to the song while I bury my nose in a book.

I line up with the other principal character skaters for the final bow, then we take one last lap around the ice and wave before heading backstage. The lights come back up as I reach the edge of the tunnel. For the first time, I can see just how packed the arena is. Another sold-out show.

Lingering for a moment in the tunnel, I watch as the families gather their souvenirs and programs and depart. Everyone is in a happy mood, talking about their favorite parts of the show. It's hard to believe that twenty years ago, I was in their shoes. I can still vividly remember the show Dad took me to. It was just like this one. Seeing how all the performers defied gravity, jumping and twirling in the air, mesmerized me.

For weeks after, it was all I could talk about. "Dad, did you see that spin? Dad, can you do that? Dad, can I have a dress just like the one the princesses were wearing?" It didn't take him long to sign me up for ice-skating classes. I wonder if I've managed to inspire any of the kids from today to follow in my footsteps.

"Lost in the past again?" My pairs partner, Fernando, squeezes my hand.

I shouldn't have favorites, but I do. Fernando is from Spain and joined the company a year or two before me. He's about six feet tall and has brown eyes and brown hair, which makes him perfect for playing the roles of a few different princes. Tonight, he was my Beast and prince. Off the ice, he's like a brother to me and a close friend.

I turn my attention away from the departing audience and glide with him down the remainder of the tunnel. "Is it that obvious?"

"Sí." He nods. "How many shows do you have left now?"

All around us, members of the company's technical team run around reorganizing props for the evening show a couple hours from now.

"Three weeks' worth?" I guess. "My last show will be in Lyon, France."

Skating over to the rim of the ice, we collect our jackets, water bottles, and plastic skate guards from the storage cubbies.

"That quick?" He lets out a low whistle. "If that's the case, how would you feel about going out with a bang?"

"That depends on what you have in mind," I tease.

"I was thinking it would be fun if we added some difficulty to our program. What if we replaced our normal side-by-side double toes in the ballroom number with triples for the final eighteen shows."

I place a hand on the wall and secure the skate guards over my blades. "Triple toes?"

He nods. "Frankie, you're one of the few skaters who can still do triples. Why not have some fun and show them off before you retire? They're gorgeous."

I inhale sharply. Yes, I can still do triple toes, but the question is, should we? I don't want to risk either one of us getting hurt. A triple jump means a lot more pounding on the landing than a double. I chew on my lip. On the other hand, Fernando is right. I am retiring. Once I leave Dreams on Ice, I won't have much of a reason to keep up my triples. It really is now or never. "Okay, we'll do it."

"Yes!" Fernando holds up his hand and we high-five one another. "It should only take us a couple tries to work out the timing. We can play around during the warm-up before the night show."

"Yes, sir." I mock salute him, and we share a laugh. Fernando is a technical expert, especially on jumps. When he retires, he'll make an excellent coach.

"I'm going to miss you a lot, Frankie." His facial features soften. "Out of all the female skaters I've partnered, you're always going to stand out as being one of the most gifted."

I snort. "Very funny."

"It's true!" He places his hands on his hips. "You're one of the rare ones, Frankie. The complete package. You can do the big jumps and sell a program to the audience with your artistry. I wish you were my partner when I competed."

"Stop, or you're going to make me cry." My body is already overwhelmed with emotions thinking about how close I am to the end. I really don't want to break down in tears yet. Especially when we have another show tonight.

"Hey, kids," my best friend Gemma calls out. I glance over my shoulder. "Are we doing a group thing for dinner? Or should I just bring back something for you two?"

Originally from Scotland, Gemma is about five-foot-four and has curly blond hair and blue eyes. She's as close to a real-life Cinderella as they come and one of the sweetest people you'll ever meet.

Fernando shakes his head. "Thanks, but that's a no for me. I have plans."

My eyes meet Gemma's. We both hold back our laughter. "Big plans" is Fernando speak for an afternoon siesta. He lives to sleep and can do so just about anywhere. If he doesn't get his nap in, there's a chance he really might transform into a beast.

"I'll catch up with you ladies in a few hours." He excuses himself and heads down the hall to his dressing room.

"Too bad. What about you, Frankie?"

"I'm in." The more time I can spend with Gem, the better. "I love Greece, and I haven't been outside the arena or hotel once since we arrived."

She arches an eyebrow and shoots me a "who's fault is that" look. "Go change and I'll order a car for us."

It's early afternoon. Gemma and I sit at an outdoor café tucked off the main street of Athens' Plaka district. Pink bougainvillea petals rain down on top of the umbrella in the middle of our table, adding a fun flash of color to the blue-and-white backdrop.

"So, you still haven't given *any* reconsideration to renewing your contract, have you?" Gemma asks as she stows her phone into her brown designer wristlet.

"Nope." I shake my head. "Three weeks from now, I'll be in California, sleeping in late, not worried about having to pack up and rush to the bus."

The truth is that every time somebody brings up my retirement, it still saddens me, but I've had four months to come to terms with it. My father needs me.

"Wow. I can't believe it." Gemma's eyes widen. "Out of everyone, I thought you'd be the last of our friend group to retire. You love this life."

"It's just my time. When you know, you know." The lie rolls right off my tongue. I reach for my cup and take a long sip of my latte, letting the spicy flavor of the chai dance on my taste buds. The truth is, I feel like I'm being forced to retire. "It's scary, but I'm at the point in my life where my priorities have changed."

I'm twenty-seven and already one of the oldest skaters with Dreams on Ice. Closing the door on show skating at my age is considered normal. Last year, we said goodbye to Michelle just after her thirtieth. The season before that, it was Gia. She'd just turned twenty-eight and suffered injury after injury. Her poor body was so broken, and I don't want that to happen to me.

Skating may look glamorous, but the sad truth is that years of practicing and performing on a surface as unforgiving as concrete takes a toll on our bodies. It's common for us to develop arthritis in our hips, knees, and ankles. I'm one of the lucky ones. Unlike Gia, I have more good days than bad. I'm able to close out my career by choice.

"Do you promise that you haven't been holding out on me and are leaving the tour to run off with a guy?"

"A guy?" I scrunch my nose. I live out of a suitcase for more than half the year. And most of the time, I don't even know what city I'm in. There's no time for guys. "Nope. Definitely not. I haven't been on a date in . . . I don't even know how long." I shake my head. "If there were a guy involved, you'd be the *first* person I'd tell."

The real reason is more personal. As we sit here, I wonder if I should say something to her about Dad's recent struggles. We've always told one another everything. I do feel guilty keeping such a large secret from her, but it's nothing personal. I haven't said anything to anyone. I don't want any of their sympathy.

"Point taken." Gemma reaches for the last piece of baklava on her plate. "My last date was with Paul, the Gaston on the South American tour. He's a great skater, but has terrible people skills."

"You're brave to date another skater. They're the worst."

Gemma snorts. "They really are."

"I think all skaters are socially awkward. If you think about it, we're only taught to focus on ourselves. We never have any teammates to worry about."

"True." She sighs. "At least as a pairs skater, you were able to work with another person. Knowing what I know now, I wish that was the route I'd taken when I was still competing. It's so much more enjoyable."

Gemma grew up as a singles skater. Like most skaters on tour, she didn't learn the basics of partnering until she joined the company.

"In theory, but not all partnerships are what they're cracked up to be. Look at me. My old partner was a first class jerk." I cringe thinking about him. "Every practice, he'd only be able to comment on what I did wrong or what he thought was best for us. I was never able to get a word in edgewise."

"It was your jumps that were your biggest problem, wasn't it?" she asks.

"Uh-huh. Puberty hit me at the worst possible time. The Olympic year. When I turned seventeen, I started to struggle with my jump consistency. He saw me as a loose cannon and didn't want to wait for me to figure it all out, so he dropped me."

Gemma inhales sharply. "I still can't believe he'd do that. You were supposed to be partners. Who does that?"

"A person who only cares about themselves," I mutter. "The harsh reality is that the guys have all the power. When it comes to pairs skating, there are about ten female skaters for every male partner. Think of it like a Regency-era marriage mart. As soon as a skating mom identifies a potentially eligible partner for her daughter, she does her best to snap the guy up for a tryout."

"Even if he's already taken?" Gemma says, sounding surprised.

"Mm-hmm. Skating moms with money will pay top dollar for the best coaches, costumes, and choreographers if it means moving a step closer to the Olympics. That gives the guy in the partnership the ability to pick and choose whom he'll skate with. For my ex-partner, it was a no-brainer. He replaced me with a female partner whose family paid for everything, including his rent."

"I take back what I said earlier. I wouldn't want to play skating politics," Gemma says.

We chat for a few more minutes, before Gemma notices the time. "We should start heading back to the arena to warm up soon."

"Good idea." I enjoy two final bites of my salad and push

my plate away. "Do you think we can spare two minutes? I just want to pop into the shop next door and pick up a magnet for my father."

Gemma signals for the waiter to bring us the check. "Is there even any space left on the family fridge?"

"Last time I was home, there were a couple gaps near the freezer."

"He'll be so happy to have you nearby again." She smiles. "What's he been up to recently? It's been a while since I've talked to him."

Thankfully, I'm saved from having to answer by the timely arrival of the waiter.

Chapter One

THREE MONTHS LATER

My turn indicator clicks while I wait for the oncoming traffic to pass. My hands grip the steering wheel tightly. A few drops of rain make a soft pitter-patter sound against the windshield. It's ironic. I swore I'd do everything I could to escape Grizzly Springs, and here I've moved back.

Driving down the town's main road, State Highway Three, I'm amazed by both how little and how much everything has changed. On one hand, all the facades of the town's historical buildings are the same. But on the other hand, many of the small mom-and-pop businesses that were here when I was growing up have disappeared. In their places are big-box retailers like Val-U-Mart and Bullseye.

Turning left, I enter into the parking lot of the Lakeside Apartment Complex and claim an open spot near my apartment, number fifteen. The skies have opened. Sheets of rain pelt down on the windshield steadily.

Taking a few moments to myself, I close my eyes and wonder what I should tell my dad. He's sure to ask how my last job interview went. I won't be able to skirt around the issue much longer. I feel the dull throb of a tension headache between my eyes.

Searching for a job outside of the skating bubble has been a wake-up call. Employers I've interviewed with may be impressed with my skating experience, but that's where the positive part of our conversation ends. According to them, I have "no practical work experience."

They turn from treating me like a well-traveled adult to thinking about me as being on par with a high school kid. I've had, "We'll be in touch if a position suited to you opens up," thrown at me more times than I can count. If I hear it again, I'll scream.

Why can't the darn hiring managers just be frank with me? If I'm not the right candidate for the job, tell me directly. It saves us both time and energy. I can handle rejection. It's being stuck in limbo that drives me mad.

I rest my forehead on the cool leather of the steering wheel. Maybe I'm just being too picky. I'm looking for any job that'll give me stable hours and insurance benefits. Is that too much to ask? The longer I sit here, the more I realize, it probably is. Why hire somebody full-time and pay out benefits when they can hire two teenagers for a fraction of the cost?

I swallow hard. Maybe I should expand my search to include part-time roles. At this point, I'm starting to get desperate. A surge of guilt floods my body. When I was growing up, even though money was tight, Dad always did whatever it took to come up with the money to pay for my ice time, skating lessons, costumes, choreography, and competitions. No matter what. He believed in me. Because of him, I've been able to live out one of my dreams. Now, it's my turn to repay him. And so far, I'm failing. Miserably.

I open my eyes and take a deep breath. If Dad could do it,

so can I. After all, I'm his daughter. Giving up is not an option in the Tomlinson household.

Pushing aside the negative feelings, I reach over to the passenger seat, retrieve a brown takeout bag, and make a dash from the car to the front door. "Dad, I'm home," I call out, shrugging off my wet coat. "Look what I have." I shake the bag. "Care to guess what it is?"

The newspaper crinkles as Dad lowers it and sniffs the air. "Soft tacos?"

"Lucky guess."

He folds the sports section of the paper and places it on the side table. "We order from the same place every Friday, Frankie. It doesn't take a detective to figure it out."

I walk around the ancient coffee table and kiss him on the cheek. The sharp edges of his beard rub against my lips. My father is in his mid-seventies, has cropped salt-and-pepper hair, and wears thick black glasses. If you ask him, he'd say he was about six feet tall, but it's actually closer to five-foot-ten.

"I'm gonna warm this up. Did you do your physical therapy exercises today?"

Frown lines appear on his forehead. Picking up the remote control, he clicks the TV on and flips it to the news. I fill a glass of water from the tap and hand it to him. "Dad?" I repeat.

"No. I haven't," he murmurs.

Not surprised. He hates them with a capital H.

I breathe deeply. "Okay. After we eat, we'll work on them together. Remember, the sooner you build up the muscles around your hip, the quicker you'll be able to ditch the cane."

I pad into the kitchen and retrieve two plates from the cabinet above the dishwasher. As the news anchor on the TV talks about record-setting heat in Australia, I wonder if that's what Gemma and Fernando are experiencing right now.

The new Dreams on Ice season is beginning in

Melbourne. It's one of the few places none of us had ever been before. "I kind of wish I were there right now too," I whisper under my breath.

"What'd you say, sweetie?"

"Nothing," I reply quickly.

"Uh-huh. Anyway, how was your interview today?" Dad grunts, changing the subject.

I grimace and resist the urge to say, "Like salt being rubbed into an invisible wound." That's the last thing I'd tell him. I can't let on how frustrated I am. I have to put on a brave face and stay positive.

"It went fine. Better than the one for Henry's Hardware." I pop two tacos into the microwave and set it for one minute. "The woman interviewing me said they'd make a decision over the weekend. If I'm shortlisted for a second interview, I'll hear back soon."

"And what position did you interview for today?" He crosses his arms over his chest.

"For the hostess at Lou's Diner," I say in a low voice, hoping he won't hear me.

"Frankie."

"Dad."

"Frankie."

"Dad."

He removes his glasses and rubs his eyes. "Honey, don't do this."

"Do what?" I feign ignorance, knowing full well what he's about to say.

"Frankie, we both know you'd never be happy as a hostess. I love having you home. You're my only child. My pride and joy—"

Here it comes.

"—but you should be doing what you love, not stuck here taking care of an old man. I promise I can manage on my own just fine. If you call the Dreams on Ice HR department, I bet there's still time to tell them you've changed your mind, and you'd like to renew your contract."

The microwave beeps. I open the door to retrieve the tacos. "Dad, we've been through this. I *want* to be here with you. I know I'm not stuck. I'm *choosing* to be here. With you. I've hit the point where I'm ready to move on from skating."

As the words leave my mouth, I realize how weak they sound. Mentally, I *am* ready to move on to the things that matter, but my heart is still back with DOI. I remind myself of the reason I'm here. My stomach muscles suddenly tighten and my mind flashes back to one of the worst days of my life.

"Is this Miss Francesca Tomlinson?"

"Yes."

"This is your father's friend, Fred Johnson. We had a lunch date today that he never showed up for."

"That's weird; Dad's always on time."

"Yes, I thought it was strange too. I gave him a call, and when he didn't answer, I went to check up on him. Are you, uh, sitting?"

"Yes."

"Good, because I'm afraid I have some bad news. There's been an accident."

A cold shiver runs down my spine. The day before I received the call, Dad had fallen and broken his hip. I'm so thankful he had that lunch date planned with Fred. When his friend showed up to check on him, Dad had been lying cold and helpless on the ground for a little over twenty-four hours.

I promised myself when I arrived at the hospital that I wouldn't ever let something like that happen again. Deciding to move home was the easy part. My father is the only family I have. Making sure he's taken care of is my top priority in life. Everything else, including skating, takes a back seat.

"Frankie . . ." Dad's voice trails off.

"There's no point in arguing with me. I'm not going to change my mind. I'm stubborn. Just like you." I plate a taco and carry it into the living room. "We've both experienced a lot of changes recently. It's been an adjustment period for each of us."

He lowers his chin, staring at the plate. "I know."

Grabbing a taco for myself, I plop down on the love seat across from him. We eat in silence, listening to the extended weather forecast for the weekend. "Do you want another? I bought six."

"Yes, please."

I stand and reheat a second taco for each of us.

"Sweetie, I wanted to ask you . . . I know in the past you haven't exactly been sold on the idea of becoming a figure skating coach, but is there any chance you might reconsider?"

I hesitate. He's caught me off guard. Growing up, I was adamant about never wanting to get boxed into the one job all professional skaters seem to take. But if my recent job-hunting experience is anything to go by, it's probably something I should reconsider.

"I think it might be the perfect job for you. You love kids, you're patient, and you have much more experience than the average skater."

He's right. I do have a lot of experience, and I do love kids. If I have to take a job coaching, at least it would come with perks like being able to skate. "I'll add it to my list. Though I'm not too thrilled about having to drive to Fresno. It's at least a two-hour drive each way, plus gas."

I also hate the idea of leaving my dad alone for so long every day. The whole point of my coming home was to be close to him.

"Fresno? No, dear, there's a rink that's closer. I thought you would've heard about it. It's been all over the news." He places his plate on the table and reaches for the newspaper, flipping through to the third page. "Here's the article." He hands it to me. "The rink where you used to skate in Sequoia Valley is open again. It just celebrated its two-year anniversary."

"It is?" My eyes skim the article. "Huh. I never thought anyone would actually buy that place and fix it up. It was in rough shape when I was a kid and probably should've been condemned. I can't believe I didn't know about this."

"It didn't hit me either until I saw the article." He smiles. "If you contact them, I'm sure they'll jump at the chance to interview you."

"I hope so. The way things have been going, I don't want to get too far ahead of myself." I sink into the soft back of the sofa. I'm not one to pass up an opportunity that's literally been placed in my lap. Being hired to work at the rink would check all the boxes I'm looking for in a job.

One, it's close to home. Two, it's something I know how to do. And three, it means I can start skating again. Sessions at rinks like the one in Fresno charge twenty bucks for an hour of ice time. That adds up quickly when you're living off your savings. It's one of the reasons I haven't been on the ice in weeks.

"Thanks for dinner, sweetie." Dad scoots forward and gingerly gets to his feet. I hold my breath, fighting the urge to help him as he adjusts his stance and takes a few steps with his cane. I can't help it—I suffer a mini panic attack every time I watch him move around, especially on the slippery linoleum floor. "I'll take care of loading the dishes."

"Dad, I'll do it."

"No. I can do it. I may still be feeling like crap, but I'm well enough to load the darn dishwasher."

His tone leaves no room for negotiation. He's won this battle. "Yes, sir." I collect the plates and stack them on the kitchen counter.

He pecks me on the cheek. "That's a good girl."

While Dad works in the kitchen, I sit back down on the couch, pull out my phone, and perform a little more research on the rink. The website loads with high-quality images of a gym, a café, two rinks, and a ballet studio.

"The California foothills' premier ice sports destination . . ." The new owners have done a great job. I'm excited it looks like they cater to more than just the hockey clientele. The management at the old rink sure didn't.

I click on the staff page. It loads, but flashes a red stop sign that reads, "Under Construction." Clicking on the pages for the skating academy, hockey academy, and birthday parties, the same error occurs. I might've spoken too soon. I don't understand why a place that's just celebrated its two-year anniversary doesn't have an up-to-date website.

"Find anything interesting?" Dad asks, glancing over my shoulder.

"Yes and no. The rink has waivers and some photos of its facilities, but a lot of the website is still under construction. I'll have to give them a call tomorrow or drop by in person to see if I can get some info."

"Sounds like a plan." He dries his hands on a dish towel. "I'm going to pop into the bath before we start the wash cycle. I'll let you know when I'm done."

I open my mouth, but Dad's already read my mind. "I'll call you if I need help. I promise."

All I can do is trust him.

Two days later, I wipe my palms against the fabric of my dress pants and swallow hard. My pulse is beating wildly against my ribs. I shouldn't be so nervous. It's just another job interview. But the difference is, I really want this one.

The big hand of the clock behind the manager's desk reaches the twelve the exact moment a heavy-set balding man in his mid-fifties enters the office. He's dressed in a navy-blue and white hockey jersey and jeans. I jump to my feet.

"Francesca, thanks for coming in on such short notice." We shake hands. "I'm Jack, the rink's manager. Please, have a seat."

"Thanks for having me. And please, call me Frankie." I sit back down. "Your timing was great. Today happens to be my day off." I cross my fingers behind my back at the small fib.

"In that case, I won't keep you long. I'm sure you have a lot of errands to squeeze in." Jack sits and folds his hands on top of the desk. "I had the chance to skim over the resume you submitted. It's impressive. You have so many accolades on there. A bronze medal in the junior pairs division at U.S. Nationals and a top-ten finish at the Junior Figure World Championships."

Okay. So far, so good. Jack seems impressed. I allow my body to relax.

"With that being said, unless you want to be a cashier, unfortunately, I'm afraid the only job openings I have right now are for part-time public-session ice patrol or for a part-time skating-school coach. Are you interested in either of those?"

Adrenaline floods my body. A job. He's offering me a job! "I'd love to coach," I blurt out.

"Great." He smiles. "During the week, most classes are taught after five. On Saturdays, we offer classes from eight 'til two. Starting pay is fifteen dollars an hour, which I know is low for you, but we do offer some limited medical and dental benefits."

My heart sinks a little. The pay is way less than I'd hoped

for, but it'll be enough to fill my gas tank and help cover what Dad's pension and Social Security check don't. It'll also give me some flexibility with scheduling his doctors' appointments since they tend to be late morning or in the early afternoon.

"If all that works with what you had in mind, I'll have our skating director email you the new-hire paperwork, staff handbook, and an availability sheet. You'll need to read it over and complete the forms by your first day on the job."

"I'd love to take the job. I'm free to start as early as next week."

"Then I guess that settles it." He taps his computer mouse and enters his password. "Do you have any more questions for me?"

"I do, actually. As a staff member, how does ice time work around here?"

"Of course. Sorry I left that out." Jack blinks a few times. "The morning ice belongs to Charlie Welch and his private-lesson students. If you want to skate before ten, you'll have to take it up with him. Otherwise, there's a gap in the schedule from ten to twelve or from three to four. You're welcome to take advantage of either of those slots."

Charlie Welch. I frown. There's a name I haven't heard in a while. Back when I was skating competitively, Charlie was one-half of the top pairs team in the country. A three-time national champion and a world silver medalist. He was on track to not only make the Olympic team, but bring home a medal.

I remember just about every major advertisement the American Skating Union put out that year had his face on it. Dad teased me about saving a couple of them. At the time, I had a major crush on him. It's funny—until now, I'd forgotten all about it. In the months leading up to the Olympics, right after my ex-partner Danny dumped me, I took an extended break from anything skating related.

It wasn't until I joined Dreams on Ice that I heard Charlie had announced his sudden retirement three weeks before nationals. I followed some of the gossip about it online, but the reason behind his retirement never slipped out.

"Charlie Welch coaches here?"

"Yes. He's the skating director. You'll meet him soon enough."

Goosebumps appear on my arm. In my mind, even if he's been retired a few years, he's still skating royalty. Nobody could make their partners float across the ice the way he could. Not to mention how handsome he was.

After promising to look out for the paperwork from Charlie, I step out of the rink and into the parking lot. I don't perform my little victory dance until I'm safely in my car. I've found a job I won't hate, and soon, I'll get to meet my skating crush! Life is looking up.

Chapter Two

A few days later, I finally receive the long-awaited email from Charlie.

To: FTomlinson@email.com

From: CWelch@email.com

Dear New Hire ________,

On behalf of the Sequoia Valley Ice Sport Center staff, we're thrilled to welcome you to the team. It's our valuable staff members like you ____________ that bring the joy of skating to the community. Attached to this email, you will find the New Hire Handbook.

Please read the handbook in full and return the last page stating you've read and agreed to the rink's rules and regulations on your first day, in addition to any other paperwork attached to this message. You are scheduled to begin on _________ at _____. You'll be working with __________.

If you have any questions, please don't hesitate to reach out to me. Again, welcome to the team.

Sincerely,

C

I stare in confusion at the message. "There are so many things wrong with this email."

Dad glances over the top of his crossword puzzle book. "Like what?"

I shift the screen of my laptop toward him. "It looks as if Charlie copied and pasted this email from a template and couldn't be bothered to fill in the details." I shake my head. "I'm supposed to have a handbook, a start date, and some other forms to fill out, but none of that has been included with the message. Everything is blank."

Dad's eyebrows knit together. "That's unprofessional. Who's this Charlie fellow? An assistant?"

"No." I shake my head. "He's Charlie Welch, the rink's skating director—my new supervisor."

"That name sounds familiar."

"He used to be a pairs skater." I don't remind him about my crush. I'd rather save myself from his relentless teasing.

"Ah." His attention returns to his puzzle book. "Well, he's certainly making an interesting first impression with you. Maybe he just forgot to attach the documents."

"That's what I'm hoping."

I hit the Reply button and begin to type.

To: CWelch@email.com

From: FTomlinson@email.com

Dear Charlie,

Thank you for your welcome email. I'm excited to be joining the team. However, I think there might have been a mistake when you sent me this message. I didn't receive any attachments, a start date, or the name of the person I'll be working with from you. If you could please clarify those items for me, I'd appreciate it. You can also reach me at (559) 555-5555.

Thanks!

Frankie

A moment later, my inbox chimes.

"Did he reply already? The man must have lightning reflexes." Dad chuckles.

I open the message and groan.

To: FTomlinson@email.com

From: CWelch@email.com

This is an automatic reply. I am out of the office and unavailable until __________. If there are any important or pressing issues, please reach out to the rink at __________.

Sincerely,

C

"It's an out-of-office reply." I rub my temples. "More blanks."

Dad's eyes sparkle with mirth. "This Charlie is firing—"

"Dad. No. Please, don't finish that sentence." My cheeks sear with heat. "I need to focus."

My father shrugs. I locate my phone and dial Jack's number.

"Hello?" he answers after the third ring.

"Hi, Jack, this is Frankie Tomlinson. Sorry to bother you. I just received an email from Charlie. There were, er . . . a few pieces of missing information on the message that I need to clarify with him. I was going to try calling his extension, but I realized I didn't have his phone number. I was hoping you might be able to help me out."

"Of course, Frankie." I hear typing in the background.

"Blanks," Dad mouths at me.

I shoot him a glare. Sometimes he acts more like a teenager than a seventy-two-year-old man. "Not now," I mouth back, pulling the phone away from my ear slightly, missing some of what Jack says. "I'm sorry; can you repeat that one more time?"

"I was saying that according to the notes I have in the

system, you're scheduled to start coaching today at five. Charlie was supposed to give you a call about it."

"Today?" My blood pressure jumps ten points. I glance at the clock. It's four twenty. "I'm so sorry," I sputter. "I didn't know. I never received a call from him. I promise, I'm not normally like this. I'll be there as soon as I can."

"Don't worry, Frankie. Miscommunications happen." Jack's voice is patient. "If you'd still like to start today, we'd be happy to have you. Come when you're able to. You'll need your skates and two forms of government ID. Stop by my office. I'll get you set up with payroll and take care of any other loose ends. After that, I'll have Leslie, our skating-school director, take care of you. Charlie just left."

"Perfect. I'm on my way."

"Don't rush. Just drive safely."

In record time, I change out of my pajamas, remind Dad of what we're having for dinner, and run out the door. By the time I insert my key into the ignition, it's four-forty. "Charlie Welch, you are not off to a good start with me," I mutter, hoping I don't run into any more trouble today.

All the tension in my body flees the moment I step onto the ice. The bright-eyed, cheery faces of the four- and five-year-old level-one students instantly fill my body with excitement, as if I've been offered an all-you-can-get shopping spree at one of my favorite shops, Hobby Land.

Each child wears a helmet, gloves, and an oversized jacket, and has a skills lanyard looped around their neck. They stand in a neat line, hugging the closest wall, their eyes wide and hungry to learn.

"And how is everyone doing tonight?" Leslie calls out

cheerily. She's the director of the skating school. She has jade-green eyes, bubblegum-pink hair, and an athletic frame. If I had to guess, I'd say she's about five-foot-nine.

"Gooooood," the children chorus.

"Are we excited to skate today?"

"Yes!"

Leslie cups a hand to her ear. "I don't think the level fives on the other side of the rink heard you all."

"YES!" they exclaim.

"Excellent." She grins. "Today, we have a special helper with me. Her name is Coach Frankie. Can you say hello to her?"

"Hello, Coach Frankie," they chorus.

My stomach performs a somersault. I was nervous about being thrown into coaching, but they're so darn cute; the kiddos help take the edge off my nerves. I lift a hand and wave. "I've heard you're all superstars. I can't wait for you to show me what you can do."

Leslie claps her hands, and the children return their attention to her. She has them well trained. I'm glad I'll be learning from her. "Who can tell me what we worked on last week?"

Two hands rocket into the air. Leslie points to a little boy in a red hoodie. "Michael?"

"Swizzles."

"Very good." Leslie nods. Michael puffs out his chest, looking pleased with himself. "Eric, can you show us what swizzles look like?" she asks the other child who raised his hand.

The little boy in a black jacket wiggles forward, pushing his skates toward each other, then away. His blades leave an S-shape indentation in the ice. The other children watch carefully and mimic Eric's movements with looks of fierce concentration on their little faces.

I can't help my giggle. They remind me so much of kids

dancing the Hokey Pokey. Each one is wiggling to their own beat.

"You're all doing an amazing job. Give yourself a pat on the back." Leslie reaches her arm behind her. The kids mirror her movements. "Now that everyone remembers what swizzles are, let's practice."

One by one, the kids come away from the wall, skating toward us. Leslie's eyes are glued to the students, watching them like a mother hawk in case they fall. I hover at her side, ready to step in, too, if needed, but for the most part I'm just here to observe.

In the blink of an eye, two hours pass. I continue to assist Leslie with a level-six class, a level-seven class, and an intermediate-level boys' hockey class. As we clean up the orange safety cones dividing the ice into different sections following the last class that evening, Leslie asks, "So how did it feel being on the other side of the boards as a coach, instead of being the skater?"

"Not as weird as I'd thought it would be. The level ones were so sweet and great listeners. I *was* scared the boys in the last class would be little terrors, but they were the best-behaved group of the night!"

Leslie laughs. "It's taken me a long time to get them there." She deposits a set of cones in one of the two hockey-bench areas near the speaker system.

I cock my head to the side. "Really?"

"Uh-huh. I've had most of those kids for two years. They know I won't take any crap from them, especially if they want to try out for the junior hockey team. I'm the head coach. Every time they step onto the ice, they know I'm watching them. They have to prove to me that they're able to listen and be respectful."

"That's brilliant." I deposit my cones next to Leslie's.

"Agreed. It works like a charm. Hockey has a lot of

moving pieces to it. I'll only work with kids who can prove they'll be team players." Her eyes sweep the ice one more time to make sure everything is put away. "Speaking of being a team player, you were late today. As a rule of thumb, I like all the instructors to be on the ice at least five minutes before class begins."

My shoulders stiffen and I bob my head up and down. "It won't happen again. I'm usually the type of person who's never late. There was a . . ." I consider my words carefully, uncertain as to how friendly Leslie is with Charlie. ". . . misunderstanding with my paperwork. Jack's aware."

"Charlie." Leslie's eyes narrow. "What did he do this time?"

I hesitate. I don't want to throw my new boss under the bus yet. But Leslie is my direct supervisor. She's the one I'll be dealing with on a daily basis, not him. Do I tell her the truth? Or take part of the blame?

"I swear on my favorite hockey stick that whatever you tell me stays between us. I promise."

I rub the back of my neck. If the kids trust her, I should too. They're usually the best judges of character. "Charlie only emailed me at four this afternoon. And it was, uh . . . missing a lot of information."

Leslie face-palms and mutters under her breath, "This is exactly why *I* should've been named the skating-program director and not my brother."

Whoa! Did I hear her right? Charlie is her brother? All the muscles in my body clench. Great. Just great. It's my first day, I've only been on the job two and a half hours, and I might be responsible for starting a fight between the siblings who also happen to be my bosses.

"Thanks for telling me. In the future, promise me that if you need anything, you'll come straight to me or to Jack." Leslie locks eyes with me. They're sharp and intense. "Charlie will take forever to get back to you, and that's only *if* he remembers."

"I will."

Leslie relaxes. "Now that that's been settled, let's get you a set of keys to the pros' room, a coaching jacket, and a schedule."

Note to self. Do not get on Leslie's bad side. She's the one who holds the real power around here. Now it makes sense why all the other coaches I met earlier were a little on edge around her. They must've been scared. She seems like the type who won't take anything less than perfection.

We skate over to the rink door and step off the ice. "Just so we're on the same page, I don't think I'm ready to teach on my own yet."

"Don't worry. You won't be." Leslie winks, lightening the mood. "You'll be shadowing me for four more weeks, then co-teaching for another four after that. If you need more time, we can talk about it then, but my gut instinct tells me you'll be ready. You seem like a natural."

"Thanks," I say softly.

Maybe all these years, I was wrong about coaching. So far, it hasn't been too bad. Then again, I have Leslie around me. The real test will be when I have a group of kids on my own. At least that's a few weeks away.

Later that week, I arrive at the rink at nine to warm up before I skate. The lobby is nearly empty. A few straggling students from the morning session, already late to school, are ushered by frantic parents to cars double parked in front of the building. It reminds me a lot of me when I was younger.

Dad was always frustrated I could never learn to tell time. I was one of those kids who wanted to stay on the ice, squeezing in one more jump or spin until I was literally kicked off the session by my coach or the Zamboni driver. Good times.

Inserting my wireless earbuds into my ears, I crank up the music and start jumping rope. My heart gets pumping, and soon, I'm warm and slightly out of breath. I move on to stretching. My body is stiff. It's my own fault. I haven't gone to the gym or skated since my last Dreams on Ice show.

That was when? Three and half months ago? Can that be right? I frown. I've gone for some walks, but other than that, I've been taking Dad to appointments, looking for a job, or running errands. So my math is right. It's been three and a half months. No wonder I feel like a worn-out rubber band that's lost its elasticity. I hope my skating isn't this rough.

At five to ten, I lace up my skates and head to the rink. Cold air greets my face. I bend my knees and focus on digging my blades into the ice. My goal is to hear a ripping noise that signifies a nice deep edge. They may not be the sexiest ice moves, but they're one of the most important and satisfying when you get them right.

Moving on, I pick up some speed with a set of fast back crossovers, and decide to test myself with some spins. I like to get them out of the way early in a session since they take more energy than jumps, and even after all these years, they still make me dizzy. Most skaters would start with something basic, like a scratch spin, but I prefer starting with my favorite spin, the camel, where I spin on one leg and have my other leg lifted straight behind me, making a ninety-degree angle.

Changing positions, I bring my back leg in front of me and snap it into a sit spin, a position that looks like a CrossFit pistol squat. Just as I lean forward to see if I can still grab my shin, a man's deep voice suddenly calls out, "Hey!"

My concentration breaks. It causes me to lean too far back

on the blade of my skate. I fall to my butt and spin around like a breakdancer. It takes a second for the world to shift back in focus and for me to catch my breath.

"Hey!" the voice shouts again.

Brushing the snow off my butt, I look up and see an angry man in a black beanie entering the ice, awkwardly half walking and half sliding in black running shoes. "Get off the ice! The rink is closed!"

Slowly getting to my feet, I wrack my brain for the conversation I had with Jack the day he hired me. I'm one hundred percent positive he said any time after ten, the rink was free. Didn't he?

The man reaches me. I get a better look at him. He's dressed in a pair of dark jeans and a black North Face fleece jacket with a few white stains on the front. A wisp of curly tawny-brown hair sticks out from underneath the beanie. His eyes remind me of green lightning bolts ready to shoot out jolts of electricity. His cheeks are red, and his forehead is knitted with tension. An unkempt, tangled beard adds to his wild appearance. "Well, what are you waiting for? Get going!"

"I . . . I was told it was okay," I say in a small voice.

"By who?" he growls. "Don't you have any common sense? It's dangerous to be out on the ice alone. What if you fell and hit your head?"

Getting over my initial fear of him, I find my voice. "I understand the risks of skating as well as anyone. I know what I'm doing." I was under the impression that this session was only for staff and coaches. And even if it wasn't, I've signed about fifty liability waivers since I was hired.

"It doesn't matter if you're an expert or a novice. Anybody can get hurt out here. So tell me, who was it?" He crosses his arms, sending me a glare so cold, the temperature drops another degree.

I glide back a few inches. "Jack," I sputter.

"Jack?"

"The rink manager."

"I know who he is," the guy snaps.

"He said staff members could skate before the public session from ten to twelve."

"Are you even old enough to work here?"

My nostrils flare. "Yes, I am!" Who does this guy think he is? How rude can you get? And another thing, how is someone so unkempt allowed to work here? I bite back the words I *really* want to say to this guy and swallow my pride. As tempted as I am to skate today, I am *not* in the mood to deal with a jerk. "Look, I'm sorry. Clearly, I was given some wrong information. I'll get off the ice now."

"See that you do. Don't let me catch you out here alone again. Make arrangements for someone to be here if you're planning to skate. I don't have time to babysit you."

Turning on his heel, he starts sliding toward the exit, exposing his back to me.

Clenching my fists together, I count backward from ten, giving him a head start. I won't let him ruin my day. I have enough problems to worry about. I just hope I don't run into him again anytime soon.

Chapter Three

The following week, I text Gemma while I'm waiting with Dad at his doctor's appointment.

> Frankie: You will never believe the kind of week I'm having.

> Gemma: About time I heard from you. Spill the tea! How's the new job going? I'm stuck on a hot bus with a broken AC, and I need something to take my mind off it.

I snort. One thing I don't miss about Dreams on Ice is the extended bus rides. Especially if the air is busted.

> Frankie: Do you remember that grump I mentioned yelling at me last Monday?

> Gemma: Did you see him again?

> Frankie: Yes. The situation's gone from bad to worse.

> Gemma: That's cryptic. What happened?

Frankie: This morning, when I arrived at the rink, I was running late. I should've made two trips to my car, but to save time, I thought I could juggle all my stuff for the day in one trip.

Gemma: Uh-oh. I think I sense where this is going.

Heat sears through my body.

Frankie: When I pulled the door to the rink open, I wasn't looking where I was going. The grump saw me and stepped aside, but I still somehow managed to accidentally whack his huge coffee with my skate bag.

Gemma: Ouch.

Frankie: Yeah.

Gemma: Where did the coffee spill? All over his shirt? Please tell me it was transparent, and you have photos of it clinging to his chest.

I roll my eyes. Leave it to Gemma to hope for a scene straight out of "Pride and Prejudice." This is real life, not a movie.

Frankie: Gemma!

Gemma: What do you expect? You know where my mind goes.

Frankie: That's true. I do.

Gemma: Anyways, get on with it. Where did the coffee end up?

Frankie: All over his jeans in the worst imaginable spot. I'll let you figure out where.

Gemma: *laughing emoji* That is bad.

I squeeze my eyes closed. I know I should've felt guilty, but based on how the grump treated me last week, I felt like the coffee accident was the universe's way of trying to teach him a lesson.

Frankie: I know.

Gemma: It was an accident. He'll get over it eventually.

Frankie: I hope so. I apologized and even offered to run out and buy him another coffee, but all he could do was glare and walk away. For a moment, I considered running back to my car.

Gemma: It could only happen to you. Have you found out who he is yet?

Frankie: I know. Just my luck, right? And no. I still have no idea. I keep forgetting to mention it to my supervisor. There is so much to focus on with coaching; by the time I remember, I'm usually in my car on the way home.

Gemma: You'll remember one of these days. I've got to get going, but are we still up for a video chat Sunday?

Frankie: Yes, ma'am.

Gemma: *Smiling emoji* Talk to you soon. Good luck with your dad today.

Frankie: Thanks!

I stow my phone into the outside pocket of my purse.

"How's Gemma?" Dad asks.

"She's good. They're in Canberra, Australia, for the next couple days."

"Is she having a good time?"

"Uh-huh, except for the heat. It's been over a hundred every day they've been there."

"Robert Tomlinson." A nurse in blue floral scrubs reads off Dad's name from a clipboard as she steps out into the reception area.

We both stand.

"If you'll follow me into exam room number four. We just need a quick blood pressure reading, then I'll let Dr. Kaur know you're here."

We enter a door near the check-in desk and are guided down the hall to a small room that smells like disinfectant. Posters display the anatomy of the hip joint. While Dad sits on the edge of the cushioned table, I take a seat on the plastic chair across from him.

The nurse makes idle chatter. I try my best to follow along, but my thoughts are elsewhere. I hope more than anything that this latest set of X-rays is better than the last ones. Last time we were here, the news was okay, but not overly encouraging. Dad was healing, but a lot slower than the doctor wanted to see.

I'm also worried about his balance. He's still unsteady and extremely reliant on his cane. A part of that is due to the fact that unless I'm home, he won't do his physical therapy exercises. And even then, it's like pulling teeth every time I suggest it. His mood darkens and I turn into the bad guy. I know they make his hip ache, but he needs to understand they're for his own good.

I squeeze my knees together and wonder if I should say something privately to the doctor. Maybe hearing about the importance of PT from a medical professional will help change his attitude.

The blood pressure monitor beeps. "One-forty over eighty-three. A little high, but it could just be because you're in the office today. BPs are always elevated in this type of environment." The woman scribbles down his numbers and unfastens the Velcro. "Any problems with your medication? Any swelling or new pains?"

Dad shakes his head. "Nope. Everything's great."

I clench my jaw. That's not entirely true.

"Great. I'll let Dr. Kaur know you're here and she'll be in shortly." The nurse leaves the room.

"Dad . . ." I start. "You've been really tired lately. Make sure you mention that if the doctor asks you."

"Frankie, it's just me getting older." He frowns. "I sleep more than I used to. You know I fall asleep in my recliner by eight right after *Jeopardy*."

"Dad. Mention it anyway, please? For me." My patience is fleeting. Why is he so darn proud?

"Frankie. There isn't any point. We don't need to worry the doctor. Like I said, it's just me—"

A knock sounds at the door. Dad stops speaking. A petite woman with dark-brown hair, brown eyes, and olive skin enters, wearing a white lab coat.

"Hello, Mr. Tomlinson. Miss Tomlinson. It's nice to see you two again." Dr. Kaur takes a seat in the corner of the room and logs on to the computer, pulling up Dad's chart. "How have you been doing lately? How are you finding your physical therapy?"

Dad flashes her a grin. "Everything's great! I've been doing my exercises every day just like you told me to."

I grit my teeth. Not every day, but most days.

"Excellent. Let me just load the images from your most recent set of X-rays and we'll see how your body is doing." Dr. Kaur swivels the computer screen, so it faces us. A black-and-white photo of the hip bone with the surgical hardware loads. "You're about sixteen weeks post-op, and as you can see from this most recent image, the fracture is nearly all the way healed, just as we had hoped."

For the first time today, I allow myself to breathe a little easier.

"That's reassuring." Dad pats his hip. "I thought I'd bounce back after twelve weeks, like when I had my knee replaced."

"Every patient heals on their own timeline. The older we get, the longer it takes. Remember, this is a marathon, not a sprint."

The doctor changes the screen. "Glancing over the notes from your PT appointment last week, I can see we haven't quite reached the targeted range of motion and increase of muscle strength we'd aimed for. Is there anything you feel might be contributing to this?"

Dad nods. "That, ah . . . may be my folly." His cheeks flush a rosy-red. "I might have missed a day or two of exercises. Everything has felt stiff."

Finally, he's admitting that not everything is picture-perfect.

Dr. Kaur shoots him a look of sympathy. "How would you rate the pain on a scale of one to ten? Ten being the worst discomfort."

"A three?"

"When it comes to the exercises, experiencing a little soreness is normal. Remember, you're rebuilding muscles that haven't been in use for a while. The goal is to be consistent. Perhaps you can try doing shorter sets twice a day instead of once a day? I'll email your physical therapist and have them contact you with some other modifications you guys can make to your routine."

"And I'll make sure he keeps doing them on a schedule." I squeeze Dad's arm. "Now that I'm home for good, there won't be any more excuses."

"Do you have any other questions for me?" Dr. Kaur asks.

"No, I think you've covered everything," Dad says.

"Excellent." She nods. "Mr. Tomlinson, I'll have my assistant set up your next appointment and take your BP one more time. Ms. Tomlinson, if I could borrow you for a second?"

"Sounds good." Curious, I follow the doctor.

"I know how stressful caring for an elderly parent can be. It's just you, isn't it?" Dr. Kaur asks candidly once we're out of earshot of the exam room.

"Yeah. There isn't anyone else. I'm an only child."

Even though the doctor is kind, I'm not comfortable disclosing more info than necessary. Dad and I aren't your conventional family. He adopted me as a baby and raised me as a single father. I can't stand the looks of sympathy people shoot me when they hear that I never grew up with a mom. Why should it matter? It never felt like I ever missed out on anything. Dad loved me more than enough for two parents.

"We have a support group I can email you information about. There may come a time when you find it helpful to speak to others in the same situation as yourself."

"Thanks." My voice comes out gravelly.

While I appreciate her offer, I know I won't be taking advantage of the group. I'm doing just fine, thank you very much.

"Did you have any questions that you'd rather ask privately?"

"I do." Pulling up my mental list, I rattle off, "Should I be worried about his balance? Do you think the fall was just a one-off? Is there a chance he has an underlying condition that caused it?"

"Take a deep breath, Ms. Tomlinson." Dr. Kaur blinks slowly and places a hand on my shoulder. "Your father is in very good overall health for his age. All the tests we've run have come back clear. I suspect at the time of the fall, he may have experienced some vertigo from a nasty inner ear infection."

I exhale. Okay, that's not new news. The emergency room doctor mentioned the same thing.

"As for his balance, it'll improve over time, but there is always a possibility that he may have to rely on a cane for the rest of his life. It's all up to him and how that physical therapy continues to go."

Her words ignite a fire within my belly. "I'll make sure I'm more vigilant with him. Thanks, Doctor."

"You're welcome." She smiles softly. "If you ever have questions for me, please, feel free to call or email."

"I will, thanks."

Dr. Kaur excuses herself. I stand outside the exam room, taking a few moments to myself. The appointment has gone as well as expected. All I need to do is keep Dad on his routine, and everything will start to fall into place. It just has to. There's no room for any other outcome.

After dropping my father at home, I make my way to the rink. I can't think of a better way to relieve the stress of the day. That is as long as I don't run into the grump.

The cashier in the booth at the entry greets me as I walk in. "Hiya, Frankie. Doing the public session today?"

"Yeah. I had some stuff to take care of this morning. Is it busy?"

"So-so. We have about thirty-five kids here on a class field trip. Sixth- and seventh-graders." I grimace. Eleven- and twelve-year-olds are giant daredevils. Especially when they're with their friends. It stinks for whoever has ice patrol duty. They won't have a moment's peace.

"Do you need any help fitting the kids with rental skates?" I offer.

"Nah. You enjoy your practice. Charlie took care of the skates. Max and Aaron are on ice patrol. They'll handle any troublemakers."

"Charlie is here?" I stand taller. It's been three weeks since I started here, and I still have yet to meet him. I wonder if he looks the same. I've been hoping to run into him, but figured he's probably long gone by the time I arrive. Especially since his day probably starts at five a.m.

"He's up in his office now, up to his ears in paperwork. I told him not to put it off, but you know men. They think they always know better than us. Just like my ex." The lobby doors open. A mom and two young kids chat excitedly, approaching the window to pay for the session. "If I see Charlie, I'll let him know you'd like to say hello."

"Thanks."

Stepping onto the ice a scant ten minutes later, I wonder if it's even worth my time bothering to skate today. The surface that was probably smooth at the start of the session is now covered in deep ruts, making it bumpy, uneven, and missing chunks in some places as I glide toward the middle.

Two of the youngest staff and members of the community college hockey team, Max and Aaron, weave in and out of public-session participants, keeping a watchful eye on all the pre-teens. They're like a pair of award-winning scent hounds. They can smell trouble before it happens.

On cue, I spy Max cutting across the ice to the area where we keep the buckets used to help the toddlers learn to skate. A trio of boys have pulled a few out and are racing one another with them across the center of the ice. As they see Max, however, they abandon the items and rush away. He hurries to collect them. Meanwhile, Aaron nods to me and puts out a set of orange traffic cones in the center of the ice where I intend to practice.

"Thanks," I call out cheerily. He holds up his hand in acknowledgment, then darts over to the other side of the rink to deal with another set of troublesome teens throwing loose shards of ice at one another.

With the lousy state of the ice and the unpredictability of who might dart in and out of the middle, I decide today is the perfect day to work on some old-school figures. It's how my long-time coach used to start every lesson. He'd draw a shape on the ice, and then challenge us to trace over it.

The goal was to get your skate to go *exactly* over what he'd drawn. It rarely happens because figures are hard. You have to use just the right amount of knee bend and control to make it all the way through the shape. Most of the time, my tracings were way off. I never took them seriously, thinking they were a colossal waste of time. I wanted to work on jumps, spins, and lifts with my partner.

It wasn't until I hit my late teens that I understood how lucky I was to have learned them from Mr. Franks. Practicing those darn shapes *had* given me the literal edge over my competitors. Before I switched to pairs, judges always commented on how the footwork and transitions in my programs were the best of any skater they'd judged.

When I joined Dreams on Ice, I got out of the habit of practicing them. But now that I'm coaching, I don't have any excuses. Claiming a small patch of ice, I spend the next hour challenging myself to see what I can still do.

"Hey! What are you doing out here?"

I squeeze my eyes shut. He's here again. The one person I

keep running into, no matter what time of day I skate. "What does he want from me this time?" I mutter to myself.

Today he has skates on and comes to a sharp stop next to me. The lines of his forehead are creased into a deep V. His jaw is clenched. It seems to be the only facial expression he can muster. Once again, he's in all black. His beard has continued to grow out with the curly locks entangled together, reminding me of a gnome. Except their beards are better maintained.

"I thought we already went over this. Didn't you tell me just a few days ago that you wouldn't practice out here alone?"

The muscles in my forehead twitch. "I'm *not* alone. This is the public session."

He gestures to the empty rink. "Public ended half an hour ago."

"Huh?" I blink a few times and glance up at the hockey scoreboard displaying the time. It's two-thirty. My shoulders hunch. "Oh, I didn't realize."

"Clearly." The grump points to the door. "Now, if you don't mind, clear off the ice. Aaron can't wait any longer." The teenager sits atop the Zamboni with an amused expression on his face. "The ice needs a cut so it's ready for the three-p.m.-freestyle session. I have lessons to teach."

The grump is a coach? Huh. Leslie did mention there were some coaches here who didn't teach any skating-academy classes. I guess it makes sense. He has no people skills. Maybe he only works with boys or hockey players. He certainly has the disposition for it.

"I'm done." I flip my hair over my shoulder. "I'm sorry. Again." I start toward the door to the ice, the grump hot on my tail.

While I collect my skate guards from the ledge by the plexiglass, he stands across from me, arms crossed, leaning against the door. It's unnerving, and I try my best to ignore him. But he makes it difficult. "That's twice now that I've caught you skating alone on my ice. I *should* take you straight to Jack's office and let him know you need to go. We don't have room on this staff for those who can't follow the rules of the rink. What type of example does that send to our students?"

I've had it with this guy. He thinks he runs the place. Words tumble out of my mouth. "You're wrong. I *do* take the rules seriously. Safety is one of, if not the most, important thing to me. Both times you found me it was only by coincidence I was alone. If you have a problem with me, feel free to report it to Charlie or Leslie Welch. I work for them, not you.

The grump takes a step closer to me. "I hate to break it to you, *hon*, but you *do* work for me. I'm Charlie Welch."

Alarm bells start ringing in my head as I notice the pocket of his jacket contains fancy white embroidery that reads "Mr. C." A wave of shock flows through my system. There's no denying that only Charlie Welch would walk around the Sequoia Valley Ice Center with a cocky swagger like he owns the place—because he does.

I gulp. My legs tremble and my voice weakens. "I . . . didn't know. I'm sorry. I need this job."

Charlie holds up his hand. "Even if I cared, your excuses wouldn't do anything for me."

"I'm sorry," I repeat in a whisper. Of all the people I had to make an enemy of, why did it have to be him?

Chapter Four

"Charlie!" Leslie shouts in a shrill voice. Both our heads turn to the left. "What are you doing terrorizing my newest instructor?" She marches right up to her brother and invades his personal space. If I weren't so traumatized, it would be amusing to see Leslie, who's a head shorter than him, standing up to him. "Well, I'm waiting for an answer."

"It's none of your business." Charlie's eyes flash. "This conversation is between me and her." He jabs his finger in my direction.

"Her name is Frankie, and it *is* my business. You're done acting like a rude, obnoxious bully to the staff. I should've called you out on it sooner. I'm sick and tired of having to deal with complaint after complaint about you. Nobody wants to work with you. You can treat *me* however you want, but the staff is off-limits. After I sort Frankie out, you and I are going to meet with Jack and have a serious talk. I should've reported your behavior to him ages ago."

"I don't have time," he hisses through his teeth.

"Yes, you do." One look from Leslie silences him. "If you're running late for your first lesson, maybe you could ask

Frankie if she'd be willing to get whoever you have started on warm-ups." She turns her head. "Not that you owe *him* anything. I wouldn't blame you at all for saying no."

All my instincts tell me to hightail it out of here. I've never been so embarrassed in my life. How could I have been so stupid as to miss that Charlie is the grump? I risk a glance in his direction. It has to be the hair and the unkempt clothing. The Charlie I had a crush on always had short hair and was clean-shaven. In the pictures I have in my scrapbook, which I won't admit exists to anyone, he's in a suit or skating costume.

I *don't* want to help him. He *has* been a world-class jerk to me. But Leslie is the one who's asking. Not him. When I was a student, I hated when my coach would cancel a lesson on me at the last minute. If I can help it, I don't want his student to have to suffer because their coach can't get along with others.

"I'll do it," I say in a hushed tone.

"Thank you," Leslie says.

"But she doesn't know anything about—"

Leslie clamps a hand over his mouth and pulls the collar of his jacket closer to her. "Stop talking and listen to me." Her nostrils flare. "Frankie may be new, but she's more experienced than almost every single member of the teaching staff except for you. You'll not only trust her with your student, you'll owe her *big* after this. Understood?"

I'm in shock and awe at the same time as I watch Leslie take on her brother. I can see exactly why she makes a solid hockey player. She doesn't take crap from anyone. She may be short in stature, but she makes up for it in attitude and spirit.

"Fine. Whatever." Charlie closes his eyes and rubs his temples, resigned to letting his sister have her way. "My first student is Richelle. She's working on her novice moves in the field. Have her warm up with forward and backward power pulls." He opens his eyes. "I assume you know what those are."

"Yes," I say, proud of my even tone.

"Quit being a smart aleck. You're only going to get yourself into deeper trouble with Jack. And believe me, I'm going to tell him *everything*." Leslie huffs and releases Charlie's jacket. "Before we leave, you owe Frankie an apology."

"No, it's fine."

"No. It's really not." She crosses her arms and taps her toe. "Charlie," she warns. "Apologize."

He takes a deep breath. "Frank . . . I, uh . . ."

"Her name is Frankie. *Not* Frank."

"Frankie, I'm sorry," he grunts.

I manage a curt nod.

"That's not even close to being acceptable, but it's a start." Leslie grips Charlie's shoulders, spins him around, and gives him a small push. "The clock says it's two-forty. I'll meet you in your office in five minutes. In the meantime, go shave and fix yourself. The beard is not a good look on you. You look like a caveman. You don't want Jack to see you like *this*."

Charlie shoves his hands in his pockets and slowly walks away from the rink, muttering something under his breath.

"He needs a shower too." Leslie fans the air. "Good grief. He smells worse than the locker room after a hockey game." Placing her hands on my shoulders, my boss studies me. "Are you okay? I'm truly sorry for the way he treated you."

"I'm fine. And I didn't know who he was." My muscles slowly started to relax. "I can't believe the two of you are related. He's so, uh . . ."

"The words you're searching for are irritable and ill-tempered." Her eyelids flutter. "Not that I want to make any excuses for him, but you've caught him at the worst possible time. It didn't hit me until this morning that the anniversary of his accident is coming up this week. He's always an emotional mess around this time of the year. I wish he'd stay home, but unfortunately, I don't have the power to boot him out of here. Only Jack does."

My eyes widen. Accident? Does that have anything to do with why he's been so anal? I think back to some of our earlier encounters. There's one in particular that stands out. *"I thought we had gone through this already. Didn't you tell me just a few days ago that you wouldn't practice out here alone?"*

Leslie rubs the back of her neck as she glances at the clock on the scoreboard above the rink. "I hate to do this, but I'm going to have to run out on you in a minute. The student you'll be working with is named Richelle."

"Richelle," I repeat to myself. "Can you tell me what she looks like?"

"Sorry." Leslie shoots me an apologetic smile. "She's about eight years old, always wears a sparkly pink headband, and carries a purple unicorn-shaped tissue-box holder. If you have trouble finding her, let Aaron know. He's best friends with Richelle's brother."

"Got it."

"I really appreciate this, and I won't forget it."

"**R**elax, Richelle. You're so stiff. Is there any way you can make your edges a little deeper for me?"

"What do you mean, Coach Frankie?" The petite skater cocks her head to the side and stares quizzically at me like a baby owl with her large eyes. "Mr. C told me I was doing a good job."

I breathe deeply. Here I am coaching for the first time on my own with a student who is light-years ahead of the ones I've been working with. If it were anyone else, I'd be panicking about now, but lucky for me, Richelle is nothing like I'd expected. She's polite and takes directions well. I wonder how she ended up with a coach like him.

Think, Frankie. Think. What does Leslie do when she's explaining things to the level ones and twos? How can I explain what I want Richelle to do? I flash back to one of my first days on the job.

"There are two tactics you can try. Show and tell. Showing is what the name implies. Visually demonstrate to the student what you want them to do. Telling is a little more complicated. You'll have to break the skill down and explain it in a way that makes sense to them. For kids, I like to use TV show references. But I'm sure you'll figure out what works for you."

"You *are* doing an amazing job, but let's see if we can make your footwork sequence even better." I motion for the tiny skater to hold on to the wall. "Let's do the inside three and rocker pattern one more time. But every time you do a new step or turn, I want you to bend your knees, like a ballerina doing a grand plié."

"Oh! I think I get it now. Mommy makes me do ballet to help my ice skating. Is it like this?" She bends her knees more than she has.

I sigh in relief. Phew, she gets it. Thank you, Leslie. "Yes! That's great. Just like that."

Richelle sticks her tongue out. "It feels weird."

"You'll get used to it."

She shrugs. "Okay."

"Go ahead and try it now."

From my position at the center of the ice, I watch intently as the eight-year-old repeats the pattern we've been working on for the past twenty minutes. Charlie still hasn't joined us, which is fine by me. I'm enjoying myself out here. Richelle is good for her age.

It's hard to believe she's already working on the novice level. It's only two below the Olympic level and one of the hardest. When she takes her American Skating Union test, I'm sure she'll pass on the first try. She won't need three attempts like I did.

"Bend even more," I shout.

Richelle takes the correction and picks up speed as she glides past me. The blades of her skates make sharp ripping noises, indicating secure, deep edges.

"Not bad," a male voice suddenly interjects.

I gasp and my hand flies to my chest. Charlie's managed to sneak up on me, standing to my left. I've been so focused on watching Richelle that I'd missed him entering the ice entirely. He looks like a completely different person. The beard has disappeared, replaced by a sharp, angular jaw and high cheek-bones. The stained jacket has been swapped for a fresh one, although it's still black. Whatever Leslie said to him in private must've been powerful to get him to change so quickly.

"Sorry," he says, eyes glued on his student. "I didn't think I'd be this late. I'll take over the last five minutes. What have you two worked on?"

I wouldn't mind finishing the lesson, but now that he's here, I'm happy to take my leave. I'm still cross with him from earlier. Keeping my tone even, I bring him up to speed. "Besides the footwork pattern, we've played with some forward and backward twizzles. She said they're the move that gives her the most trouble."

"I'd say she tends to struggle more with her forward loops, but her twizzles did need some work."

Stop the presses; he's admitting I did something right. I *never* thought I'd be on the receiving end of a compliment from him. A small amount of pride wells up in me. All things aside, from a professional standpoint, hearing that I've done well from the skating director boosts my confidence in my ability to coach.

"She's a gifted skater, just a little rough around the edges. I enjoyed working with her. I'll, um . . . just head out now."

"Wait." He glances in my direction. "She'll want to say goodbye to you."

"Oh, okay."

I stand next to him in silence, out of things to say while we wait for Richelle. She completes her last skill and heads back toward us. The moment she spots her normal coach, she lets out an ecstatic, "Mr. C!" and sprints over. Her small arms wrap around his legs, causing my heart to melt. Just a little. "Coach Frankie said you might not make it today. It made me sad because seeing you is my favorite thing about Mondays." She releases him and frowns. "Where did all the hair on your face go? I hope it stays gone. I didn't like it when you looked like a lion."

"I'm glad you approve." He runs a hand across his jaw. "My big sister made me get rid of it."

"Is she bossy? My big sister is." Richelle wrinkles her nose. "She's always telling me what to do, but Mommy says I don't always have to listen to her. Maybe you can tell your mommy to tell your sister to not be bossy to you."

I cover my mouth with my hand to bite back a giggle.

"I'll keep that in mind. Your footwork looked better today."

"Thank you, Mr. C." Her large brown eyes dance. She clearly looks up to him. "Coach Frankie told me to just bend my knees more. It's hard."

"Yes, it is." Charlie nods. "But Coach Frankie is right. If you bend your knees more, it'll help you make the jump to the junior level quicker."

I take advantage of the opportunity to say my goodbye. I kneel down so I'm even in height with her. "Richelle, now that Mr. C is back, it's time for me to go. I just wanted you to know that you did a great job today. I hope I get to see you again soon." I hold up my hand for a high-five.

"Are you leaving?" A look of distress crosses her face. "Mr. C, can you make Coach Frankie stay a few more minutes?"

Charlie blinks slowly. "Richelle, Coach Frankie might have places to be. We can ask her nicely, but we can never make anyone stay," he says, looking away from me.

She turns to me. "Coach Frankie, can you please, please, stay until the end of my lesson? I like you and I don't want you to leave yet."

I hesitate, glancing at the clock. There are four minutes left in the session. "Um, I guess I could."

"Yeah!" She smiles widely.

Charlie stands and focuses on Richelle, ignoring me. "Okay, tiny mite, your choice. What do you want to end with?"

Richelle tilts her head. "Uh, double loops?"

"Good choice. We don't have enough time for the harness today, but if you want to try one or two without it, we can. Do you remember the drills I showed you?"

Richelle nods and walks through the jump. I watch from the background, more confused than ever by Charlie. There's no trace of the grump. He's a different person as a coach.

"Okay, kiddo, show me what you've got."

Richelle makes a horseshoe pattern around us. Taking a long edge, she bends her knees and jumps. Her tiny body lifts into the air and rotates one and three-quarter times around. She's so close. I jump up and down, wanting her to land it badly.

"That's the best her double loop has looked," Charlie comments.

Richelle skates back over to us for some corrections.

"Slow down your takeoff. Your goal is to press deep enough into the ice that you can spring up and off your toe pick like a bunny." Charlie walks her through the motions of the jump, making sure she hits each position.

"You've told me that before, Mr. C, but I don't get it."

He puffs his cheeks out. "Any words of wisdom, Coach Frankie?"

Remembering what worked earlier, I decide to take a gamble and try a visual approach. "Richelle, watch what my legs do when I do a double loop." I push backward into a slow, short entry and exaggerate my takeoff. My knees bend so low that I'm sure it looks like I'm trying to sit in a chair. Loops have always been the easiest jump for me. Even moving at a glacial speed, I can easily crank out a double.

Landing the jump, I glide back over to the pair.

"I think I get it now." Richelle's eyes glimmer in excitement. "Can you do a triple?"

"I can." Or at least I could a few months ago.

"Cool! Can I see?"

Charlie clears his throat. "If Coach Frankie tries a triple, that means no more double loops—you only have one minute left."

"Time's up already? I wanna do one more."

"Okay, then get going. This is your last attempt; make it count." Charlie holds out his hand and offers her a fist bump. Taking his phone from his pocket, he discreetly starts recording her.

I hold my breath, wanting this badly for her. Richelle starts forward, then changes direction. Lining up her body on one of the circles, she copies my exaggerated knee bend, spins around like a top two times in the air, and lands sideways, but on one foot.

"I'd count that as clean." I grin.

"Yes!" Charlie shouts, shoving his phone into his pocket and racing over to his young student. He kneels down and hugs her. "You did it! I am so proud of you, tiny mite."

"Wait until I tell Mommy!" she brags.

I cross my arms, running my hands over my forearms. As I watch Charlie speaking to her softly, I wonder how the man in front of me can go from being a supportive, approachable coach to a person who makes me want to run out to my car and cry. What did Leslie and Jack say to him?

Charlie releases Richelle. She turns around and looks for me. "Coach Frankie, did you see? Did you see?"

"I did," I say, going over to them. "That was so good!"

Richelle hugs me tightly. "Thank you, Coach Frankie! You are the second-bestest coach ever!"

"You're welcome." I wink.

"Okay, kiddo, time's up. You'd better go grab your stuff before your mom gets out here," Charlie says.

A moment later, a woman in a tan parka and plaid Burberry scarf rushes over to the door of the rink and points to her watch. "Richelle, come on. We have to get going. We'll be late for your piano lesson."

Charlie lets out a slow breath, his expression reverting to the sour one I'm keenly familiar with.

"Mommy, guess what I did?"

"You can tell me about it in the car. Let's go!" Her mother frowns.

Richelle's face falls. "Yes, Mommy."

"You can take your skates off and change in the car. I'm parked in the usual spot."

Stepping off the ice, Richelle collects her unicorn tissue box and rolling bag, and waves goodbye.

"Go, I'm right behind you." Her mother urges her forward. "Mr. Welch, please make sure you're on time next time. I pay you for a thirty-minute skating lesson, not thirty-one minutes. I've told you this before. We're on a tight sched-ule. If you can't keep track of time, I'll find a coach who will."

Charlie's lip curls. "Yes, ma'am."

Richelle's mother huffs and quickly walks away.

"That was rude."

"She's a tiger mom." Charlie shrugs. "Thanks again for the help. I'm late for my next lesson."

Not waiting for any sign of acknowledgment, he rushes off to a teenage boy who appears to be about fourteen or fifteen years old.

Hmm. Maybe Charlie is only good with kids? Whatever the answer is, I'm happy to be leaving before the grump returns.

On Tuesday, Leslie gives me the green light to lead the level-five class. I've officially been here for four weeks.

I skate up and down the line of teenage and adult students practicing their Salchows, the first single jump most skaters learn. "After you turn backward, kick your leg, just like you're aiming for a soccer ball. Then jump."

This class is different from all the other ones I've assisted with. The students aren't here because they have a parent who's convinced they'll be the next Olympic champion. They're here because they chose skating. The vibe in this group is unlike anything I've experienced so far.

Everyone is encouraging one another and exchanging tips on what works and what doesn't. I'm hardly doing anything. I thought I'd want to primarily teach young kids, but actually, I think working with adults might be my ultimate goal.

When class ends a few minutes later, Leslie and I skate over to the boards to collect the roster for the last group of the evening.

"You've really started to come into your own. You're

impressing me, and that doesn't always happen easily," she teases.

"It's all because I've had you to learn from. You taught me that half the battle is about finding the right words to use to explain to the students what to do."

"That's right." She nods in confirmation. "It is. Let's talk more about the mental side of coaching. One of the biggest problems you'll have to navigate is figuring out how to help students deal with mental blocks and frustration. Take the adult class we just had, for instance—" Leslie stops speaking as a student approaches us.

"Hi, Leah. Did you forget something?" I ask.

"No. Mr. Charlie was by the door and asked if I could grab you. He said it would be quick."

I glance in the direction she's just come from. Sure enough, there's Charlie, lurking in the shadows. "He wanted me? Not Coach Leslie?"

"Yes."

Okay. I don't know what he could have to say to me, but I guess I don't have much of a choice. Why is he even here so late? "You can tell him I'll be there in one second."

"Okay." She glides back to the exit.

"I can't believe he can't wait thirty minutes. He knows classes end at eight." Leslie huffs in frustration. "Tell him you only have two minutes. The next class starts in ten. Oh, and if he gives you any trouble, just call for me." She busies herself with checking in with one of the other coaches near us.

I lazily push my skates and make my way over to the door, taking a few moments to compose myself.

"Frankie," he greets me, hands shoved into his pockets.

"Charlie. Leah said you had something to talk to me about?"

"I wanted to start out with a big apology for all the times

I've been awful to you. It's been rough lately." His voice comes out raspy. "I'm ashamed of how I've been acting."

This could've waited until after class, but at least he appears to mean it this time. "Apology accepted. Was there anything else you needed? Leslie's given me two minutes."

He lifts his chin, his Adam's apple bobbing up and down. "I, er . . . wanted to know if your offer to help me out still stands?"

I arch an eyebrow. Was the apology only a ruse to get what he really wants? As I stand there, I realize there's dark purple shadows under his eyes. Messy strands of curly hair poke out at odd angles from under his signature beanie. He looks terrible. Like a guy who hasn't gotten a good night's sleep in a long, long time. I decide to give him the benefit of the doubt. "Yes, it does."

"Are you able to stay after your last class tonight? I understand if you can't."

I chew on my lip. "That depends. How late is late?"

"An hour? I screwed up and I know Leslie can't stay tonight to help me fix it. I thought I'd ask you instead. You're one of the few staff members who's on speaking terms with me."

I believe that. "What do you need help with?"

"Paperwork. I read my calendar wrong. There's a test session scheduled for the Sequoia Valley Figure Skating Club's members this weekend." He pinches the bridge of his nose. "I thought it was next weekend. All the kids have to be registered by midnight tonight. I know it's short notice. If you can't stay, I get it. I'll ask someone else."

He just admitted there probably isn't anyone else. I'm really *not* in a mood to help him. I'm tired and I'm hungry. All I want to do is change into my PJs, lounge on the couch with a slice of pizza, and watch TV with Dad. But I see Charlie's slumped shoulders. His eyes are dull, and his hands hang limply at his side. I doubt he'd ask for help if he didn't really need it. I can't bring myself to say no to a person in trouble.

"I'll stay."

"Thank you." He inclines his head. "I better let you go before my sister sends out a search party for you. I'll be in my office. Come on up when you're done coaching."

I return to Leslie. Her eyes lock on to me, like a sharp-eyed falcon. "What did he want?"

"Just some help with paperwork."

"Huh. He did? That's unlike him. I wonder why he didn't ask me."

"He said you're busy."

"Technically that's true. I have plans. My boyfriend is in town for a short visit. I haven't seen him in a couple weeks. He'll understand if I tell him my bro needs me though."

I know exactly what it's like to be on the road all the time and only have a day or two with your loved ones. Leslie works hard. She deserves a little downtime with her man. "It's no biggie. I can do it. Besides, it'll give us a chance to clear the air."

She doesn't seem too convinced by my words. "Are you positive?"

"Yes." I nod.

"All right, then. I'll be available by phone or text if you need *anything*. When we finish this class, you can go straight to his office. I'll take care of the cleanup." She takes a deep breath and says under her breath, "In spite of all his flaws, Charlie is a good guy. I hope everyone will come to see that eventually."

I'm not sure if she intended for me to hear her last comment, but I believe her. After seeing how soft Charlie was with Richelle, I believe he does have a few redeeming qualities. Rumor has it he was one of the nice guys back when he skated. I wonder what happened to change him so much.

At eight, just after the last child has cleared the ice, Leslie approaches me. "You're good to go if you want. But a word of warning—Charlie is one of the most disorganized people you'll ever meet. We cleaned his office last week, but it doesn't take long for it to turn into something you might see on a hoarding show. Nothing is going to be where he claims it is."

"Got it."

"Oh, one more thing—Don't let him keep you all night. He'll also lose track of time."

What am I getting myself into? I hope I won't live to regret this.

Chapter Five

I rap my knuckles on the door of Charlie's office. His voice is muffled, but I take it as a sign to enter. As the door swings open, I gasp. Leslie wasn't kidding. It looks like somebody's raided an office supply store and tried to create some abstract modern art.

The room has a similar layout to Jack's office. There's a desk, computer, printer, bookshelf, and two chairs for visitors. Except that's where the similarities end. Every available inch of flat surface space is covered by binders, stacks of paper, books, coffee cups, boxes, and other assorted items. Crumpled balls of paper that have missed the recycle bin litter the floor. Photos that should be hanging on the wall are propped against the bookcase.

If this is a week of mess, I'm glad I didn't see it before it was cleaned. At least there aren't any takeout containers on the desk. Coffee cups are bad enough. If I saw any bugs, I'd freak and hightail it out of here as quick as my feet could carry me.

Charlie jumps to his feet, sending the desk chair crashing into the wall behind him. His face slowly turns a shade of candy-apple-red. "Is it eight already?"

"Uh-huh." I nod, still staring at the mess.

He walks around the side of his desk and tosses the jackets piled up on the visitor's chair onto the printer. Thrown off balance, the items on top of it crash to the ground. Charlie groans.

My body shakes with laughter. "I'm sorry, I shouldn't laugh." I clutch my stomach and wipe a stray tear from the corner of my eye. "It's just, this room is so filthy."

Charlie scratches the back of his head. "I know."

The neat freak in me can't stand it any longer. Before I know what I'm doing, I tie my hair up into a messy bun and offer, "I know I'm here for the paperwork, but I can at least help you get rid of all the trash first, if you'd like."

"No," he says a little too quickly. "It's a pigsty, but it's the only way I know where everything is."

Must. Stay. Quiet. As much as it pains me to work in a cluttered area, at the end of the day, this is Charlie's space and not mine. I take a deep breath and remind myself that I'm here to make sure he gets all the people testing this weekend registered.

The American Skating Union, which oversees competitive ice skating in the U.S., has eight different levels that range from pre-preliminary to senior. In order to compete in one of these levels, a skater has to pass two different tests.

One involves performing a series of predetermined technical moves and patterns called Moves in the Field, while the other asks the skater to put a program together with music. There's usually between six to eight different required elements that have to be included, like a double Lutz or camel spin. That test is called the Free Skate test. In order to take a Free Skate test, a skater has to pass the Moves test first.

"Okay," I say, taking a seat in the now-empty chair. "So, um . . . how many people do you have testing? Are they all kids or do we have adults?"

He sorts through the pile of papers under the computer monitor. "Twenty-five participants. All kids."

"Do you mind if I write on this notepad?" I hold one up.

"Knock yourself out."

I scribble the information down. "And of those, how many are testing singles? Any ice-dance tests?"

"Yes, to both of those. Two kids are doing the preliminary-level solo dances. Everybody else is doing their singles Moves or Free Skate tests."

"Perfect." I glance up. "If I remember correctly, each participant is going to need a waiver and the corresponding judging form for the level?"

"That's right. Good memory." He appraises me with the same look he gave me when I was coaching Richelle—respect. "Lower-level tests only need one form. Anything past level three needs three forms."

I tap my pen against the desk. "Um, not to overstep here, but have the judges you booked been able to change their dates to this weekend?"

"So far, so good. I have two judges confirmed. There's still one I haven't heard back from yet." Charlie taps his mouse. The computer glows to life. "I'll just pull up the American Skating Union's website so we can start printing everything." He starts typing slowly with his pointer fingers, glancing from the keyboard to the screen every few keystrokes.

I drum my fingers on the desktop. What could possibly be taking so long? It's literally just AmericanSkatingUnion.com. Is he doing this on purpose? A surge of resentment begins to well up inside of me. Maybe this is his way of paying me back for the two times he caught me on the ice alone, and tonight was a setup. I glance up at Charlie. He's squinting at the monitor, mouthing letters to himself. It doesn't *look* like he's messing around.

"Do you need some help?"

The nape of his neck flushes a shade of deep red. "My . . . ugh, my computer is running slow."

"Is it updating? Or is it frozen?"

He sits there several long moments. "Uh . . . actually, I'm not good with computers. I don't know what it needs. Would you mind taking a look?"

He stands and walks over to the window overlooking the parking lot, his back turned to me. I plop down into the vacant chair. The ASU site is open, but a big red message reads: **The number of log-in attempts has been exceeded. Please enter your email to reset your password.**

I frown. Why didn't he just say he didn't remember his password? It's not a big deal. I open and close my hands a few times, keeping my anger in check. I glance over the top of the monitor at him. "What's your email address tied to the ASU page?"

"My email? It's, uh . . . the skating club's name."

"Can you tell me the whole thing?"

"Sequoia Valley FSC."

My eyes twitch. "You spelled it wrong in the log-in box."

"I did?"

"Yes, you did." My tone is flat.

"I'm sorry," he quickly apologizes, shoulders hunching. "I've made more stupid mistakes than I can count. Nothing is going right today."

I decide for the moment to cut him some slack. He does look exhausted. That could be why he's not thinking straight. "I'll tell you what. I'll take over the computer side of things if you tell me what needs to be done. It'll give your eyes a chance to rest."

He looks me up and down uncertainly. "Are you sure?"

"Positive." And with that, I become Charlie's secretary. "What's your password?"

"Split double twist."

"All one word, no caps?"

"Yes."

"Are there any special numbers or symbols?"

"No."

I log in, then head to the forms' library.

A while later, my stomach growls loudly. "I'm sorry." I place a hand on it, hoping to silence it, but it only growls again. We're almost done. I want to finish this, but I'm also starving. I need some sugar in my system to be able to keep going. "Do you mind if I run to the pros' room? I think I have a granola bar in my bag that'll do the trick."

Charlie fights a yawn and covers his mouth with his hand. "When was the last time you ate?"

"Right before I left for the rink? Two-thirty?"

"That was hours ago. It's eleven." His eyes widen. "You haven't eaten dinner? Why didn't you *say* anything?"

"I usually eat when I get home. I guess I just lost track of time."

"Come on." He stands and stretches. "I already owe you for helping with Richelle, and after tonight, my debt's grown even larger. The least I can do is make you something to eat in the café. Are you okay with pizza?"

"I'll eat anything, but if you have it, pizza is perfect. It's my favorite food."

We walk down the hall. The ice complex is eerie at night. Through the glass, the two rinks are inky black. The only sound is the electric hum of the vending machines. Charlie leads us through the door next to the skate-rental room and taps the switch, flooding it with fluorescent light.

Opening an industrial-sized stainless-steel refrigerator, he pokes his head inside and removes a bowl of dough, as well as tomato sauce and cheese. "We can fight over the toppings in a minute." He preheats the oven, then searches for a pan and rolling pin.

"I'm not picky, but my favorite type of pizza is Hawaiian, if you're asking."

Charlie's face sours. "Pineapples do NOT belong on pizza."

So he's one of those people. I place a hand on my hip. "Says who?"

"Me."

We share a laugh. It's the first time he's loosened up.

"*I* prefer supreme pizzas with everything on it," he says, "but if you want pineapple, how about a compromise. We can do a half-Hawaiian, half-supreme."

"Let's just make a supreme pizza and I'll add my pineapples separately. I don't like them hot."

Charlie washes his hands and flattens a handful of dough. He gestures his head toward the fridge. "Would you mind pulling out some toppings? We should have a decent number of choices." He spreads the sauce with a ladle.

"I see mushrooms, olives, bell peppers, onions, pepperoni, and pineapple. No bacon though." Retrieving the plastic containers, I line them up on the counter and remove the lids.

Charlie is sprinkling some cheese over the crust. "Any food intolerances or allergies I need to be aware of?"

"Nope." I wash my hands in the sink. "How did you know you'd be able to find all the ingredients in here?"

Charlie opens the pepperoni and randomly places them on top of the cheese. "Who do you think prepares the pizzas for the weekend birthday parties?"

"Oh." I pass him the mushrooms and olives. "I thought you guys might have an events director or have the pizzas delivered."

"Nah." He shakes his head. "Events directors are expensive. And it's cheaper to make pizzas in-house. It's just Jack, Leslie, and me. Jack takes care of the business side of things. I'm supposed to do skating side of things . . ." He hesitates. "But most of the time it's Leslie who steps in."

Hearing this, I'm surprised that Leslie doesn't have Charlie's job. She runs the skating school and is clearly much better organized than her brother.

"Twelve minutes should do it." Charlie walks over to the oven and slides the tray inside. He checks the time and temperature. "There are some bar stools over here."

We sit across from one another. I rest my head on my arm, suddenly exhausted. I've been going all day nonstop, and I've hit my wall. Tired of discussing skating topics, I change the subject. "So how much older is Leslie than you?"

"We're actually twins."

Twins? I picture the vivacious woman with multicolored hair standing next to Charlie. Physically, they have a slightly similar build, but that's where the similarities end. "I'm having a hard time seeing it."

"Doesn't surprise me. We're the complete opposite of one another in every way imaginable. Leslie's always been the type of person who hates fitting in, hence the zany-colored hair. But me . . . I'm the twin who doesn't like to cause any trouble. It was hard enough being bullied in school for being a figure skater."

My shoulders droop. I've seen that happen before, especially growing up as a pairs skater. "I'm so sorry. Kids can be so cruel."

"It *was* painful, but at least when I was at the rink, none of that mattered." He rests his hands on the counter. "I could just leave the outside world behind. The girls *loved* me."

Not surprised. "Let me guess, you were tall for your age and one of the very few male skaters at your rink."

He smirks. "Correct."

I can picture the hormone-crazed teenage skaters taking notice of him and worshiping the ground he walked on. Especially since most of them were likely homeschooled and boy starved. At my old rink, all the girls had crushes on the ice-dance guys. They were in their twenties when we were all under fifteen.

I remember thinking how cool it was when the guys would actually take notice of me and say hello. They didn't ignore us like most of the adults. Not to mention they were gorgeous to look at when they were in the gym working out, usually shirtless. We'd look for any excuse to walk by the gym windows to peek inside.

"I hope you treated your female admirers decently."

"You have too much faith in me. I was arrogant and cocky and the center of my own universe. I'll let you fill in the blanks on how I acted."

I hold in a laugh. It's all Dad's fault. I'll never be able to take the word "blanks" seriously again. I clear my throat. "Somehow, I can't see Leslie letting you get away with that."

"You're right. She made sure my ego was cut down to size when it needed to be."

"She's never taken crap from anyone, has she?"

"Nope. It's one of the reasons why Les is an outstanding hockey player. Our rink back home near Vancouver, Washington, didn't have any hockey teams for girls, so growing up, she was forced to play with the guys. It toughened her up."

"Uh-huh." I look him up and down. "So you two both have type-A personalities."

The timer goes off. Charlie returns momentarily with a piping-hot pizza and sets it on a cooling rack. I soak in the sight of the golden-brown crust and the perfectly curled pepperonis. The cheese has melted, now soft and gooey. My mouth waters and my mind goes blank. All I can focus on is eating. He slices the pizza and plates two pieces for each of us. "Don't forget to add your pineapple."

I snap my fingers together. "I almost forgot." Grabbing the container from the counter, I pop off the lid and sprinkle some over the pizza.

"So good!" I say after taking a large bite.

"Eat up. There's plenty more."

"I haven't been able to have pizza in a long time."

"Why?" Charlie chuckles. "You don't skate competitively anymore. Having a slice or two won't hurt you. When I retired, I couldn't wait to be able to eat whatever I wanted."

"It's not that. It's my dad. I try not to have pizza in the house. It's too tempting for him. His doctor wants him to try and eat healthier while he recovers. If it were up to my father, he'd live on frozen entrees and takeout."

Charlie's face sobers. "I'm sorry to hear he hasn't been well."

"Thanks." I sigh. "He's doing better now. He fell and broke his hip recently."

I shove the pizza into my mouth and chew slowly, not believing that I've shared something so personal with him. Nobody knows about Dad. Not even Gemma. Why did I pick Charlie, of all people? Is it the exhaustion? It has to be.

"Is it just you two, then?"

I've already shared about his hip, so I suppose sharing a little bit more won't hurt. "Yeah, it is."

"Your father is lucky to have such a caring daughter like you around." He reaches for another slice of pizza. "Thank you again for all your help tonight. I won't forget it."

"You're welcome." I pat my mouth clean with a napkin. "Just promise me one thing—You'll try to not be so grumpy the next time we see one another."

"I'll try. I'm at my worst around the anniversary of the day that I . . . that is my, er . . . accident. Let's just say it brings out some painful memories."

He removes his beanie and touches a silvery-white scar that runs along the length of his forehead and disappears into his hair. It's healed, but at the time, it must've been painful.

"I'm ashamed of myself for acting like a beast this week. I need to find a way to make it up to everyone," he says softly.

"I think if you bought lunch for everyone, it would go a long way in showing that you feel guilty. Food is always a way to win people over."

"Maybe I will." He nods slowly, thinking the idea over.

We eat the remainder of the pizza in comfortable silence. This relaxed version of Charlie is a man I like and can see myself possibly even becoming friends with. I've caught a glimpse of him while he was coaching, and again as we're chatting over dinner tonight. I can only hope he'll stick around.

Chapter Six

Dad sips his decaf coffee and lets out a long sigh over breakfast the next morning. "Not strong enough."

I hate being the bad guy. He's trying to guilt me into giving him the non-decaf stuff, but it isn't going to work. No matter what he does. The doctor said giving up regular coffee would help his blood pressure, and so far, it has. So, I'm sorry, Daddy, but your health is more important than your wants.

I pop open the box of cereal and pour the honey flakes into a white ceramic bowl, pretending not to show how difficult it is for me to deny him his favorite beverage. "It tastes identical to your old favorite blend from Norma's Cafe."

"I survived on coffee for fifty years. I can tell a light roast from a dark. A blonde roast from a french roast. It doesn't taste anything like it should." He pushes the cup aside. "Maybe I should just switch to tea."

"Drama king," I giggle.

He ignores my remark and changes subjects. "You got in late last night. Was it a date? Any young men I need to give 'the talk' to?"

I almost drop the milk. "Daaaaaaaaaaaaaad."

"What?" He schools his face, so his features remain neutral.

"I wasn't on a date, and I don't have any plans to enter the dating scene. I had to work late."

He pops a piece of bread into the toaster, clearly not believing a word I say. "Uh-huh."

"It's true. My boss had some paperwork he needed help with. I offered to stay and help out. That's it." I pour myself some of the supposedly nasty decaf and take a sip. "I can't taste any difference."

"Mr. Blanks?"

"Please don't call him that." I grimace, remembering how I could hardly keep from laughing when Charlie mentioned the phrase "fill in the blanks." If that continues, it's going to cause trouble.

Speaking of Charlie, I hope he managed to get some decent sleep after last night. I wonder what he's up to right now.

Looking over to Dad, I see he's giving me an "I know you're hiding something from me" look. I push all thoughts of Charlie aside. "I'm being serious. Dad, there is nothing going on when I'm not home. Quit looking at me like that."

"Like what?"

"You know what." I blow out air. "This is too much before I've had my second cup of coffee."

The toast pops up in the toaster. He places it on his plate. "Your cereal is going to get soggy if it sits there much longer." Opening the butter container, he dips a knife in and spreads it over the bread. "Have I told you that Gemma sent me a few links to that dating show you two young ladies are obsessed with, *Cupid's Fate*?"

"You mean *Cupid's Arrow*?" Is that what he was so wrapped up in last night? He was still awake when I got home.

Which is weird for a man who's usually snoring his head off by eight.

Cupid's Arrow is a reality television show Gemma discovered and introduced me to last year. It revolves around a bachelorette who's been unlucky in love, her two best friends, and twelve guys living in a mansion.

Unlike other shows, the bachelorette doesn't control her fate—her friends do. Every week, they set up a series of dates with the guys and ultimately decide who goes home. As cheesy as it sounds, it's addicting. The besties have access to all the cameras in the house. Nothing escapes their notice.

"That's the one." Dad bobs his head up and down. "I watched the first two episodes last night. What I don't understand is why Selena and Mackenzie opted to send TJ home. It should've been Mike. He seems more like the type of young man Yvonne might like. Gemma agrees with me."

I chew a bit of my cereal slowly. This is what my life has come to. Dad watching a dating show and texting my best friend about it. Things have changed so much in the last few months. He's no longer interested in attending book clubs, going out for a long walk or swim, or even running errands. He used to be so much more independent. But now, all he wants to do is stay home. I really need to find him some new hobbies.

Choosing not to comment on the TV show, I move on to a new topic. "Dad, I'm going to go grocery shopping, then skate in the public session. I'll probably be home around two-thirty. Is there anything you need while I'm out?"

"Nope. I've got everything I need here."

"What are your plans for today?"

"I'm gonna binge *Cupid's Arrow*. Maybe we can discuss it when you get home."

My eyebrows twitch and my face tightens. Today is going to be a very, very long day.

"Great."

On the way out to the parking lot, I text Gemma.

Frankie: You really had to get my dad hooked on our show? Gah. He's going to be so annoying until he catches up to where we arc.

Gemma: You're welcome. I never thought he'd get into it, but he's sent me some hilarious texts. I have some screenshots I can send you. *Smiling emoji*

Frankie: You're awake! And no thanks. Whatever you and my dad talked about can stay between you two.

Gemma: It's not anything earth-shattering. Going to bed soon, I promise. And the texts are mostly harmless.

Frankie: Mostly?

Gemma: Let's just say it makes me wonder how your dad has stayed single all these years.

Frankie: He was married once. It was years before he adopted me.

Gemma: Have you thought about having him try out senior dating? It's a thing. It might be nice for him to find somebody to spend some time with who's closer to his age.

I stare at my phone screen blankly. My immediate thought

is to completely dismiss Gemma's suggestion. Dad is fine on his own. He has been for the twenty-seven years we've been together. But what if I'm wrong? What if I've been blind all these years and he has been lonely? Senior dating could be the perfect opportunity for Dad to leave the house for a few hours, and maybe even make some new friends.

Frankie: I'll run it by him later.

Gemma: If it would be easier for you, I'll personally volunteer to help him set up his dating profile.

I snort.

Frankie: I feel like senior dating could make an amazing concept for a reality TV show.

Gemma: I'd watch it. *Winking emoji*

Frankie: Leaving for the rink now.

Gemma: Good luck with Mr. Blanks today.

Frankie: *Eye-rolling emoji*

Gemma: You know you love me.

I skate a couple laps around the rink to warm up, weaving in and out of the handful of recreational skaters here today. Making a game plan in my head, I decide to play with some jumps.

I change directions and step onto an outside edge. Making sure I'm far enough out of the way from everyone around me,

I swing my right leg up into the air, pull my arms in, and do an easy double Axel.

I land on a solid edge and hold it. A few of the skaters clap. Others stare openly. I give them a small nod of acknowledgment. Admittedly, I haven't worked on my jumps in a while. If I were to try something harder like a triple flip or triple Lutz, I'd probably fall flat on my face.

A twinge of sadness fills my body. I worked so hard to learn my triple jumps, but now, there's little point in practicing them. I'm retired. All I'd be doing is risking injury. For now, I'll just work on the jumps I know I can do on autopilot, like my double Axel, and maybe a triple toe loop.

Repeating my entry pattern for a second double Axel attempt, I set up again for the middle of the ice, pick up speed, and launch my body into the air. From the corner of my eye, I spot Charlie observing me. Butterflies flutter in my stomach, although I'm not sure why.

Just like the last jump, I hold the rotation for two and a half revolutions, and kick out for another decent landing. As I approach the boards, I see Charlie has moved and is now standing at the door to the ice. With a frown, he points at me, signaling that I should meet him there. I *thought* my jump was pretty good. Does he see something I don't?

My body deflates as I skate over to him, feeling like a naughty child caught doing something wrong. After last night, I'd thought we'd started to find some common ground and had moved past the point of him being testy with me. I've changed my entire schedule around to coincide with the public session where there are plenty of people around to "supervise" me.

I let two kids cross in front of me, then exit the ice. "Hi, Charlie," I say in a neutral tone.

His hands go to his hips. "What do you think you're doing?"

My face falls. The grump has returned. So much for any progress we've made. "Skating?"

"A public session is *not* for doing big jumps like double Axels. There are too many safety hazards and liabilities out there. What if a kid darts in front of you when you're taking off for a jump and you don't see them or can't stop in time?"

I tilt my head back and stare at the ceiling for a split second, supremely frustrated. "What do you want me to do? Skate before public or during? I've tried both options, and apparently neither works for you." I lock eyes with him. "Help me out a little. What should I be doing?"

"Skate in the morning freestyle session," he states matter-of-factly.

He makes the solution sound so simple. "I thought you didn't want anyone but your students in those sessions."

"I changed my mind." He relaxes. "It's the quietest time of day and the ice will be freshly cut. I cap the number of skaters on the morning ice at twelve. Unlike the public session, *my* students are all experienced and trained to give the jumping skater or the skater running a program the right of way."

I guess I could skate before Dad wakes up. It just means going back to early mornings like when I was a kid and no more sleeping in. "What time would I be able to stop by?"

"Anytime between four and eight," he offers.

I nod slowly. "What's the catch?"

"No catch." He fidgets.

"In that case, I'll be here around six."

"Great." He lifts his chin and gestures to the ice. "You have textbook technique. Who was your coach?"

"Thank you." I smile brightly. "John Franks."

"You skated with Mr. Franks?"

"I did, for fourteen years."

He lets out a long whistle and leans casually against the door frame. "And you were a show skater too, weren't you?"

Heat sears my cheeks. He should know this. Didn't he read my resume? Maybe not. Jack's the one who hired me. "Mm-hmm, with Dreams on Ice."

"Do you have any experience doing pairs?"

That answers my question. He definitely doesn't know my past history. But he's making an effort, so I guess that counts for something. At least the grump has been tamed and sent back to whatever cave he crawled out of. "I did. Through the junior level."

"Interesting." He strokes his jaw. Before I can ask just what he means by that, he snaps his fingers. "Oh, before I forget, breakfast, lunch, and dinner this entire week are being catered by Millie's Steakhouse. You might want to take something home for you and your father. There's plenty of food to go around."

"Thanks, I will."

"See you Friday morning." He turns and makes his leave.

I can't believe he took my suggestion, and the meals are being prepared by a steakhouse. That won't come cheap. I shake my head in disbelief. Dad will be one happy camper when I come home with a takeaway container of meat. It's nice of Charlie to think of him.

Gathering my belongings, I head for the pros' room, where I can smell the food and hear the excited chatter of the coaches. My lips curve up in a smile.

<h1 style="text-align:center">Chapter Seven</h1>

I shouldn't be nervous. It's just another freestyle session. I arrive at the rink at six on Friday morning. Watching skaters through the glass windows of the lobby, I recognize Charlie and the two coaches from the afternoon session where I worked with Richelle.

All three coaches are bundled up in multiple layers for warmth. Metal thermoses, likely filled with coffee, are balanced on the edge of the boards between the water bottles and boxes of tissues belonging to the students.

This morning session has eight skaters on the ice. When I join the group and stroke around the perimeter, I wave to my fellow coaches, who greet me right back. Zipping up my puffer vest, I rub my forearms and pick up some speed, willing some warmth to return to my body. One of the worst things about skating in the mornings is not being able to feel my toes when I'm this cold. I woke up late and didn't have time to warm up.

Finding a patch of space in the center, I take a deep left outside edge entry and set up for a layback spin. It was one of my favorite moves when I performed as Belle. I put in a lot of effort to get the turnout of my leg and arch of my back just right. Since I was never a singles skater, it was something I had to learn as an adult. And let me tell you, learning to look at the ceiling as you spin is much scarier than being lifted ten feet up into the air.

About halfway through the skate, as I'm grabbing a drink of water, Charlie hollers at me, "Hey, Coach Frankie, can I borrow you for a moment?"

I screw the top of my bottle back on and glide in his direction. A young teenage pairs team looks on with wide eyes. The girl has silky strawberry blond hair and appears to be about fourteen years old. The boy is much taller, with curly jet-black locks. I'm guessing he's about seventeen.

"Kaylee, Steve, this is Coach Frankie. Please say hello."

They greet me softly.

"Coach Frankie was a junior-level pairs skater," he tells them, then turns to me. "We're working on learning some new elements, but they're having a hard time understanding the takeoff and catch of a split double-twist. They've mastered it off the ice, but on the ice is where they're struggling. We were wondering if you wouldn't mind watching them and seeing if you could offer a few words of advice on the skill."

"Of course. Split twists are super tricky. I remember it being one of the hardest elements to learn. Nothing can really prepare you for it. What entry are you guys using?"

"We're doing a Lutz entry," Kaylee responds.

"Okay, great. Let's see it, then."

"You heard her, you two—go on, show her your best attempt." Charlie's voice is light and encouraging.

The duo nods and takes off from the boards.

"Thanks for doing this." Charlie's eyes track his charges. "You were great with Richelle. I hoped if I asked you again, you might be able to give Kaylee and Steve some helpful advice. You'll see what I mean in a minute."

"Of course," I sputter, slightly stunned by his compliment. That's the second one this week.

Kaylee and Steve perform their footwork into the skill. She turns backward and he places his hands on her hips. Tapping her right skate into the ice, Kaylee pushes off her toe pick just as Steve vaults her into the air. She crosses her legs, rotates twice, and comes down for the landing. Up until this point, it looks good, but as soon as Kaylee heads back down to the ground, both skaters tense, anticipating the landing.

"The technique is all there. I'm guessing it's just a trust issue on that landing you wanted me to see?"

"You've got it," Charlie says with approval. My body grows warm. "They've heard me tell them a thousand times to relax, but it never sinks in." He inclines his head. "I've tried every training trick I know of—trust exercises, visualization drills, journaling, and the harness. I don't know what else to do."

Kaylee and Steve return to where we're standing, cheeks rosy, catching their breaths.

"Sorry, Mr. C, that wasn't our best. We know we can do it better," Steve apologizes.

"I know you can."

I puff out my cheeks. What can I say? Trust is one of the most important things in pairs skating. Without it, a team won't get very far. "Kaylee, once you finish your rotation position, what's freaking you out?"

"I don't know." Her shoulders sag. "Mr. C has told us if I clear my mind and let my muscle memory take over, we'd be able to do this skill. I just can't seem to let go of the memory of the last time I fell. I hurt my shoulder and was off the ice for six weeks."

Bingo. There it is. She has a fear of falling. Every time she goes up, she overthinks what she's doing.

Steve rubs the back of his neck. "It's not just you, K. I know it's my fault too. My timing isn't consistent when I'm trying to catch you."

What Kaylee needs is a distraction. That way, she won't have to think. She'll have to just react. "Show me your arm position again." Kaylee crosses her wrists and brings them into her chest, as she might for a jump. "What would happen if you tried rotating with your arms over your head?"

"I don't know?" She fidgets. "I've always done split twists with my arms pulled in."

"What do you say we give it a try off-ice, K? We could go to the gym and play around. I promise I won't let anything happen to you," Steve says.

"We can also put you in the harness to try a few single twists if you'd like," Charlie adds.

The men have solid intentions, but that won't work. As the one being tossed into the air, Kaylee, like Richelle, needs to see the skill being done before she'll agree to try it. Especially since trust is the issue. My pulse begins to increase. This might be taking a bold risk, but what I'm about to suggest needs to be done if Charlie wants these kids to move past the mental block. "What if Mr. C and I were to show you how it's done? Would you try one then?"

"I haven't done any pairs elements since I, um, retired." Charlie's face pales. "I don't know if I remember how."

I play Ms. Confident, although hearing him say that has just freaked me out even more. "I think we can manage a simple single split twist. That *was* one of your signature skills back when you competed, if I remember correctly. If it'll make you feel better, we can use the harness."

"Please, Mr. C," Steve pleads. "Every time we ask you to show us something, you always say no."

Several unreadable emotions pass over his face. Finally, he

says, "Only a single. And only once." He swallows hard. "The harness won't work for us. Neither of the other coaches here has ever tried using it with a pairs element. And I don't think now is the best time for them to try experimenting."

"No, definitely not."

He removes his jacket. "I need a minute." He sits down on the bench in the hockey box, rolls up his pant legs, and tightens the laces on his skating boots.

I know I shouldn't have put him on the spot like that, but this *is* the best way. It's the ultimate test. If Charlie's students can see that I can trust him to toss me up and safely catch me after never having skated with him, they'll see they can do it too.

Kaylee and Steve clap their hands together gleefully and start chanting, "Mr. C. Mr. C. Mr. C."

The other skaters and coaches turn their heads to see what the commotion is about. As Charlie steps onto the ice, he slowly peels off two more layers of clothing. Soon, he's down to a long-sleeved compression shirt.

As I strip my own vest and jacket, I can't help but admire how in-shape Charlie still looks. The grump hasn't let himself go. He still resembles the man in the ads in my secret scrapbook. I quickly turn my head away, hoping he doesn't notice.

All action on the rink ceases. Skaters and coaches huddle together, watching the scene unfold with amusement.

Charlie's face is still ghostly white. He takes several deep breaths. I start to second guess myself. This was a bad idea. Why was I dumb enough to even suggest it? He's clearly not in the right frame of mind to do this. "Let's forget it."

"No." He straightens his posture. "I can do this. I need us to walk through this first."

I turn my back to him. Tentatively, he places his hands on my hips. A jolt of electricity surges through my body. It's been so long since I've skated with a partner. We slowly glide backward. Feeling his arms and knees bend, I relax my body and let him do all the work, lifting me up and down as if I'm a feather floating in a gentle breeze. He may not have done much in five years, but his body still remembers what to do.

We face one another again. "I've only ever done a split twist with my old partner. How was my touch and pressure to you?" Charlie removes his beanie and scratches his head. I've started to notice that it's a nervous habit of his.

"It was perfect." I grin. The teenage me would be giddy that I'm about to skate with *the* Charlie Welch. I would've given anything. But the adult me is on edge. I take a deep breath, pouring yet more confidence into my words. "You're in luck. I used to perform a split double twist with different partners daily at Dreams on Ice. As long as you push me up into the air and promise not to drop me, I can do the rest. I have the experience to get us through this."

"That's good because we're going to need all that experience," he says seriously. "We'll take a lap around the ice forward, then change to a slow set of back crossovers for a second lap. When you're comfortable, give me the word. We'll cut across the center and set for a long entry edge into the skill."

"Got it."

Adrenaline pumping through my body, I take the lead. Charlie matches my speed as we skate side by side. When we reach the corner, his hands lock on to mine. His grip is firm. Despite the reservations he voiced a few moments earlier, there's no trace of any uncertainty in his hold.

"Change," I direct.

Our bodies glide backward. I grip his wrist. The only sound in the arena is our blades pushing against the ice. The world slowly blurs as we pick up speed. I extend my left leg. The electric energy from a few moments ago is still there. It's energizing me. I've never felt more certain about a first-time partnership.

"Change," I command. We both move into position, his hands on my hips. "On my count. Three, two, one, go."

My knees bend. I tap my foot into the ice, and Charlie pushes me up and overhead. I have good height. I feel like I could float up here for ages. Holding my arms over my head, I rotate once. My body wants to continue spinning, but I fight it and hold tightly for the landing. As Charlie's hands wrap around my waist and assist me back onto the ice, he lets out a deep sigh.

We come to a stop and stare into one another's eyes for several moments. His are a lovely shade of green. They're filled with the same excited energy coursing through my veins. That's when I know he felt the same jolt I did.

The coaches and skaters catcall and clap. We step apart and head back toward Charlie's students.

"Not bad . . . for a retired guy," I tease.

"That *was* pretty good. The only bad thing is that my arms are going to pay for it later." He shakes them out. "I'm so much weaker than I was back in the day."

My eyes linger on his biceps. I find that a little hard to believe. He might be a little weaker than his competitive days, but he's still much stronger than the average person.

Kaylee and Steve stare at us with wide eyes.

"That was so graceful," she says. "I love the look of the arms overhead. And you really haven't done that since you stopped skating, Mr. C?"

"No. I wouldn't lie to you." Charlie reaches for his jacket.

"Can we try a single twist on the harness now?"

He glances at Steve. "How does that sound to you?"

The teenager has a glint of determination in his eyes. "Let's rock it."

"Coach Frankie, will you stay and watch us a little longer?" Kaylee asks hopefully.

"Guys, Frankie—Coach Frankie is here to skate, not be put to work."

"It's okay." I reach for my jacket. "I'd love to stay and watch. Pairs is my thing."

"Thank you!" Kaylee wraps her arms around me.

Charlie chuckles. "I'll go release the harness."

He skates off, more relaxed than I've ever seen him. I swallow hard and brush my fingers over my wrist where we held hands a few moments ago. It's still warm to the touch.

"Here we go," Charlie says, coming back toward us.

I quickly drop my hands and shove my vest on, busying myself with fastening the zipper. Why did I just do that? It's not like I have a crush or anything on the man. I did as a teen, but not anymore. He's my boss. And let's not forget the grump. He's off-limits.

Later that morning, I meet Leslie in the neighboring town of Lake Wakahanra, located between Sequoia Valley and Grizzly Springs.

I pull my car into the spot next to her sunshine-yellow VW bug just as she climbs out, excited to have a girls' day. "You made good time," she says as I open my door. "My color artist said she could take us early if you've made a decision."

"I have." I click my car alarm button. "I'm not ready to commit to anything *too* dramatic, but I'm willing to try having the ends of my hair colored."

Leslie slaps me on the back. "Once you see how fun it is to have colored hair, you'll never go back."

As we enter the salon, I'm immediately struck by the cool

vibe of the place. The furniture is all sleek black leather. Each station has a circular mirror and funky light fixture hanging above it. In the middle of the salon is a large planter box with tall succulents that look to be part of the aloe vera family.

My gaze continues to sweep the room. Three of the walls are white, but the back wall, made up of exposed brick, has an illuminated neon sign that reads "The Mane Event." The logo is a male lion in a red boxing robe, with a silky mane and crown. Classic eighties music is playing.

"Frankie, this is Alyssa. Lys, Frankie." I shake hands with a curvy woman with seafoam-turquoise hair, ruby-red glasses, and oversized gold hoop earrings. There's a tattoo of the salon's logo on her forearm. "Lys is the best in the business and the only person I'll ever trust to touch my hair."

Alyssa laughs and sets us up in two chairs adjacent to one another, offering us sparkling water and chocolate-covered strawberries.

"These are the best!" Leslie immediately reaches for one. "Lys's husband grows them himself. I don't know what he does to them, but they're the sweetest things ever."

Alyssa wraps a smock around my neck. "It's not a state secret. My hubby is just obsessive about checking the pH of the soil, the temperature, the humidity levels, and whatever else might affect their growing conditions in his greenhouse. It drives me insane, but that's what I get for being married to a plant biologist."

Leslie nods. "He's a professor at Fresno State."

"Ah." I pull my hands from under the smock and reach for a chocolate-covered strawberry. The chocolate is dark, rich, and creamy, and melts the moment it touches my tongue. I groan. "I need a basket of these."

"I'll pack one up for you before you leave." Alyssa pivots my chair, so it faces the mirror. She distributes my shoulder-length copper-colored hair evenly on both sides of my shoulders. "What would you like to have done today?"

That's the question of the day. I've been going back and forth on this since Leslie suggested today's adventure. It's time I pushed myself to try something new. "I've never dyed my hair before. So I'd like to start with something simple. Maybe purple and teal streaks?"

Alyssa studies the ends of my hair. "If I were you, I'd start with just one color. We could lighten your lovely hair one shade and have the very ends be a subtle violet. If you like it, in a few weeks we could add some more color to it."

That's much more in my comfort zone and still counts as a change. I let out a deep breath. "I'd love that."

Alyssa walks over to Leslie. "What about you?"

Leslie grins. "Since spring's coming up . . ."

"Which means you want an extreme makeover." Alyssa chuckles. "I'm afraid to ask. What's your latest and greatest idea?"

"I'd like you to chop off my hair so it's Twiggy short. Let's do a tangerine orange with some daffodil-yellow highlights."

"You can't do subtle, can you?"

"Subtle is boring." Leslie bites into another strawberry.

As Alyssa sets to work washing my hair, I chat with Leslie about the time I've spent with her brother over the last few days. She's no replacement for Gemma, but it's nice to be able to get out and away from my apartment and the rink. We're on our way to becoming fast friends.

"I cringed the entire time I was in Charlie's office. It stresses me out having a sink full of dirty dishes. I'll never understand how people can let their stuff pile up like that."

"Charlie has a one-track mind. Once he starts something, if he gets interrupted, it's game over. He'll just move on to something else."

"He could write things down. Maybe even keep a to-do list."

Leslie shakes her head. "It wouldn't help. He's dyslexic."

"He is?"

Things suddenly make much more sense. If he's dyslexic, that must be why he kept squinting at the computer and giving himself a headache on Monday night. And why he's always behind on his paperwork. "He could've saved us both a lot of time if he'd just said something about it from the start. It's not like it's that big a deal. All sorts of people have to work through learning disabilities."

"My brother is too proud to ask for help most of the time. I have to force his hand to let me step in when I know he's in over his head." Leslie frowns. "We've talked about delegating, but it's in one ear and out the other. Uncle Jack says to let him be, but it really makes more work for both of us."

More surprises. "Back up. Jack . . . is your uncle?" I sputter.

"Yup. Our mom's brother and the financial backer of the rink," Leslie says.

"I would've thought your parents would want to run the rink."

"It's not their style. Mom and Dad don't like to be settled in one place for too long. They made their fortune in real estate and took an early retirement to travel the world. My brother and I had other ideas. It's always been my dream to run our own rink."

Alyssa massages my head. I relax and close my eyes, processing all the information. "Hearing that makes me so happy. Few people are ever lucky enough to have their dreams come true." Like me.

"Yes and no. It's not all it's cracked up to be. There's a saying that you should never go into business with your friends and family for a reason." Leslie's voice is flat and emotionless. "Working with my brother and my uncle as business partners has been stressful, and it's strained our relationship."

"Basically, Leslie's uncle is a blockhead," Alyssa grumbles. "He named Charlie the skating director over her because he has an established name in the skating world. Supposedly, putting a recognizable face on the rink's marketing materials is the key to bringing in business."

I open my eyes and wrinkle my nose. "That's not true. When I was training in L.A., there was hardly anyone outside of the students who knew who the top skaters were. How did your uncle expect the public to know who Charlie is? If he'd won a gold medal at the Olympics, I can see the marketing having some measure of success, but without it, he's a no-name."

It hurts me to have to be so blunt about Charlie, but it's the truth. He *is* a nobody to younger skaters and the general population. Even me, a pairs skater and a girl who had a crush on him, had forgotten who he was until I started working here.

"Exactly. Around here, people don't care about having a big name. It's about having good facilities and skating classes that are affordable. Everyone who wants to learn to skate or play hockey should have a means to."

"The skating school is also what pays their bills," Alyssa adds.

Hearing Leslie's passion makes me proud to play a small part in helping to fulfill her vision. She's brilliant with the skating school. She'd make an ideal director. "Why did Charlie even take the role in the first place? Do he and your uncle know how you feel?"

"Charlie's never liked confrontation. And he's always been scared of Jack. He does whatever our uncle asks." Leslie draws small circles on her thigh. "I've tried to tell Jack that I want

Charlie's job, but he just brushes me off. He thinks my brother is doing fine."

"Leslie is afraid to antagonize him. He's the majority owner and holds the purse strings to the rink. She needs a bigger budget to expand the hockey program," Alyssa says.

"And Charlie?"

"As much as I complain about him, I'd never want to force him out of the role. He's had enough things taken from him."

Alyssa repositions my chair and gently combs my hair, prepping it for a trim. "Les, you almost single-handedly run the rink," she says. "You do so many things that aren't officially part of your job description. I wish you'd talk to Charlie. He might surprise you."

"I can't." She shakes her head vehemently. "At least not now. This weekend is five years since the accident. I'm on standby to make sure he doesn't do anything stupid. I know he's not sleeping well. The last thing he needs is extra stress."

I inhale sharply. "I'm guessing you don't know the rink is hosting skating tests this weekend?"

Leslie bolts upright. "What?"

"All that paperwork I helped Charlie sort out was test applications. He misread his calendar."

"Of all the possible weekends for a test, it had to be this one? His stress levels are going to go through the roof between all the crazy parents, judges, and kids." Leslie face-palms. "Charlie, Charlie, Charlie. You're going to be the death of me."

She holds her face in her hands for several seconds, then takes a deep breath. "Frankie, I feel horrible asking you this, but do you mind if I have you come in early Saturday to help out? I'd do it myself, but I don't have anyone to cover my classes."

"You can count me in."

I should've known the day I met Leslie that she would

keep my life from being boring. She's definitely one of the most outgoing and outspoken people I've ever met. Just what does she have in mind for me? Is it working with her brother?

The thought of being his assistant for the day causes a few goosebumps to form on my arms, and I can't help but smile to myself. Skating together this morning ignited something within me that's long been dormant. Was it a fluke? Or is there a chance I *still* have a crush on the man? There's only one way to find out.

Chapter Eight

Leslie and I arrive at the rink an hour and a half before the first classes on Saturday morning.

"Oh good, there's already a table set up here." She runs a finger over its surface. "It needs a good scrub though. It's still sticky from the last birthday party."

"I'll run and get some cleaning supplies." I set the box of breakfast items down. "Anything else you need?"

"If you could also grab a tablecloth from the back too," Leslie shouts.

"On it." I start to walk backward, and collide with a solid wall of muscle. Two arms steady me with a light touch. A touch my body remembers all to keenly. I tilt my head back. It's Charlie. He's dressed in business-professional clothing today. A white button-up shirt and fitted black trousers. "Um . . . hi."

His eyes met mine. "Hi." He helps me regain my balance and gently pushes my head into a neutral position. "I know I'm good-looking, but try not to strain your neck."

I laugh nervously, trying to play off my misstep. Leslie said he'd be stressed today, but he's able to crack a joke first thing. That's a good sign.

"You two are here early," he says.

"We're here to set up for the test session." Leslie shrugs.

"I've got it covered," he says firmly. He releases me and looks over my head to his sister. "The forms are in the judging area with pens and clipboards. I'm just waiting for them to arrive."

Leslie rolls her eyes. "Have you set up their hospitality room with food and snacks? What about the parents' hospitality room? The table for check-ins?"

Charlie's brows knit together. "It may have slipped my mind."

Leslie blinks slowly. "Bro, go and collect five of the best-looking clipboards the rink owns, the waivers you and Frankie printed out, pens, and a cup to put them in. I'll take care of putting out the coffee and breakfast pastries we picked up. It's ten to seven. The judges could start arriving at any time."

His gaze darts from Leslie to me and back to his sister.

"Chop-chop." She claps her hands together. "We can talk later."

"Thanks for being here," he says quietly to me.

"You're welcome." I shoot him a coy smile.

One he half returns. Yes, I won't mind being around Charlie at all today.

A short while later, I bemoan ever volunteering to scrub the check-in table. "Ugh . . . why isn't chewing gum banned from the rink?" I cringe and use a scraper to remove another leftover gift from one of the birthday parties.

"It is banned. But trust me, it's better you find it there than have it stuck to your skate," Leslie says, passing through the lobby to pick up the extra plates and cups from Norma's Cafe.

"True." I wipe the back of my hand against my forehead. "At least this is the last of it."

"Do you need me to pull any more chairs?" Charlie inquires.

"No, bro. I think we're good." Leslie slides a navy vinyl tablecloth over the table and places the check-in supplies just as the first sleepy-eyed judge enters the lobby area. "Vera, good morning."

She nods in response to Leslie's welcome. "Good morning, Miss Welch. How are you doing?"

"Good. Thanks for asking. Let me show you where your home base is going to be for the day. We have you set up in party room number two."

"Is there coffee?" Vera asks.

"Of course. We have a full spread for you this morning."

"That's one reason I always say yes to working here. You and Mr. Welch know how to treat us judges right."

Right behind her, two nervous kids and their parents approach the table. Charlie perks up and greets them with a smile—the first one I've seen. My pulse picks up a few beats. "Jake, Emily. Are you excited?" he asks. "It's your big day. You're going to do so well."

"Answer your coach, Jake," his mom says.

"Yes, Mr. C."

"You too, Emily," the second mother adds.

The girl, who appears to be about seven years old, squeezes her mom's hand and nods.

"I think we have some club jackets for you two as well." I elbow Charlie. "Leslie said they're in her office, next to the doorway."

"Oh, um, right. Be right back." He stands and jogs over to his sister's office.

"Our club jackets are here?" Emily says.

I smile widely. "Yes, they are, and it even has your name on it."

She tugs on her mother's sleeve. "Mommy, can I wear it to school on Monday? I want all my friends to see it."

"We'll see. It might be too warm."

"But Mommy . . ."

Charlie returns with the boxes. Setting them down on the ground, he kneels next to it. Discreetly, I watch him go cross-eyed as he stares at the names on the order forms. But somehow, he manages to pull out the right jackets for the two youngsters. "Here we are." The children's eyes dance. "Emily, you have a youth small, and Jake, a youth medium?"

I hold my breath, ready to step in if needed. Both parents nod. They all grin like Cheshire cats. Phew. He's chosen correctly.

Emily rips off her school sweater. "Mommy, I have to wear this right now."

"Me too. If Emily is going to wear hers, I want mine too," Jake says.

"Let's step off to the side. We have others waiting to check in," Jake's mom says. Jake and Emily are shepherded out of the way, and we help the next set of parents and kids.

Over the next few hours, Leslie pops in and out of the lobby between classes, keeping an eagle eye on the hospitality rooms, while I take charge of check-ins and retrieving the feedback forms from the judges.

Charlie, in my opinion, is given the toughest tasks. He has to ensure that the students make it onto the ice at the correct times and is also responsible for letting the kids know whether they've passed or failed.

Emotions run high, and by late afternoon, all three of us

are exhausted. The lobby is nearly empty. A few students from the adult class linger, chatting about their plans for the week. There's no public session scheduled for the day.

"That was it. We're done!" I say gleefully. "All that's left for us to do now is log the results."

"Let's do it later. I'm drained." Charlie rubs his temples and sags against the wall. "I still don't understand why Kaylee failed her test. It crushed me to have to tell her she missed passing by one point. Maybe I should go talk to the judges and see if they could make a one-time exception for her."

Having worked with Kaylee the morning before, I agree with him. It was painful to see the teenager so upset. I place a hand on his elbow. "I know you mean well, but that won't do any good."

"How do you know?" he snaps.

I back up a few steps and hold up my hands. All morning, he's done well to hold his temper in check. It doesn't surprise me to see it flare now. Unlike previous encounters with it though, I'm prepared. I use my coaching voice. "From past experience, I think the judges won't change their marks. Kaylee *was* super prepared, but sometimes there are other factors, like nerves, at play. Skaters can't be on all the time."

"Vera is friends with Kaylee's grandmother . . ."

"I know where your brain is going with this. Don't ask for any favors," I shoot back. "You'll just end up hurting her chances more than helping her."

For several heartbeats, he breaths. The copy of Kaylee's test crinkles in his hands as different emotions play out over his face. "I guess you're right. This is the hardest part about being a coach. I want the best for my students. I want them all to be happy."

Crisis averted. I'm impressed by how quickly he checked himself. "I know you do. You're doing a great job. I wish I'd had a coach who would fight for me like you back when I was competing." I start folding up the vinyl tablecloth. What can I say that's a positive? "Overall, you should be really proud. All your kids did well. Congrats."

His shoulders hunch. "It doesn't feel right to celebrate unless everyone passed."

He's taking it too hard. That's when I remember—virtual testing is an option! "When is Kaylee's next lesson with you?"

"Monday morning," he murmurs.

"Why don't you guys use the time to film and submit a virtual test?"

He leans against the table, and it scoots a few inches to the side. His cheeks pink as he recovers his balance. "That's an option?"

"Yeah. It's new for this year. I was looking at the ASU website. The only downside is it might take a couple extra days to hear back, and you don't know which judges are going to view it."

"That won't matter. She's ready."

"What time is her lesson?"

"Six-thirty."

I nod. "I'll make sure I'm here, and I'll even volunteer to be the proctor."

He cocks his head to the side. "You would do that for her?"

"Not just for her, for the both of you. I can see how important this is to you."

Charlie wraps his arms around me. As our bodies touch, an electric spark similar to yesterday's shoots through me. My body is supercharged and anxious for more. I never thought I'd say this, but I don't want him to let go. He smells so good, like a campfire in the woods first thing in the morning. But like all good things, nothing can last forever.

"Thank you." He releases me and sets off in a quick walk down the hall. "I have to call her parents and let her know."

I move a stray piece of hair behind my ear and wave, still in a daze.

"Did my bro just hug you?" Leslie says with disbelief.

I nod.

"Who would've thought you'd be the one to crack the code on him. You have the magic touch, Frankie. I haven't seen him this excited in a long time. When he gets back, tell him I volunteered to stay and close up. You guys can get going."

I find my voice. "You could tell him yourself." It comes out scratchy.

"And ruin the good mood he's in? No. He's still cross with me and doesn't want to talk more than he has to. You be the hero." Leslie's eyes glaze over for a moment. "Actually, I have another favor to ask you."

"What's on your mind?"

"Would you mind taking Charlie out to dinner? He needs a night out. Millie's Steakhouse, the place that catered for us, is his favorite."

I pivot slowly, not believing I heard her correctly. "You want me to go on a date with your brother?"

"Not a date. Think of it more like babysitting or taking care of a puppy. He needs to be socialized." Leslie sighs. "In all seriousness, I'd like to see him have a night out where he forgets himself. I don't know how you managed it so quickly, but you're the first person in a long time he's bothered to open up to. He needs you as a friend more than you know."

Without a second thought, I agree.

Chapter Nine

"What did Leslie bribe you with to get you to have dinner with me?" Charlie asks as he pulls into the parking lot of Millie's Steakhouse. He turns the ignition off and glances at me.

I raise an eyebrow. "You really think your sister would resort to bribery?"

"Yes. I know exactly how her mind works. It's a twin thing."

It's hard to tell if he's being serious or sarcastic.

"She didn't bribe me." I unbuckle my seat belt and open the car door. "I came willingly. As a friend."

Charlie slides out of his own side. "So she guilted you into it?"

"Is it so difficult for you to think that I might *want* to have dinner with you?"

"Yes." He nods. "Few people can handle me."

"If you must know," I huff, "Leslie called it babysitting, but that isn't at all how I see dinner tonight."

"How *do* you see it?"

We close the doors, and he clicks the alarm to his truck.

We carpooled from the rink to Millie's since I wasn't one hundred percent sure where I was going. I know Grizzly Springs well, but I haven't spent enough time in Sequoia Valley to know where all the newer restaurants and shops are. It just goes to show that I need to spend more time venturing outside of my bubble.

"I spend all my time with my father or at the rink. I'm there so much that at some point, the staff is gonna become my second family. So I see tonight as the perfect way to melt some of the ice between us," I answer truthfully.

"Okay. That I can get on board with."

So far tonight, Charlie has been more talkative and at ease around me. Skating and coaching together has caused our relationship to shift. I no longer have the urge to avoid him or hide. In fact, it's the complete opposite. I truly want to be around him and get to know him better. All the signs are telling me that we're on the path to becoming friends.

We walk up a pathway lined by a string of tea-light lanterns to the historic wooden cabin that houses Millie's. They shimmer like golden fireflies dancing against the backdrop of the evening. The air is thick with the scent of cooking meat.

"I hope we can get a table. I knew they'd be busy since it's the weekend, but not this busy," I say, eyeing the crowded dining room through the window.

"I'm on good terms with the manager. If it's going to be a long wait, I'll use my VIP status to bump us up on the list. He'd do it for me."

"How often do you come here?"

"At least once a week. I enjoy the vibe."

Charlie holds the door open for me, and we step inside. A roaring fire burns in a glass fireplace behind the hostess' podium. Soft piano music plays in the background.

"Welcome back, Charlie. How are you and your friend doing tonight?"

"Great, thanks for asking. I'd like a table for two," he says.

"Sure thing. Anything for you!"

Charlie puffs out his chest as the hostess taps her tablet. "It'll be about fifteen minutes before you're seated. This buzzer will go off when your table is ready."

"Thanks, we'll wait in the lounge," he says.

Walking deeper into the building, I count a total of five rooms. Each one has its own distinct animal theme and color.

"This structure dates back to the 1860s and is the original Sequoia Valley schoolhouse," Charlie says.

"It's large. I would've thought it might be one or two rooms max. That's how the buildings in Grizzly Springs are."

"Good eye. It *was* a one-room schoolhouse. There's a picture I'll show you on the way out. The owners had an extension built around it."

"Wow. I'd never be able to tell."

We sit across from one another in plush maroon chairs. Everything in here is art-deco themed, from the Tiffany-style lamps down to the soft blankets draped over the chair. My favorite feature is the gray stone fireplace, where a hearty fire is crackling away. Fast asleep in front of it is a chocolate-colored Great Dane.

"The atmosphere really does feel like we're sitting in a lodge in the middle of a forest." Looking out the window, all I can see is the darkened silhouette of pine trees.

"That's why I keep coming back here." Charlie grins. "Millie's is my escape from the outside world. I can come in here at any time of day, find a spot in the lounge, and pretend I've gone back in time to the 1920s. When life was simpler."

So Charlie enjoys the craftsman-style aesthetic. I don't blame him. It's cozy in here. I can see myself wandering in for lunch, curling up with a good book in the corner, and not wanting to leave. It's crowded tonight, but I wouldn't know it from being in this room.

I nod toward the Great Dane. "Who is that cutie over there?"

"That's Millie. The restaurant's mascot."

"Do you have any pets?"

"No. I don't have time for one, but someday, I'd like a dog." Millie's ears perk up, but she doesn't move from her warm bed. "What about you?"

"No pets. It's against my apartment's policy."

"And if it weren't?"

"I'd be happy with either a dog or cat. Growing up, I always wanted one of each, but my dad said I'd have to be the one to take care of it. Like you, I didn't have the time. I was always training. And as an adult, I was constantly on the road, living out of a suitcase."

"Maybe things will change now that you're here," Charlie muses.

"Maybe, but not until things settle down with my father."

We sit in silence for several moments.

"I should've asked, do you want anything from the bar?" Charlie scoots forward in his seat. "I'm driving, but don't let that stop you from having a drink if you want one."

"I don't normally drink, but I wouldn't mind a Shirley Temple." I reach for my wallet.

"Got it. Tonight is on Leslie. I'll have her expense it as a work dinner." He hops to his feet. "I'll be right back."

I relax into my seat and watch Charlie cross the room to the bar. His back is turned, giving me the opportunity to enjoy his form-fitting jeans and navy cable-knit sweater. His legs and backside are massive compared to his trim waist. I wonder how he's managed to find jeans that fit over his bubble butt. I can get away with wearing leggings most of the time, but men have it more difficult, especially as skaters.

He turns and catches me staring. I quickly look away to find that Millie has repositioned herself at my feet, her tail wagging and paws in front of me. She whines. I lean forward, scratching the dog's ears. Her fur is silky soft. Millie licks my hand. "I don't have any treats for you. Sorry, girl."

"Millie, you know better than to beg." Charlie chuckles. She sits up at hearing her name. "Your drink is on the side table." The dog lets out a second high-pitched whine. He crosses his arms. "Nope. If you want a treat, you'll have to go find your mama."

The dog huffs and slowly saunters back toward the fireplace.

"She definitely understands you."

"I speak dog fluently. It's one of my many gifts," he jokes.

How should I play this? I reach for my drink and take a long sip, letting the cherry flavor settle on my tongue. I mentioned to Charlie when we came in that this was going to be an icebreaker dinner, so he shouldn't mind a few personal questions. I'll just have to make sure they're generic. If he starts to pull back, at least there's always skating as a topic of conversion.

"So, um . . . when I was with Leslie yesterday, she said you guys have lived in the area for a couple of years. I never asked, but what drew you to it?" I take another sip my drink.

"Family?" He strokes his chin. "My grandmother doesn't live too far from here. I've always enjoyed the area whenever I visited her. When I retired from competitive skating and needed a place to lie low for a while, Nan invited me to stay with her. A few weeks in, I just knew this was the place for me."

"Gotcha. I thought you were going to say it was because of the rink. Leslie mentioned it was always her dream."

"No, that happened a little later. The day Leslie and I signed our apartment lease, if you want to get specific."

"Whoa." I cross one leg over the other. "Talk about ideal timing!"

"I know, it's almost like my sister planned the entire thing, but it was all luck." He chuckles. "We were taking a drive through town and Les discovered there was a rink for sale a five-minute drive away. Because of the amount of repair work it needed, the listing price was dirt cheap."

"I believe it. I skated at the old rink twenty years ago, and it was in rough shape even then. The roof used to leak, the air and heating systems didn't work, and half the time the compressors under the ice were broken. It closed when I was thirteen, and I think it must've sat vacant until you guys bought it."

"Yeah. When we did the initial walk-through with the property agent, it was bad. Really bad. We were at the point where we thought we might have to knock the whole building down and start from scratch. And that wasn't going to be possible with our budget. But as it turns out, the contractor we ended up using was able to work miracles. And because of that, with Leslie, me, and Jack pooling our resources together, we were able to buy it. A few years later, here we are."

"That's one heck of a story," I say.

"I wouldn't believe it myself if I hadn't lived through it. What about you? Why did you decide to move here?"

"I grew up here. I never thought I'd move back until my dad needed me." I stare at the floating pieces of ice in my glass. I can't bring myself to look Charlie in the eye.

"You mentioned the other night that it's just the two of you."

"Uh-huh. It is. Dad's lived in Grizzly Springs most of his civilian adult life."

"Was he in the military?"

I nod. "The navy."

The buzzer goes off. We stand and make our way back to

the reception area. The sound of many conversations fills the room. While the lounge felt like our own little world, the main area of the restaurant is like a big city. The hostess takes the device and places us at a table in a room themed after the red fox.

We order fried artichokes to split as our appetizer. Once we're alone again, we continue our conversation. "How have you been finding life as a retired figure skater?" Charlie asks.

I drum my fingers on the table as I consider his question. "At first, I was so occupied getting settled and moving that I didn't have time to think much about it. But now that I have more time on my hands, I miss my old life," I admit to him.

"I understand," he says softly. "When I was training, my day revolved around going to the gym, working on and off the ice with my coach, and physical therapy. When I retired, it was up to me to pick and choose what I'd do on any given day. It was like an out-of-body experience not having to be at a set place at a set time."

"Exactly. I'm the type of person who needs to stay busy. I love my father dearly, but I feel like I'm wasting time when I'm sitting around the apartment watching TV during the day. Thankfully, being able to practice and coach has helped me feel productive again."

"Are you coaching with us part-time or full-time?" Charlie places a napkin on his lap.

"Part-time. Jack didn't have any full-time positions open."

"Would you like more hours at the rink?" He pauses, locking eyes with mine. Under this lighting, his are the color of emeralds. "I know you're still new to coaching, but I'd like to invite you to help me with some of my students. You were great with Richelle, Kaylee, and Steve. They all keep asking about you. I have a few other kids I think you'd work well with."

My throat goes dry. I'll take any extra hours I can get in a heartbeat, but is he sure he wants me? "You do know I don't have any prior coaching experience? I've only been at it less than a month," I say carefully.

"I do, and I'm impressed by what I've seen. You're doing much better than I was when I started out," he emphasizes, still looking directly at me. "Remember, everybody has to start somewhere. We learn along the way as we gain experience. It's all about trial and error."

I hear what he's saying, but I'm still having a difficult time computing it in my brain. "You have the pedigree of being a world-class and international-level pairs skater. I don't. If we're looking at this realistically, how much do I have to offer your students? Not much."

"That's where you're wrong. You're selling yourself short. I looked at your resume again last night. You have more performance experience than anyone else on the staff, plus a natural coaching instinct."

My heart thumps against my ribs. Charlie is fired up, and it's one of the most attractive things I've seen from him.

"You also forgot to mention that you were a national medalist. One-half of one of the three best junior teams in the U.S. That's a *huge* accomplishment. How many people can lay claim to that?"

"Not many," I mutter, reaching for my water glass.

"Exactly. So don't tell me you aren't experienced." He chuckles. "Once Kaylee and Steve hear you were with Dreams on Ice, they'll never stop pestering you with questions. Being hired by the company is one of their long-term goals. Kaylee especially. That's the entire reason she switched from singles to pairs. She was inspired by one of the shows she saw."

My heart swells. Maybe it was one of the shows I performed in.

"I do have a question for you," Charlie says.

"Sure." I focus my attention back to him.

"Do you mind if I ask why you never moved up to the senior ranks?"

My mood shifts from happy to resentful. Charlie's hit on a sore spot. I rub the back of my neck and lower my chin. My voice grows quiet. "I never had the opportunity."

His eyes widen. "Why not?"

"My partner ended our partnership when I hit puberty. I lost my jumps, then I lost him."

Charlie frowns. "What blockhead were you skating with?"

"Danny McDonald."

"I vaguely remember that name. Was he the guy with a wonky double Axel and a triple toe he used to fall on at practically every competition?"

"That's him."

"And he dropped you?"

I nod. Thinking about him still leaves a bitter taste in my mouth. "I tried to find someone to replace him, but nothing ever worked out. You know how it is . . . There are way more female skaters out there than male skaters."

"I wish that weren't the case." He grimaces. "I'm sorry you had to go through that. For what it's worth, he was the weak link in your partnership, not you."

"Thanks." Hearing Charlie say that gives me a warm glow in my chest. Although I doubt he's ever seen a video of Danny and I skating. "It worked out okay in the end. Free from Danny, I turned pro and started my touring career."

Charlie strokes his jaw. "Answer me this—Given the chance, would you go back and skate competitively?"

"Definitely. I had so many goals that were left unfulfilled. The feeling of having unfinished business in the sport will always leave me wondering what-if. But none of that matters now." I scrunch my nose. "My window of opportunity has passed. I'm too old and I have other responsibilities to worry about."

The waitress brings out our appetizer, giving me a moment to compose myself. My hands shake as I take a piece of the artichoke and munch on it. Thinking about the past has stirred up a lot of painful emotions I've had carefully boxed up for several years.

People always say that you control your own destiny, but I'm living proof that that's not always the case. I know the Olympics were always a long shot for me, and I probably would never have qualified, but there was still always a one-percent chance. Or at least there was until my selfish partner dropped me. I did everything in my power to try finding another partner, but eventually I had to come to terms with the fact that it just wasn't going to happen.

"Are you two ready to order?"

Charlie glances in the server's direction. "We need a few more minutes."

"No problem. I'll circle back around to you two."

He thanks her and returns his attention to me. "You all right?" he asks softly.

I manage a weak bob of the head. "Just a few painful memories. I promise, I'm not normally like this."

"Like what? I don't see anything wrong."

"Emotional."

"Frankie, never apologize or be afraid to show your emotions. I understand how powerful memories can be, and that they can inflict just as much damage now as in the past." He reaches for my hand. It's larger than my own and warm. His fingers are long, and the tips calloused.

"Your accident?"

"Yes."

Our chests rise and fall. I'm struck by his compassion and how much he's trying to comfort me. I close my eyes and take a few deep breaths. He doesn't let go until I open my eyes, back in control of myself.

"So, um, your students. How would—"

He holds up a hand. "We'll get back to coaching in a minute. First, I need to know—what did you leave unfinished in the sport?"

"It's nothing."

"Humor me."

I swallow hard. "I don't know, there's a lot of things on my list."

"Such as?"

"I would've liked to have taken my senior test. And skate as a senior at nationals," I start. There's one other big-ticket item, but sitting here with a former national champion and world medalist intimidates me. I decide not to share it, and look out the window at the darkened trees.

"I can see it in your body language. There's something else, isn't there?"

"It's what everyone who skates wants. A trip to the Olympics. I wanted to be an Olympian." My shoulders droop. "Saying it now, I know how unrealistic it was. It's stupid. I was never all that great of a skater." I shake my head. "Forget I ever mentioned it."

"It's your dream," he says slowly. "It's not dumb. It was something *I* wanted once upon a time too." I return my attention to him. His Adam's apple bobs up and down. "What if I told you that at least one of those items on your list could be accomplished?"

He's playing with fire. "I'd be tempted to say, tell me what to do and I'll do it."

"What if you could take your senior test?"

"I'd say I'm interested but . . ." I shake my head. My stomach is tying itself in knots. "No. I can't. Let's be realistic. Who's going to skate with me, knowing full well that the partnership would never go anywhere? I don't even have all my skills anymore. Not to mention even if I did find a partner, at this point in my life, I'm not willing to relocate."

All this can ever be is a dream. Nothing more. I appreciate Charlie trying to be Mr. Positivity, but it's not going to happen. Period. I have Dad to think about. He's my priority. Not skating. I'm an adult with responsibilities. Not a teenager who can shove everything to the side and hope things magically work out.

"I know a guy who lives locally, and I can say with full confidence that he'd skate with you if asked, and would help you get everything you need in order to pass that test." Charlie sits up taller. "I can't promise you'd get a trip to nationals out of it, but you could at the very least cross one item off your bucket list."

Before I can stop myself, I whisper, "Who?"

"Someone I know can be trusted to get the job done."

"Who?" I repeat, scooting to the edge of my seat.

"Me."

"You?"

"Me," he confirms.

Anger floods my body. "This isn't a joke to me. Is this your way of getting revenge on me for our first few meetings?" I stand. My entire body is shaking. I slam my napkin onto the table. "Well, it worked. The joke's on me. Haha. You got me to buy into the farce. I can't believe I was stupid enough to tell you about all those things." I fumble with my purse. "Tonight was a mistake. I should've just gone home instead of listening to Leslie."

Charlie jumps to his feet, reaching for my arm. He spins me around and stares directly into my eyes with a challenge. "I *am* being serious. This isn't a joke. I don't do revenge. Every single thing I said is *true*. I'm willing to skate with you and help you take your test."

"Now you're just rubbing salt into the wound." I rip my

hand away from him and clench my fists by my side. "I had to talk you into doing a single split twist. You haven't skated seriously since you retired."

"I won't sugarcoat it. I *haven't* skated in years. Until yesterday, I didn't have a reason to." He takes a step closer to me. "But when we started stroking around the ice together, it was like you flipped a switch in my body. I felt something that's been missing for a long time. That spark. That excitement. That energy that used to make me hungry to skate."

He takes a deep breath. "I know you felt it too! When you went up into the air, you can't tell me you didn't feel as if we were skating together like a seasoned pair. When we were together, everything clicked. I can't explain it, but it's like fate is trying to give us both a second chance."

I bury my head in my hands. "I felt it," I mumble.

"The entire rest of the day, it was a challenge for me to keep coaching. All I wanted to do was keep skating with you. Even last night, I couldn't stop thinking about the possibility of us as a team. You were in my dreams."

My hands slip down by my sides. I study Charlie, still breathing hard, trying to rein in my emotions. "In your dream, what did we skate to?" I ask.

"*My Fair Lady.*"

My legs go weak. I sink down into my chair. How could he have known that's what *I've* always dreamed about skating to? The music, the costumes, the choreography—my dream program has lived rent-free in my head for ten-plus years.

For my twenty-first birthday, Dad even had a pink skating dress made up for me inspired by costumes in the film. It's the only one I still own. All the fight leaves my body. Can this really be fate?

"You're a busy man. You wouldn't have the time for me," I say weakly.

Charlie sits back down too. "For you, I'd make the time."

I'm fighting a losing battle. "What would you get out of all this?"

"My own closure." He tugs at his shirt collar. "Having unfinished business is the worst feeling in the world. I never got to end my career on my terms."

"I can't believe I'm even considering this. It's madness." I stare at the ceiling, then back at Charlie.

"It wouldn't be all that crazy. We'd start small and work up to a full program, step by step. I can see the easier elements like the spins, footwork, and death spirals starting to come together quickly. But other elements like the jumps, lifts, and split twists would take a lot more time. We can start working on them off ice, but realistically, I need time in the gym to build up my physical strength."

"Who do you envision coaching us?"

"Starting out, we would coach ourselves. We both have the experience. When the time comes, if we decide we need one, we can ask our friends for recommendations."

What Charlie is saying is true. I've been coaching myself most of my pro career. Touring with Dreams on Ice, I had to skate with different people every night. It was always up to me to figure things out. The show always went on.

I take a few more deep breaths. This is all so much to wrap my head around. He makes it sound so easy, but it seems too good to be true.

He reaches for a piece of fried artichoke. "What do you say?"

"I'll think about it."

"That's all I ask."

Chapter Ten

I relax as dinner goes on. Our appetizer has been eaten and our steaks cleared away. The tea lights on the table have burned to the end of their wicks. There's only one other couple remaining in the red room.

We've spent the last few hours talking. A bubble of excitement rises higher up in me the longer we're together. "We can't spend the entire meal talking about work. Leslie made me promise I'd help you relax. There has to be something besides skating we can talk about. What's your favorite TV series?"

"I don't own a TV." Charlie leans against the back of his chair.

"Okay, what about your favorite book?"

His neck flushes red. "I, erm, don't have time to read much."

I'd forgotten about his dyslexia. Gah. Rookie mistake. "That's right. You pretty much live at the rink," I say, playing off my faux pas.

"I do, but that doesn't mean I don't enjoy *listening* to books. I stream audiobooks on my drive home or when out

I'm running errands. My favorites are thrillers, especially if there's a treasure hunt involved."

I soak in the information. You can tell a lot about a person's personality based on the type of books they enjoy. "Treasure hunts, huh? Do you mean like an Indiana Jones type of adventure?"

"Is there any other kind?" Charlie laughs.

I picture him dressed in Indiana Jones' signature hat, white shirt—open at the neck, of course—and brown leather jacket, skating around the rink. It's the perfect ensemble for a man who enjoys a rustic aesthetic. Warmth spreads through my veins from my head to my toes like a pleasant heat wave.

"I live vicariously through the characters just like Indy. In an alternate universe, if I weren't a skating coach, and didn't have problems with computers and reading, I probably would've been a middle-school science teacher. I love working with kids."

The image I have in my mind shifts to Charlie, still dressed as Indy, in a classroom wearing goggles, helping a child mix baking soda and vinegar for one of those stereotypical exploding volcanoes. He's gone from athletic sexy to nerdy sexy. "Science?" I squeak.

"Uh-huh. It's the only subject where you can go outside and do hands-on activities. I hated being inside the classroom as a kid. You should see my friend Tim. He's always coming up with these crazy experiments for his middle-school students." He studies my face. "Not a fan?"

"Science is okay. I was homeschooled, so everything was done online or with a tutor. I'm more of an art gal. I love sketching, painting, really any form of arts and crafts."

"I'll be sure to let Leslie know. She'll be thrilled to have a new person to drag along to Hobby Land. Nobody in the family will go with her anymore. She can spend hours going up and down the aisles, looking at every single new thing."

"That's my favorite store." I giggle. "She can't be that bad, can she?"

"Oh yes, she can." Charlie groans. "It's gotten to the point of being embarrassing. All the cashiers at the Sequoia Valley location know her by name. She's their best customer. And half the stuff she buys she doesn't need. It's always for a just-in-case situation."

I tilt my head. "Where does she store all her craft supplies?"

"At the rink. I'll show you her storage closet the next time we're there."

I'm willing to bet the room is bursting with decorations and other odds and ends for every holiday, especially Halloween and Christmas.

Our waitress approaches the table. "Sorry to interrupt, I just wanted to ask if you'd care to look at the dessert menu. The kitchen is getting ready to close."

I default to Charlie. "I'm game if you are."

Without a glance at the menu, he says, "We'll split a piece of the pineapple upside-down cake."

A few bubbles of excitement well up inside of me. He remembered I like pineapple.

"Sounds good, Charlie. I'll be right back with it." The waitress gives me a knowing smile. "Do you want a scoop of ice cream on the side too?"

"Lady's choice," Charlie says.

"Vanilla, if you have it."

"Perfect, I'll be right back." The waitress scribbles our order down.

"Vanilla is so plain." Charlie shoots an amused glance at me. "I thought you'd go for the chocolate or the strawberry."

"Chocolate would overpower the pineapples and cherries."

"And strawberry?"

"Same. I don't like too many flavors competing against one another. What flavor would you have chosen?"

"Chocolate. I'm a sucker for anything chocolate."

"You didn't want a chocolate cake?"

"No. I've had it plenty of times before. Tonight is about you."

"Thanks for ordering the pineapple cake, then." The bubbles inside of me continue to fizz to the top of my stomach in happiness. "I just hope you'll enjoy some. I know *you're* not a fan of pineapples."

"I don't mind them. It's only when they're on pizza."

We share a laugh, giving me a chance to admire his cheekbones and how youthful he appears when he's not a grump.

It hits me then that we're alone. The other couples in the room have all left. I glance at my watch. "It's ten-thirty already," I gasp. "I didn't realize we've been sitting here for four hours! It's a good thing tomorrow's Sunday."

Charlie reaches for his water glass. "What happens on Sundays?"

"Sunday is my lazy day. It's the one day a week I allow myself to sleep in past six. The only things I have on my to-do list are to call my best friend Gemma, catch up on *Cupid's Arrow*, do laundry, and pick up a few groceries."

"Six sounds like a luxury. I wake up every day at three."

"I must be keeping you up way past your bedtime."

"If I'm in bed by eleven, it's a victory."

"Are you part vampire? How can you run off four hours of sleep?" I'm genuinely curious.

"You get used to it." He shrugs. "Even if I wanted to sleep late, I don't think I could. I'm on autopilot. My body is used to early mornings."

"Even on your days off?"

He nods. "I'm only off on Sundays."

"And your Sunday routine is . . .?"

"Hiking." His eyes light up. "Weather permitting, I try and get out on a different trail every week. There's no better way to clear your mind than being out in nature."

"Where are you planning to go tomorrow?"

"I'll probably take it easy and do the King's Summit loop. It's a nice flat trail, plus I haven't been up to the waterfall in a while."

I rest my elbows on the table. I did that trail once with Dad about ten years ago. "That takes about five or six hours round trip, doesn't it?"

"Give or take."

"In that case, as soon as the server comes back, let's ask her to box up our dessert. You really should get home and get to bed. I can call a cab and have it take me back to the rink."

"We're fine on time. I'm enjoying your company. And don't worry about the cab. I'll drive you back. You're on my way home. I promise." Charlie's tone doesn't leave room for negotiation.

"Are you sure?"

"I'm positive."

The server returns with our dessert. Anticipation courses through my body at the thought of spending more time with Charlie.

The next morning, I text Gemma.

Frankie: I've never been more confused in my life.

Gemma: ???

Frankie: I got an offer I don't think I can say no to.

Gemma: Call me right now!

Frankie: It's like two in the morning in Auckland!

Gemma: There's no show tomorrow and I'm waiting for the season finale of Cupid's Arrow to drop. I only have another hour.

Frankie: Only you.

I shake my head and giggle. "Gemma, you're crazy."

Frankie: Do you want to do a video chat, or chat-chat?

Gemma: Either one.

Frankie: Do you have your own hotel room?

Gemma: No, but it doesn't matter. I'm sharing with Vivian.

Frankie: Even a thundering herd of elephants wouldn't wake her.

I snicker.

Frankie: Let's do video.

Gemma: *Thumbs-up emoji*

I send my bestie a video request. A moment later, she picks up. The background is dark. Gemma holds up a finger to her lips, takes her phone into the bathroom, and shuts the door.

"Hey, pretty lady, how are you getting on?"

I've missed hearing Gemma's thick Scottish drawl. Lying

on the couch, I bring my knees to my chest and rest my phone on them. "Good?"

"What's this about a crazy offer you've received? I'm dying for details. Spill," she commands.

"Last night, I had dinner with my boss," I begin.

"You had a date with Mr. Blanks? Whoa. Reverse the train back into the station. How did *that* happen?"

"Call him the grump, or Charlie, but please no more Mr. Blanks." Luckily the lighting is low enough that Gemma probably can't see how red my face is. I clear my throat. "There's nothing to read into us having dinner. It was *not* a date. It was a getting-to-know-you thing."

"Sure. If that's what you're going to call it," Gemma says dryly. She signals for me to continue.

I roll my eyes at her. "Anyway, you're never going to believe this, but guess what, Gem? He's offered to become my pairs partner. He wants to help me take my senior pairs test." Saying it aloud still doesn't make it feel more real. I resist the urge to pinch the skin on my forearm.

"What did you tell him?" She brings the camera closer to her face.

"I said I'd think about it."

"What's there to think about? Isn't this something you've always wanted? Tell the bloke yes and crack on with it."

"It's not that simple."

"Why? What's holding you back?" She scrunches her nose. "Are you worried about your dad?"

I listen carefully for any signs of him stirring. But luckily, I hear snoring. "Yeah. There are some things that have been going on that I haven't told anyone about."

Except for giving Charlie a few hints. It's time for me to come clean with Gemma. "Do you remember earlier this year when I took two weeks off while we were in Spain?"

"I do." She nods. "I knew something with up, but I didn't

want to ask too many questions. I knew you'd share whatever it was with me when you were ready."

That's why Gemma is my best friend. She knows me and my limits better than anyone. "The thing is something did happen." My breath hitches. "The reason I took off had to do with Dad. A little over five months ago, he suffered a bad fall and had to have surgery to repair a broken hip."

"Frankie! Why didn't you tell me?!" she gasps. "I would've come with you to help you with whatever you needed."

A stray tear runs down my cheek. "I don't know. Everything was happening so fast. I didn't have time to think. I did everything on autopilot. If I pretended everything was okay, it didn't seem real. And then afterward, I didn't want people feeling sorry for me and treating me any different."

"Is that the real reason why you quit DOI? Because you're caring for your dad?"

"Yeah." My body curls in on itself. My voice trembles as a few more tears sneak out. "I don't have anyone else, Gem. I'm terrified that the next time something happens, I might not be around."

As I share the details of what happened with Gem, reliving one of the worst days of my life, the floodgates burst open and a dam of tears erupts. All this time, I've had to put up a facade and pretend everything is fine when it isn't. It's taken a huge mental and emotional toll on me. "Dad had been alone for over twenty-four hours. I don't even want to think about what would've happened if—"

"Frankie, don't say it. Don't think it. Your dad *was* found. He's on the road to recovery now. It's okay to cry. We all need to cry sometimes."

The waterworks keep flowing.

Gemma stands and paces the bathroom. "You're one of the strongest people I know. But I want you to remember that when things get tough, you aren't alone. You have friends like me who are always going to be right by your side. All you ever have to do is say the word, and I can be on the first plane out to California. Your dad is like my second dad."

"I know you would be."

It takes me half an hour to calm myself down. I'm lucky. Gemma is a patient listener and instinctively knows the exact words I need to hear. "Take one more deep breath for me. Hold it. Hold it. Hold it. Now exhale. Feel better?"

"Yeah." I dry the corners of my eyes with my sleeve.

"Good. Now here's my two pence. If you don't give this pairs skating thing a shot, you're always going to regret that you had a second chance and didn't take it. Everything happens for a reason. Skate with Mr. Bla—er, Charlie for a couple of weeks. If you're still feeling like you made the wrong choice, *then* you can walk away."

I nod.

"I also think you should have an open conversation with Charlie about your dad. Let him know the full extent of what's going on. From how I'm guessing dinner went last night, I have a feeling he'll be another helpful person for you to have around. Oh, and don't forget, there's always that support group for people with senior parents that Mr. T's doctor mentioned too."

"I should do both, but I'm a big chicken. I can handle letting Charlie in on my situation, but I don't think I could talk to a room full of strangers about my life."

"Fair enough." She sighs and blinks slowly. "Opening up is never easy, but if anyone can do it, you can. If you aren't ready to go to a meeting, don't. Just be mindful that you have that resource available to you should you need it."

I want to hug her tightly and spend more time with her, but she's on the other side of the world. "You're the best friend I have."

"That's why I'm irreplaceable," Gemma teases.

Suddenly, there's a rattling sound. The pipes in the apartment creak and the hot water heater kicks on. "Sounds like Dad is getting up."

"You better get going. Tell Mr. T I said hello and I'll be ready to discuss the finale of *Cupid's Arrow* whenever he's up for it."

"We'll probably watch it together after breakfast. We'll call you later."

Gemma waves goodbye, and we disconnect. I stand and stretch, picking up the discarded blankets and pillows I kicked off the couch sometime during the night. I'm going to do it. I'll skate with Charlie. Gemma's right. This is the second chance I never thought I'd get. "Carpe diem," I whisper to myself.

When Dad joins me a little later, he sniffs the air. "Blueberry pancakes this morning? Somebody must be in a good mood."

"I thought we could both use a little change of pace today."

Dad takes a seat at the kitchen table. "Did I hear you chatting on the phone earlier too?"

"It was Gemma."

"That's right." He snaps his fingers. "The finale of *Cupid's Arrow* comes out today. I hope you girls didn't watch it without me!"

"Don't worry, Dad. I told Gem I was planning to watch it with you once you were up."

"Phew." He fakes a sigh of relief.

"We can stream it right after breakfast." Turning off the stove, I set the small stack of pancakes I've created in front of Dad.

"These smell great, sweetie." He pecks me on the cheek as I join him. "After the show, I have a favor to ask of you."

"Oh?" I glance up. "What's on your mind?"

"Would you help me set up a profile on the Golden Years senior dating platform afterward?"

My knife and fork fall with a clatter. "You want me to sign you up for a dating app?"

"I've already signed up. I need help setting up my profile."

When did he have time to sign up for that? Is this Gemma's doing? "If that's what you want. Sure." My voice comes out higher than normal.

"It is. I've been hit with Cupid's arrow. If these young twenty-somethings on the show can find love, maybe I can too."

Dad sounds so hopeful. There's so much I want to say to him. Is this platform legitimate? Does it vet who it lets sign up for it? I need to do some research on it before I let him get too far. For now, however, I'll let him enjoy the moment.

Chapter Eleven

Wednesday morning, I watch and wait for Charlie as he drives the Zamboni off the ice. I bite my lower lip. Today is the day. I can do this. I won't let my nerves get the better of me. Walking toward where the machine is stored, I call out, "Hey, Charlie, do you have a second?"

He glances up, hands resting on the handle of the broom used to sweep the stray chunks of ice left behind by the machine. "Sure, what's on your mind?"

"I did a lot of soul-searching this weekend. I made a four-page long list of all the potential pros and cons, but it didn't help because I already knew what my answer was going to be. If the offer still stands, my answer is yes."

He stares at me with a dazed expression. "What are you talking about?"

"The proposition you made me at dinner this weekend. My answer is yes. I want to skate with you."

He drops the broom. The folds of his eyes crinkle. "You do?"

"I do."

"You've just made my day."

He flashes a full-on smile at me. I resist the urge to run over and give him a huge hug, trying to play it cool. "I'm glad. Um, no hurry, but sometime this week, I have a few details I wanted to figure out with you about how our partnership is going to work."

"I'm free now if you are?"

"Sure."

"Great, give me two minutes to finish up here. I'll meet you in the kitchen."

"The kitchen?"

"My office is worse than normal. I'm having a hard time opening the door. Normally Leslie helps me clean up on Saturdays, but with the testing and all, I let it go. It's on my list of things to do; I just haven't gotten to it yet."

It sounds like the warehouse from the Indiana Jones movies where all the stuff he discovers is stored. "The kitchen it is."

When Charlie joins me a few minutes later, I'm scribbling down some more notes I want to cover with him during our meeting. "Do you mind if I multitask while we talk?" he asks.

I glance up. "Nope. Do whatever you need to do."

He washes his hands, then bends down, retrieving a cutting board, knives, and an apron from the storage shelves in the central island. "I was going to make myself some grilled chicken, broccoli, and baby carrots for lunch. Can I interest you in some?"

"Only if you have enough ingredients."

"I bought enough chicken to last three weeks." His body shakes with laughter as he opens the freezer. It's packed full of meat.

I blink slowly. "Was there a big sale on meat at the grocery store? Or did you raid Millie's kitchen?"

"Neither." He chuckles. "I cleaned out my fridge on Sunday and did a huge grocery run. I may have gone a little overboard on the meat. I had to store the stuff that wouldn't fit in the freezer here. But the only things I have left now are fruits, veggies, and lean meats."

All healthy food. Those are things only a skater in training would have. A lightbulb clicks on. "You're eating clean?" I guess.

"Ten points to Frankie," he confirms. "I had my first gym session yesterday too. When you gave me your answer, which I'd hoped would be a yes, I wanted to be able to show you that I'm throwing myself all in to this. I'm committed to you." He lifts his left arm and winces. "See? I'm so sore that I can't even lift my arm above my head."

"And what if I'd said no? That I wouldn't skate with you?" I lean against the counter.

"It wouldn't make any difference. I still would've started my meal plan and working out this week. I need to get myself back in shape. If not for you, for my students." He pulls out a green basket of baby carrots from the fridge. "I'll never admit this to anyone else, but catching you and helping Kaylee with the harness last week left me so stiff that I had a hard time getting myself out of bed and moving around for two days. Everything hurt."

"You looked fine on Saturday."

"I'm a talented actor."

I cover a laugh with my hand.

"Don't believe me? It's true. Well, at least that's what the TV commentators used to say about me on the ice," he cracks.

"Suuuuuuuuuuuuure."

"Anyway, both pair teams I coach are ready to start learning riskier, more difficult elements. Sooner or later, that means I'll have to step in and help them with the harness, spot them on lifts, et cetera, et cetera. When it happens, I want to be ready."

His voice is full of sincerity. He wants his students to have the best coaching he can offer them. They're lucky he's so dedicated to them. I hope that's the type of partner he is too. He's off to a good start, but can he maintain it?

"You've let me rattle on long enough." He starts slicing the carrots into small equal pieces. "What's on this list of yours?"

"Oh." I flip my notebook back a few pages. "Um . . . number one was picking out the days and times we could skate together."

"Hmm . . . would mornings work? Right now, the first freestyle session of the day is scheduled from four to five. Hardly anyone ever shows up. If you have a day in mind, I could adjust the schedule, and we can use that hour for us. My first lesson usually isn't until five-thirty."

"That would be awesome. I can do any morning Monday through Friday. You pick."

"Those are dangerous words," he says ominously. "How ambitious are you?"

"When it comes to skating, I'm *very* ambitious."

"Then how about we skate every morning."

Whoa. He wants to get out of the starting gate with a bang. I'm all for it. Especially since it means more time with Charlie. "As my bestie Gemma would say, that's brilliant." I smile widely. "That brings us to item number two. What does your afternoon schedule look like? I'd like for us to try and fit in some off-ice training too."

"On a normal day, I coach until ten. Then from ten to one, I try to catch up on paperwork and any other admin duties." His voice grows softer. "I usually end up needing all three hours."

I glance up. "What about asking Leslie to help?"

"I'll talk to her later," he mumbles.

I'm happy he's willing to accept some help. He's just earned himself another brownie point. "Great, just make sure you do it sooner rather than later."

He grunts. I take that to mean "yes."

"Let me know if she says she's too busy. I'll help you out. That way, we could reallocate one of those hours to off-ice prep."

"As you know, the ice is open from ten to twelve. Why don't you pencil us down for ten to eleven?" Charlie wipes his hands against his apron and places the knife down, turning to face me. "If we go much later than that, it gets too chaotic. I usually help cover staff lunch breaks."

"No problem." I turn the page. "This is really starting to come together! I'm so excited. Now, next item—"

"Just how many things did you write down?"

I hesitate. "Six?"

"Well, at least you're like my sister—organized." He chuckles. "What's number three?"

"Action item three has to do with developing our artistry. I know you and your former partner were known for your presentation. And I certainly gained a lot of experience touring with Dreams on Ice, but since we're a new team and haven't developed our own style yet, I think we'd still benefit from some type of dance class. Do you guys have a ballet teacher at the rink?"

"We do, but neither of us needs ballet. We both have good lines and carriage."

"Uh-huh. Then what do you suggest?"

"Ballroom dancing." Charlie walks over to the stovetop and pours some oil into a frying pan. "We need to work on building our connection to one another." He places the first chicken breast in the pan, and it starts to sizzle. "If you find a class that works for us, I'll join you. I'm free after eight during the week or after noon on the weekends."

Wait. Did he say eight? I perform a few mental calculations and frown. "Something's not adding up for me. Charlie, how many hours a day, on average, are you here?"

He stares into the pan, mumbling something so low, the sound of the cooking meat drowns him out.

"What was that?"

"Fifteen hours, give or take?" He hunches his shoulders. "I know. It's bad." He refuses to meet my eyes.

I inhale sharply. "When I come in to coach during the evenings, you're exhausted. How do you expect to survive on three or four hours of sleep a night when we start adding in gym, skating, and off-ice training sessions?" I challenge.

"I don't know . . ." He trails off.

"That's not an acceptable answer." I close my notebook. "Pairs skating is already dangerous. I won't risk my safety and go through with this if you're not going to change your sleeping schedule. You need at least six or seven hours of rest a night for your body to recover."

"I would never take a chance on you getting hurt." He turns, looking directly at me with a fierceness similar to Leslie. "I promise, there won't be any more long days starting tonight. I'll find a way to kick myself out by five."

Whatever I say sets the tone for how this partnership is going to go. I inhale deeply and decide to trust he'll keep his promise. "Thank you."

He returns his attention back to the pan. "I've lost count —the last item was number three or four?"

"It was number three. We can skip over items four and five, but number six is important." It's the one I've been dreading.

He turns off the stove, plates the meat, and leans against the island. "You've got my full attention. Shoot."

"Do you remember I mentioned the other night that I live with my dad?"

"I do."

"My dad is, um . . ." My chest tightens. Why is finding the right words so difficult?

"Your dad . . ." He nods encouragingly.

"He isn't in the best of health." I drop my chin to my chest, staring at the sparkly cover of my notebook. "There might be times when I need to cancel a practice with you so I can take him to a doctor's appointment. Or days when I have to stay home because he isn't having a good day. I mean, he's gotten a lot better, but there's still a lot of unknowns ahead. Is . . . is . . . that going to be a problem?" I sputter.

"No. If something comes up, take care of your dad. You do you."

I raise my head. Charlie's eyes are wide with understanding. A voice in the back of my head is telling me to trust him. Tell him the full extent of the situation. But I can't. There's still a little part of me that isn't ready to share something so personal with him.

"If there's ever anything you need, I want you to let me know. Like I said earlier, we're partners now. That relationship extends beyond just being on the ice together."

"Only if you promise me the same," I croak.

"It's a deal."

Chapter Twelve

I lie awake on the couch, waiting for my alarm to go off at any moment. As much as I want to stay nestled under the warmth of the covers for several more hours, it isn't going to happen. It feels as if my head has only just touched the pillow. How could it be 2:40 in the morning already?

A moment later, my phone chimes. Groaning, I swipe to turn it off and sit up, rubbing my eyes. At least today's Thursday. I don't have to worry about coaching until eight tonight. I love my students, but despise the idea of having to put in a long day with only a couple hours of sleep. I have no idea how Charlie managed to function like this for so long. Just doing it once a week is a struggle. I'm glad he took my ultimatum and has changed his ways.

Wrapping my blanket around my body like a cape, I shuffle over to the kitchen, pour myself a cup of the coffee I brewed last night, and stick it in the microwave. The machine hums to life with an electric buzz. Pulling open the refrigerator, I find my bowl of vanilla yogurt topped with strawberries, blueberries, and granola and set it down on the table just as the microwave chirps.

Over the last two weeks, I've gotten my new morning routine down to an exact science of twenty minutes. It takes me ten minutes to eat and scroll through social media on my phone, five minutes to get dressed, three minutes to do my hair and brush my teeth, and two minutes to write a note to Dad letting him know what's for breakfast and that I love him. By three a.m., I'm out the door and on my way to the rink.

Pulling into a parking spot parallel to Charlie's truck, I take out my phone and send him a text message.

Frankie: I'm here.

Three dots blink. He's typing.

Charlie: On my way.

Even though I feel safe walking across the well-lit parking lot, Charlie's made it clear I should always wait in my car with the doors locked until he arrives to escort me inside. We've had several conversations about it, but I've given up trying to change his mind.

Tap. Tap. Tap. Charlie raps his knuckles against the window and waves, pointing to a coffee. "Good morning, sleepyhead," he calls out in a chipper voice. "Are we ready to skate this morning?"

I open the driver's door, take the cup, and clutch it to my chest. "Thank you," I grunt. "Not yet, but I will be." I take a nice long sip. It's sweet. Not like the coffee I had at home. "The barista got the ratio perfect this morning."

"Yes! About time." Charlie pumps his fist. "What are you going to do for warm-up? Jump rope? The elliptical? Stationary bike?"

"I need to wake up, so a jog around the rink? The cold air should do the trick."

Charlie holds open the door to our storage room turned private locker room. "I'll join you."

"Aren't you already warm from your gym session?" I raise an eyebrow as I slide my coat off my shoulders, hanging it up on one of the metal pegs lining the wall.

"I need the extra cardio."

"Ooooooooooook. No complaining this afternoon when you start to fall asleep at your desk."

"That won't happen," he says smugly.

Don't say I didn't warn you, I think. I exchange my trusty Converse for my running shoes, tie them, and stand. "Let's go."

Charlie and I glide forward on the ice. Our bodies are pressed in close to one another. He grips my waist firmly, applying just the right amount of pressure to be snug, but not uncomfortable. I push my skate down deep into the ice, then lift my right leg to initiate a throw double Salchow just as he tosses me into the air.

Charlie claps. "You had so much hang time on that. That was the best one we've ever done."

"It's gotten so easy." I place my hands on my knees. "I lost my breath a little on it."

"It won't be long before we're ready to try a throw triple Sal. We'll have to start thinking about what jumps we should put in our program." He skates over to the boards to grab a quick drink of water.

"I used to do a throw triple loop and double Lutz. Right now, I'm thinking Sal and loop." I stand upright and adjust my ponytail. "They're the jumps that are the easiest for me. How much time do we have left in the session?"

Charlie glances at his smartwatch. "Five more minutes."

My pulse pounds in my ear. Adrenaline rushes through my veins. "Let's try a triple Sal."

"Now? We only started doing throw doubles on the ice this week." He shakes his head. "It's too soon."

By this point, we've already been on the ice for forty minutes and done some throw double loops and Salchows. I'm tired, but I'm dying to see if I can still do a throw triple. All my other skills have come back pretty easily.

Fernando and I always talked about doing it on tour during the last few weeks of my contract, but we had problems getting on the same page. As a leftie, he jumped and spun in the opposite direction as me.

With Charlie, it's different. He has the experience of being a top-level skater. It's scary how quickly we've managed to meld our styles. We're already nearing the point where I don't have to count out our setups. Charlie intuitively knows when I'm ready to rise up into the air.

"You're giving me more than enough height and power on the jump. Plus, I've been doing solo triple Sals without any problems since we started training together. I know I can squeeze out another rotation on the throw."

"No." His hands fly to the scar on his forehead. "Remember, we're running a marathon, not performing sprints. Doubles might be easy, but with triples, there are a lot more things that can go wrong. I don't want there to be any doubts about you being able to complete the jump. I want us to be able to do the double on autopilot before we think about a triple."

We can do that almost every time now. What's the harm in doing a triple? His lips make a thin line. His face is stoic. I sigh —his stubborn mind is made up. It's like throwing a ball against a wall. The wall wins every time.

"Then how do *you* want to fill these last five minutes?"

"How about a compromise? We could try some side-by-side jumps."

My lips twitch. "Now you're talking."

We debate what to try before settling on double Salchows. Excitement swells inside me. I've been waiting for us to have a go at trying some side-by-side jumps. We're about to hit another milestone. Taking hold of one another's hands, we fly across the rink into powerful back crossovers.

Approaching the opposite corner of the ice, we drop our hands and position ourselves about eight feet apart. "Turn," I call out. Keeping my attention on Charlie's body, I aim to match his timing and keep our spacing as close as possible. "One, two, three, jump."

Rising into the air, I keep my body open and only perform a single so I can focus on Charlie. He has so much speed and attack going into the jump. As he pulls his arms in and crosses his feet, his body whips around two and a half times. Before he can manage a third rotation, he opens up and crashes hard onto the ice.

I rush over to his side. "Are you okay?"

"I'm fine." He sits on the ice for a moment, slow to stand. He slams a hand on the ice. "Gah. That was awful. I was thinking double, but my body was ready to do a triple."

"Muscle memory is powerful."

"I have to try that again." He brushes the dusting of snow from his pants. "My pride won't let me leave the ice until I land a clean one."

An amused grin crosses my face. We're on the same page. "Try to relax when you take off. Your body was so tense that it almost looked like your shoulders were trying to hide your ears."

I skate over to the boards and watch Charlie skate off for his second attempt. On his own, his timing is much better. This time, he lifts off the ice with more air, rotates, and lands with a swoosh. I shouldn't be jealous, but I am. It looked so effortless.

I slow clap. He bows.

With that, our time is unfortunately up. Our first set of students will arrive at the rink in the next half hour. We need the time in between to have a snack and change clothes.

"What solo jumps did you use to do with your old partner?" Charlie asks.

I drape my jacket over my shoulders. "We competed double Axels and double flips. Had we moved up to seniors, our plan was to swap the flips for triple toes. What about you?"

"We did the same standard side-by-side jumps everybody else does. I'd hoped Camille would be up for trying something different, like a loop jump, but she wasn't ever interested in learning something new."

"What other triple jumps can you do?"

"All of them!" He puffs his chest out and strikes a pose with his hands on his hips. "Or rather, I used to be able to. And not an Axel." He scratches the back of his head. "I skated singles until it got to the point where I couldn't be competitive without it or a quad. That's when we decided I'd be better off switching to pairs. Best decision I ever made."

"As soon as you get your triple loop back, we're so making that our signature move."

"I'll think about it."

Charlie is so different than Danny ever was. He used to always blame me when our jumps went wrong. Charlie stays positive and points out little corrections we can each make. He's an excellent technical coach. I'm learning that if anyone can break a jump down and figure out how to fix it, it's him.

"You'll get it back." I move my legs, trying to loosen my quad muscles. With every step I take, I can feel the fibers pulling in the front and on the side of my leg. I need to cool down and stretch if I hope to be able to skate again in the afternoon. Charlie was right. It's probably a good thing we didn't go for the throw triple Salchow. My body is spent.

We stop outside the locker room. "Do you mind if I ask you something?"

"You just did," he says.

I tap his arm playfully. "That wasn't what I meant."

"Ow." He flinches jokingly.

"I didn't hit you that hard." It isn't lost on me that his arm has gotten firmer.

"I know. Go ahead. Ask me anything."

"You don't have to answer this if you don't want to, but I'm just curious. What made you retire from competitive skating?"

Charlie's face pales. A look of weariness passes over his face, and he doesn't say anything for a long moment; I didn't think such a simple question would set him off. Why did I have to open my big mouth and ask?

I step in closer to him and place a hand on his shoulder. "Hey, it's okay. Like I said, you don't have to answer. Forget I ever asked."

His green orbs lock on to mine. His jaw is clenched. "I'll tell you," he says slowly, "but not here and not now. It's a long story, and I'd rather be in a place where we can have a little privacy."

As if to prove his point, the front doors to the ice center open. "Hi, Mr. C. Hi, Coach Frankie," Steve belts out.

"Hi, Steve," we both respond automatically, attention still on one another.

"We'd better hurry. The kids are here." Charlie opens the door and enters the locker room.

I linger in the doorway, wondering just what had happened to cause such a reaction from him.

Chapter Thirteen

Sunday morning arrives. I hover near Dad with a lint roller, going over his black cable-knit sweater one final time as he studies himself in the mirror. I can smell the almond and whiskey scent of his special-occasion cologne lingering in the air.

"Dad, you look dapper. You're going to make your date swoon from how handsome you are."

A light tinge of pink appears on his cheeks. "I doubt it, but I appreciate you saying so." He kisses the top of my head and straightens his glasses. "I just hope I'm not making a colossal mistake."

I set the lint roller down on the hallway side table. Time for a pep talk. "I think once you get to Norma's Café and meet your date, all the nerves will flee your body. Are you ready to head out? You have your wallet and your cell phone?"

Dad taps the pockets of his charcoal-gray dress slacks. "Check and check."

"Great! I just need to grab my purse. I'll lock up and meet you in the car."

He grabs the car keys and heads out the front door. The

moment the coast is clear, I whip out my phone and text Gemma.

Frankie: We're about to leave for Dad's date.

Gemma: Well? How is he? Excited? Anxious?

Frankie: A little of everything? He woke up extra early to make sure his shoes had a visible mirror shine. I think it's his way of relaxing.

Gemma: What outfit did he finally settle on?

Frankie: The white dress shirt, blue and gray striped tie, black cable-knit sweater, and gray dress slacks.

Gemma: *Thumbs-up emoji* Do you have any photos?

Scrolling through my camera roll, I send her one of the snapshots I snuck when he wasn't looking.

Frankie: Sending it to you now.

Three dots blink. Gemma is typing.

Gemma: Oh, looking sharp, Mr. T! He looks like one of those distinguished older chaps you would find back home in Glasgow.

Frankie: He hogged the bathroom all morning, showering, shaving, and ironing his clothes. Did I mention he took extremely detailed notes from the Dating for Dummies book you sent him?

Gemma: Oh no. *Laughing emoji*

Frankie: You created a monster. He wasn't happy until he made sure he followed every suggestion from the "Dress for Success" chapter.

Gemma: Wish him luck from me. Not that he needs it.

Frankie: Will do. He'll enjoy hearing that you thought he looked distinguished.

Gemma: *Winking emoji*

I click the phone off, tuck it into my purse, and jog out to the car to meet Dad.

"Sorry for holding you up." I buckle my seat belt. "I had a message from Gemma."

"Oh?"

"She said to wish you luck."

"That girl is too good to me. I owe her a box of chocolates. Maybe some flowers too."

"Her favorites are pink peonies and chocolate mints." I click the blinker and turn out of the parking lot. "She'll be stateside in two months. I was thinking we could invite her to visit."

"By all means. It would be wonderful to see her cheery face in person, instead of over a computer screen."

From the corner of my eye, I watch Dad fidget in his seat. He's nervous. I need to keep the conversation flowing. "Remind me again . . . what do you know about Suzy?"

His lips curve. "She's a former nurse and widower about my age. For the last two decades, she's lived on the outskirts of Lake Wakahanra with her oldest son."

"And what attracted you to her profile?"

"She's the one who made the first move." Dad chuckles.

I don't remember him telling me that. A dull pang of hurt fills my chest.

"We've only exchanged emails a handful of times, but we both love crossword puzzles, and she's also a fan of *Cupid's Arrow*."

"She sounds like a good match for you."

"I hope so, but the book Gemma sent me said not to set the bar too high. Online profiles can be misleading. Did you know that more than half of people who use dating sites digitally alter their profile photos?"

"I didn't." I turn into the parking lot of Norma's and pull into the disabled parking spot near the restaurant's entrance, turning off the engine. "Dad, you'll do great, but I'm available if you need me to serve as your wingman or swoop in and rescue you. Just send me a text."

His eyes narrow. "Don't you have plans today?"

I fidget in my seat. "Charlie and I are going to go for a hike up toward King's Summit, but he knows you always come first."

"You and Mr. Blanks are getting awfully chummy. You're always spending time with him."

Dad may be implying something, but we're just friends and skating partners. Besides, Charlie would never be interested in me romantically. He's my boss, and I doubt I'm his type. He probably has a strict no-dating policy when it comes to other skaters.

"Dad, our relationship is strictly professional. I, um . . . we . . . what I mean to say is that we've been skating together. If everything keeps going well, he's going to help me take my senior pairs' test in a couple months."

Dad opens and closes his mouth. "Where did this come from?"

I blink twice. "It just sort of happened."

"Oh, how long have you been working with him?"

"Not long." I feel as if I'm a kid again and I've been caught doing something I shouldn't have. My fingers grip the steering wheel tightly. "Three weeks?"

"Is he a good partner?"

"Yes. The most talented man I've ever worked with," I answer honestly. "He brings so much experience to the ice, not just as a skater, but also as a coach. We've picked up a lot of pairs elements quickly."

"What happens after your test? Are you two going to become a competitive team?" Dad asks.

"I don't know. It's always a possibility. We haven't really discussed the future."

His face lights up. "I'm so happy for you. Why did you hide it?"

"I didn't want to tell anyone in case it didn't work out."

"Well, I'm glad you told me. Who knows, your dream was always to make it to the Olympics. Maybe with Mr. Blanks, your dreams could become a reality."

Not likely. We have so many factors working against us, like age. If we made it to nationals, and that's a big if, we'd likely be the oldest team in the field. The judges wouldn't want to take a risk on us. At this point, I'd just be happy to say I made it to the highest level of the sport. I don't want to over-reach. I learned that lesson the hard way.

Dad continues, "And don't worry about crashing my date. Enjoy your time with Charlie. I'll take a taxi home from Norma's when we're finished."

"Do you need my credit card or any cash?"

He shakes his head. "No, everything I need is on my phone in my digital wallet."

Hearing Dad say that is surreal. I shoot him a skeptical glance. "If you say so." He climbs out of the car, and I watch him stroll inside Norma's to meet a woman with a stylish scarf and short silver hair.

"Good luck, Daddy," I say under my breath before driving away.

"I meant to ask when you picked me up, but I don't think I've ever seen you in this truck before," I say to Charlie a little later.

"It's Jack's. My battery was dead. We swapped cars for the day. He had some errands to run with my grandma and said he wouldn't mind dropping it off at the body shop for a couple hours while he waits for her."

"What's he going to do while he waits?" I ask.

"Your guess is as good as mine. I didn't ask."

As we leave Sequoia Valley for the King's Summit trailhead, the road changes from being smooth and well-maintained to bumpy, uneven, and full of potholes. My body jolts up and down in the passenger seat like clothing tumbling inside a washing machine.

My hand grips the side of the door. "Please tell me that we're almost there and that the trail we're hiking isn't in as bad of shape as this road."

"We'll be there in two seconds and it's not. I checked some of the hikers' forums last night. The section we're going to explore had a green check mark next to it, meaning the park rangers have already cleared any hazards that were out here."

Charlie parks the truck, jumps out the driver's side, and walks around to the back to retrieve our backpacks.

"That's a relief." I exhale, still able to hear my teeth rattling as I climb out of the vehicle.

He chuckles and hands me my bag.

We walk past two other vehicles in the parking lot. Dry pine needles and gravel crunch under my feet. I breathe in the fresh air, enjoying the scent of the pine trees and mud. A symphony of birds chirps.

"I'm excited. I haven't been hiking in years. I just hope I don't slow you down too much."

Charlie matches my stride. Today, he's wearing khaki cargo pants, hiking boots, a hunter-green windbreaker, and a baseball cap. "The beauty about hiking is we can take all the time we need."

"Who knows, if this ends up becoming a regular thing, maybe I'll work my way up to hiking in a place like Yosemite. I've always wanted to visit."

"You've never been to Yosemite?"

"I know. It's a running joke between Dad and me. We've always talked about going, but neither of us has ever done anything about it."

"Do you want to go next weekend? I have a National Parks pass. If you aren't up for hiking, there are tons of other things we can do there. This time of year, it would only take about an hour and a half to get there."

"Can I get a rain check? I know it's not too far, but I don't want to leave my dad alone that long." At least until he's fully healed.

"Sure thing. Just tell me the day before you want to go, and I'll make it happen," Charlie promises.

We stop walking. The silence is filled by the sound of a woodpecker tapping into a dying tree trunk. We're surrounded by a thick canopy of tree cover. Few of the sun's rays reach us.

"If you don't want to go out too far, maybe we can do the Sequoia Valley Nature Preserve next week. There's a ten-mile-long stretch of trail that runs parallel to the Merced River. Not too many people take the time to seek it out. It's always empty."

"I'll see how today goes first." I adjust the position of my backpack. "Who do you normally go hiking with?"

"Me, myself, and I?"

I frown. That doesn't sound right, especially coming from a man who's crazy about safety. "Isn't one of the number-one rules of hiking not to go out by yourself?"

"Well, if you want to be technical about it . . ."

"I do. You gave me a hard time about skating alone when we first met," I fire back.

"That's different." His voice grows defensive.

"How so?"

"It just is." He removes his hat and scratches his forehead. "When I'm hiking, I make sure to text the trail I'm taking and share my location with Leslie or Jack."

"But that's not enough. It's like you said to me out on the ice—what if you fell and got hurt out here and you were all alone. Who'd help you?" I picture Dad lying on the ground after his own fall. If I can prevent history from repeating itself, I will.

He takes a few steps ahead of me. I can see him beginning to get worked up. His face is flushed, and he's touching the scar on his forehead again. I pull back. "Charlie? What's wrong?"

His eyelids flutter. He doesn't answer me.

"Hey, look at me."

His Adam's apple bobs up and down. His eyes travel from the ground up and lock onto mine.

"Look, I'm sorry for whatever I said that set you off. You're my friend. I care about you. I just want you to be safe." I take a tentative hold of his hand and squeeze it tightly. He needs some time and space to calm down. "Let's keep walking. Clear your mind. Focus on your breathing."

We resume our hike, albeit at a slower pace than when

we'd started out, still holding hands. After several minutes, his breathing shifts.

When he finally speaks, his voice comes out slightly hoarse. "I'm sorry about all that. Hearing what you had to say has brought up some painful memories from my accident."

I freeze. "Charlie, you don't have to talk about it. I understand if there are some things you want to keep private."

"No, I need to get this off my chest. We're partners now and it's time you knew." He exhales deeply. "Besides, my therapist said the more time that passes and the more people I talk to about the accident, the easier it will be to move on."

He lets go of my hand and grips the straps of his backpack. "So here goes . . . five years ago, during a practice session, just as I was lifting Camille into a star lift, I tripped and hit my head on the ice. It took less than three seconds for my life to change forever."

Chapter Fourteen

I let out an audible gasp at Charlie's words.

Over the years, I've taken thousands of spills, not just on jumps, but also on spins and footwork. Falling is after all a part of skating. In pairs skating, however, a fall is a whole other matter. Being dropped on a lift is one of the worst possible things that can happen. There's a high probability both skaters will get hurt.

Imagine being up on a ten-foot-tall ladder, then being knocked over. Now replace that ladder with a person holding you up over a sheet of concrete and two sets of sharp skates. There's little to cushion your fall. All you have available to you are your reflexes. The chances of having a major injury increase tenfold. That's what it's like in pairs.

"When we went down, I had the oddest sensation that everything was happening in slow motion. I had just enough time to use my body to shield Camille from hitting the ice. Everything that happened after that is still fuzzy. She was shaken, but physically fine. For myself, I remember having this searing pain in my head. I couldn't hear or see straight. It was like I was having an out-of-body experience."

Charlie's voice grows softer. "Leslie had been watching us practice. She knows a lot about head injuries from playing hockey. Our coach kept telling me to shake it off so we could get on with practice, but it didn't sit right with Les. She knew I needed to be checked out for a concussion. From what I was told, they got into a nasty argument that ended with Leslie firing our coach before she dragged me to the ER. I told myself if I ever became a coach, I'd always make sure something like that never happened to my students."

My nails dig into the tender flesh of my palms. Anger bubbles inside of me. I don't understand. How could a coach, a person you are supposed to rely on, just tell somebody to shake it off? Shouldn't he have been watching out for Charlie's well-being? We're taught from an early age that head injuries and concussions are serious. There is no way Charlie's former coach should have been that clueless.

Charlie's face remains grim. "At the ER, I had to get about ten stitches for this cut on my hairline here." He brushes his bangs back. "The medical staff also confirmed I had a concussion. The treatment was to get lots of rest and avoid any strenuous physical activity for a couple weeks until my symptoms subsided, but that was only the beginning of the nightmare."

My stomach muscles are tying themselves in knots as I listen to this, knowing that things are about to go from bad to worse. But I'm also morbidly curious to know more.

"After six months, I continued to have problems with my memory. There wasn't a clear timeline of when I'd be cleared to skate again, so Camille decided it would be best if we ended our partnership. She didn't want to miss her shot at going to the Olympics, which I can't say I blame her for. Meanwhile, I spent another eighteen months off the ice doing specialized therapy."

"Oh, Charlie, that's horrendous," I say, my voice breaking down and betraying my emotions. I can't imagine having to sit in limbo for so long with an injury, not knowing if I'd be able to return to doing what I love.

He hangs his head. "Finally, two and a half years after the accident, I decided enough was enough. I had to come to terms with the fact that I was as recovered as I was ever going to be. I'd developed what's called acquired dyslexia and issues with my short-term memory. While I was medically cleared to skate again, I didn't see a point. I was damaged goods."

We reach one of the vista points on the trail. It affords hikers the first glimpse of the King's Summit waterfall through the trees. If we opened our ears, we might be able to hear its far-off sound, but right now, our focus is elsewhere.

"I went from being a top contender for the Olympics to having my identity taken from me. I didn't know what I'd do next. I hadn't skated in almost three years, and with my memory issues, a normal job was out of the question." Charlie sits on a nearby wooden bench. "Looking back, it's Leslie who saved me. I'll forever be grateful I have a twin who refused to let me drown in self-pity. She conspired with our nan, and convinced me that if I moved here, I could have a fresh start." He shifts his backpack, so it rests on his chest, reaches for his water bottle, and takes a long drink.

I cautiously sink down next to him, processing all the information he's just shared. Hearing about the circumstances of the accident, everything makes sense now. It's no wonder he doesn't want anyone being alone on the ice. It's just like with my father. I never want him to be alone either. Poor Charlie. Having an experience like that would turn most people away from skating forever, but not him. Charlie is much stronger than he looks. He's obviously worked hard to turn himself around and move forward from the past.

My first instinct is to offer him a hug, but I sense it's not what he needs right now. I settle for placing a hand on his knee, reaffirming I'm here to support him. "That's a lot for a person to have to go through both physically and emotionally."

"It was. I became bitter and depressed. I don't know how my sister could stand being near me. I was such a beast to her." He sits quietly for a moment, playing with the top of his water bottle. "Ironically, what turned me around was becoming a skating coach. You'd think it would be better if I stayed away from people, but the opposite ended up being true. I needed a sense of purpose and a way to redirect all my negative energy. I still have days where I struggle, but the good days normally outweigh them."

"You're so good with the kids," I say.

"It's hard not to love them. They're so innocent and always eager to learn, like Richelle. Working with them reminds me of why I originally started skating all those years ago. It was never about medals or money. It was about racing my sister to the other side of the rink and seeing who could land an Axel first. It was an activity I loved."

"For me, it was the same reason as Kaylee. I wanted to become a princess." I smile. "I saw a Dreams on Ice show when I was little. The skaters fascinated me. I wanted to be just like them."

"I can see that. You'd make an excellent princess." We watch a pair of large birds soar through the expansive blue sky and enjoy the sound of the waterfall. Finally, Charlie asks, "How did you move past your own broken heart?"

That's a strange question to ask. I furrow my brow. Why does he want to know about my romantic life? I mean, I guess I don't mind sharing a little bit since he's been so open with me. I have nothing to hide. But it really isn't any of his business. "I wouldn't know. I've, er . . . never been in any serious sort of relationship."

"No, Frankie. I guess I worded that badly." He shakes his

head, a smile tugging at his lips. "What I meant was when your pairs partner ended your skating relationship."

"Oh!" I sit taller, my cheeks burning. "I didn't have too much time to dwell on it. Right after it happened, my father gave me an ultimatum. If I wasn't going to skate, he told me, I'd have to find a job and start paying rent. Dad was in the navy for over thirty years. When he gives orders, he means business."

"And you applied for Dreams on Ice, just like that?"

"No. I looked for retail jobs, but after about a week, Dad intervened." I rest my hands behind me and lean back. "He told me we were going on a road trip. I assumed it would be a camping trip to the Grand Canyon to help me clear my head. It's another place we'd always talked about going to. He made a big show about packing up the car and all our gear.

"Well, sometime after we passed L.A., I fell asleep in the car. When I woke up, instead of being most of the way to Arizona, we were in Las Vegas, where Dreams on Ice was performing."

"Did he take you all that way to see a show?"

"No." I giggle. "For an audition."

"Whoa." Charlie's eyes go wide with shock.

"Yeah. To this day, I still don't know how he managed to arrange it, but I skated for the casting director after a show, and they hired me on the spot."

"Wow. It shows how much he loves you. He sounds like a character." Charlie chuckles.

"He is. Believe me." I nod. "You'll enjoy meeting him and my best friend Gemma. She's due to visit in a few weeks. She wants to see us skate."

"I'm looking forward to it."

When Charlie's ready, we continue our hike up to the waterfall. As we leave the vista point and begin ascending one of the steeper points of the trail, there's no denying that our relationship as friends and partners has just reached a new level. He's continuing to share things with me that go beyond a casual relationship. I just don't know what it means yet.

Soaking our feet in a small tide pool below the falls, Charlie and I enjoy a light lunch. We munch on sandwiches with turkey bacon and egg that he cooked earlier this morning. Droplets of water rain down from the falls, cooling down our overly warm bodies. Small fish swim near my feet, tickling my toes.

"Charlie, I was thinking." I mull over my next words carefully. "Would it be for the best if we reevaluated our long-term skating goals?"

He chews slowly before answering, "And by that you mean . . .?"

"I still want us to skate together," I throw out quickly. "Maybe we should consider pursuing something safer than pairs skating, like ice dance. I don't *need* to take my senior test. I can—"

"No." His shoulders become rigid.

"Hear me out." I finish my sandwich and brush my hands against my leggings, bringing my knees to my chest. "I don't think it's worth the risk of you suffering another concussion."

His nostrils flare. "I'm tired of having the fear of another concussion rule my life. Ice is slippery. Every time I step out there, we *both* take the risk of suffering an injury."

"Charlie, I didn't mean it—"

He stands and walks away. "Are you worried about my ability to be a competent partner?"

I open my mouth, but he cuts me off again.

"I'll have you know I had a full physical and psychological

evaluation from my doctors this past weekend. They gave me a clean bill of health." His brows knit together. "If for a single moment I felt I was putting you at risk, I wouldn't take the ice with you." His chest heaves up and down.

"Charlie, I trust you." I slowly pull my feet out of the water and approach him with even, steady steps, placing a hand on the crook of his elbow. "I'm only bringing this up because I don't want to see you get hurt again. I . . . I've had a lot of experience with it happening to the people I love and care about recently."

He freezes and whispers, "Your father."

"Yes," I say quietly. "He had a similar experience to yours." I stare at the waterfall as I recount the full story of his injury and the entire reason behind my moving home. "You're one of the very few people who knows. I'm sharing this with you so that you'll understand where I'm coming from. You're an amazing partner and I fully trust you. I just can't help but worry."

He wraps his arms around me tightly, pulling me to him, my head resting on his chest. I hear the sound of his heart beating and take in the scent of his woodsy cologne. I've started to think a lot about this man recently and what it would feel like to be held by him. Now, I know. It's like being enveloped by a soft blanket on a chilly evening. It's warm and comforting.

"I'm sorry, Frankie. I didn't mean to overreact." He swallows hard and releases me. "I've pushed away so many people. I'm not used to having anyone who'd want to be by my side."

Hearing him say that breaks my heart.

"Thank you for trusting me with your dad's story. We're partners now in every sense of the word. If you need anything, I'll be there for you."

"Thanks," I say.

"Come on, we'd better get going. It's a long hike back."

Walking over to the tide pool to retrieve my shoes and socks, I think about his hug and our conversations from earlier. That's when it hits me. I'm starting to develop feelings for this man in a way that goes beyond friendship. I gulp. I can't let this happen, can I?

Charlie remains semi-quiet on the ride back to Grizzly Springs. As he pulls up to the parking lot in front of the Miller School of Dance, I realize I'd forgotten it's still Sunday.

"I'm exhausted from the hike, and I bet you are too. Are you sure you don't feel like skipping our ballroom class and grabbing a bite to eat instead?" he says.

His suggestion sounds much better than a dance class, but we've made a financial commitment to ballroom lessons. There's no going back now. "Nope. We're doing this. You're the one who wanted to pay for the full twelve-class package in advance to get the ten percent discount."

He pinches the bridge of his nose. "I know. I'm regretting it."

We climb out of the truck. I walk ahead of him and yank the door to the dance studio open. "After you, Mr. C." He grumbles under his breath and walks inside.

"You don't see me complaining," I whisper behind him.

Once in the lobby area, we check in with the receptionist. I plop myself down on the ground and exchange my street shoes for a pair of ballroom dance heels. "You're lucky men's ballroom shoes are comfortable." I point to the two-inch heels. "These things are torture devices."

"It can't be all that different from wearing a skate boot, can it?"

I wince as I stand. The leather on the front of the shoe is

stiff and not yet broken in. It puts an uncomfortable amount of pressure on my poor pinky and big toes. I should've listened to my gut and ordered a half-size larger. "You can try my heels on after class, then tell me what you think."

He zips his mouth closed. We tuck our belongings and shoes into the storage cubbies and walk out onto the dance floor. The room is similar in size and shape to a ballet studio. Three walls are covered with floor-to-ceiling mirrors. The fourth wall contains the studio's sound system. The floor is made of polished cherrywood.

"Welcome back, everyone." Madame Miller, the studio's owner, claps her hands together. "Let's get right to work. Last week, we started learning the basic step, the chase step, and the proper posture for ballroom dancing. Has everyone been practicing?"

Madame Miller stands about five-foot-three and has her curly black hair secured in a bun. She's about sixty years old, but a person would never know that based on how she moves and carries herself. Today, she wears a black leotard, red shawl, red chiffon overskirt, black leg warmers, and black ballroom shoes.

There are a few grumbles from the men and a few half-hearted "no" answers from the women.

"I see we are going to need a quick review of the steps. First is the basic step." She walks out to the front of the room to demonstrate. "Do we all remember now?"

We stare blankly. "I see." She laughs. "Well, let's give it the old college try and see what happens. You all mastered this step at the end of last week. I'm sure your muscle memory will return quickly once you settle in."

She clicks a button on a remote, and Spanish guitar music fills the room. "Don't worry about adding any arms. Footwork only. The tempo is quick-quick-slow, quick-quick-slow." She claps her hands together again. "Ready, go."

Madame Miller increases the music's volume. Charlie and I both step toward one another with our left feet. We laugh.

"Have you forgotten already?" he asks.

"My brain is in skating mode. I normally lead with my left skate."

"Ice would be a lot easier than this. Let's try this again," he says.

"Five, six, seven, eight," I count off, just as I do during our practice sessions.

We quickly find our rhythm.

"This reminds me of a cha-cha, except there's one less step," I muse.

"Switch!" Madame Miller calls out. "Ladies, this time you try leading. Men, you follow."

We reset and I take the lead.

"Wait, isn't this step in a mambo? Think about the ice dance pattern Richelle was practicing all last week for her solo dance test."

I glance down to my feet. "I guess you're right. I don't know ice dance that well."

Madame Miller sweeps around the room, offering a few helpful corrections. When she reaches us, she says, "Try not to look at your feet. Keep your eyes up and chin up. You have a handsome partner who should make the job all the easier."

As she walks away, Charlie cackles with laughter.

"Not a word," I warn.

He holds his hands up.

"Let's try the pivot step. Men, you'll turn to . . ."

I pivot away from Charlie as if I'm practicing while Madame Miller explains. My hands fly to my cheeks. Why did she have to bring up how attractive he is? Gah. It's been on my mind for at least the past two weeks.

I turn back around. Charlie is facing away from me. My eyes travel to his strong back and firm butt, which has become even more toned over the last few weeks. The days of wearing baggy, stained clothing are gone. He's started to favor more fitted clothing to show off his new physique.

Not paying attention to what I should be doing, I stumble. As I try to catch myself, Charlie is right there to steady me. His hands touch my body, and a warm tingle radiates up my spine. "You, okay?"

My face has to be crimson by now. "Fine. It's these heels."

"Amazing how you can glide on a metal blade an eighth of an inch thick, but you can't manage to walk in a straight line."

"Yeah, amazing."

"Excellent job, everyone. You looked great." Madame Miller pauses the music. "I see we already have a couple in here who's eager to get a start on reviewing how to partner one another. Fantastic."

All the heads in the room swivel in our direction.

"See how nice and upright they are? This is exactly what I'd like you all to aim for. The only thing that could use improving is for them to be closer. You two should almost be touching. Ballroom dancing is about creating nice long lines and intimate connections."

I groan internally. How am I going to make it through the next hour with my body on fire?

Chapter Fifteen

It's Sunday morning. Charlie and I are in downtown Laka Wakahanra, where white-tented booths are packed tightly together, displaying vintage trinkets, antique furniture, delicate porcelain dolls, weathered books, and jewelry. The air is filled with the scent of aged wood and lavender.

"An antique market?" I tease.

"Blame my nan. Antiquing is one of her hobbies. She uses me as the muscle"—Charlie flexes his biceps—"to carry whatever she ends up buying."

My body shakes with laughter. I try picturing what his grandmother might look like. She has to be a sweet older woman with a short silver bob. I know both Leslie and Charlie are close to her.

"Uh-huh." I gesture to the tables. "I bet ninety percent of the things for sale here weigh less than five pounds."

"Okay, so maybe it's wishful thinking."

"Mm-hmm." I shake my head and laugh some more. "Is there anything specific we're looking for today?"

"A birthday gift for Nan." Charlie runs a hand through his hair. "Les and I wanted to get her something unique. Whenever she's brought me here, we've found some unexpected things. I thought it might be a good place to start."

If we don't find anything here, I can ask my dad. I could've sworn I'd caught him researching antique shops on the internet a few days ago, but when I asked him about it, he brushed me off. Dad has been extra secretive lately. His dating life with the woman he met online has taken off. Today, he's taking her on yet another date to a sip-and-paint class.

"What type of things does your grandma enjoy?"

Charlie strokes his jaw. "She has eccentric taste, but the one thing she always tells us is that it's best to come to an antique market with an open mind and a budget. She looks for items that appear as if they have an interesting story to tell."

"And your budget is . . .?"

"A grand?"

I stumble. He steadies me with the refined reflexes of a skater. "Whoa, careful. I need you in one piece."

"Thanks." I blush, a mix of embarrassment and gratitude rushing through me. I dry swallow. It's getting increasingly more difficult to ignore the signals my body is sending me every time our hands touch. Turning a blind eye to it on the ice is easy enough—we're there to work—but outside the rink, it's another story. Finding my voice, I manage to say, "A grand is a *lot* of money."

"It is, but this is my grandmother. I don't want to cheap out if we see something amazing."

As we near the end of the aisle, I spot a red-and-green jukebox. "Charlie, look!" I exclaim, flinging my arm out to stop him. I accidentally hit his ribs.

"Ow. That hurt. What did you have to do that for?" His gaze travels up to the machine and he lights up. "Oh. Oh! Good eye! That's it! That's what we need for Nan."

I speed up my walk to match his long strides. Somebody's eager. "I wonder if it still works."

"Even if it doesn't, I bet I could find someone who could outfit it with new hardware or a turntable. Vinyl records are making a comeback."

He's right. Dad was over the moon when we discovered some at the downtown Grizzly Springs bookshop. He bragged the entire way home about how his collection of vinyl records and eight tracks was original and might be worth a lot of money.

We enter the tent. Up close, I see the machine has chrome accents and colorful buttons. Charlie and I exchange excited glances.

"Hi there." A vendor in a Fresno Flying Squirrels baseball cap, T-shirt, and jeans approaches us. "How can I help you?"

"What can you tell us about that?" Charlie says.

The vendor leans over and turns on the power strip connected to a generator. The jukebox buzzes to life. "This belonged to my gramps. It used to sit up in his office at the Lucky Dog Diner. It's in pristine condition and still has all its original records."

Charlie rubs his hands together. "My nan would *love* this. There's a spot in the living room near her bookcases where it would fit perfectly. I can see her dancing around, enjoying a glass of wine to the Bee Gees or Elvis when no one is home, just like she used to do with Gramps when he was still alive."

Behind us, there's a few other people starting to take note of the jukebox. We can't lose this to them. I jump in. "How much are you asking for it?"

The vendor eyes us, then returns his gaze to the machine. "Why don't you tell me how much you're willing to pay for it?"

Charlie reaches into the back pocket of his jeans to retrieve his wallet. Opening it, he glances inside the cash section. "I can do five hundred in cash and five hundred on my credit card."

The vendor's face falls. "That's a lot lower than I'd hoped to get for it."

Charlie frowns. "You asked us to make you an offer. What figure did you have in mind?"

I do some quick mental math. "I can throw in another two hundred on my credit card if it would help."

Charlie sucks in air sharply. "Frankie, that's a lot."

I place a hand on his. "It's for a good cause."

Technically speaking, it's a lot more than I can afford, but with the extra coaching hours thanks to Charlie, I can just squeeze by. I'll have a month or two to pay my credit card balance down.

A couple listening in to the conversation approaches the vendor. They throw out their own offer. "We'll give you twenty-one hundred for it."

Charlie clenches his jaw. "I'll match it."

"We'll do twenty-two hundred."

"I'll do—"

"Charlie, remember what you told me when you walked in?" I interrupt him. "The budget."

His shoulders deflate. "You're right. Nan would kill me." He turns to the vendor. "The best I can do is two grand. Otherwise, you can give it to them."

The man strokes his chin. "Credit cards charge me a five-percent fee every time. Do you folks have any cash?"

"No," the man bidding against us says.

The vendor turns to Charlie. "Cash is still king to me. If you give me your five hundred bucks and settle the rest on your card, it's yours."

"Done." They shake hands.

Grumbling, the other couple leaves the tent.

Charlie hands his money to me. "Would you mind double

checking this is five hundred and helping with the transaction?" His big eyes plead with me. "Numbers . . . I have trouble reading them with the you know. . ." He trails off.

"I've got your back."

"Thank you," he says softly. "Here's my credit card. I'm just going to inspect Nan's new toy."

I organize Charlie's cash as he leans forward to study the machine.

"Thank you. This means more to him than you know." I pay the vendor. "It's for his grandma."

"That's why I'm happy to have you two take it. I'd like to see the jukebox get some use. To anyone else, it's a collector's item and would probably just get resold." He takes hold of Charlie's credit card. "I'll be right back with this."

Suddenly, the rich sound of Elvis' voice rings out from the machine. I close my eyes and let the music fill me, swaying side to side.

Charlie clears his throat. "You know, a slow song like this is perfect to practice our ballroom dancing to." My pulse increases as he extends his hand to me. "Shall we?"

"Oh, um, sure."

He pulls me in close to him, places one hand on my waist, and holds the other hand gently in his. Our bodies move in perfect sync, just like when we're on the ice. The world around us fades into a blur as we dance.

"You're a natural," Charlie says. "So talented in everything you do."

"It helps that we've been taking lessons."

"Touché." He chuckles. "Thanks for all your help today. Nan is really going to enjoy this."

"Who knows, maybe once you give it to her, she'll insist on having a dance party."

"You know what, Frankie, she just might."

As the man returns, we break apart, brought back to reality. I know it won't be long before I'll have to tell him how I really feel about him. I don't know if I'll be able to hide my feelings much longer.

The following day, Charlie and I meet Leslie for dinner at Millie's, where he tells her about our find.

Leslie claps her hands together. "A jukebox! Are you serious? That's amazing!"

"It is, isn't it?" I smile, my eyes fixed on Charlie. "Your brother fought off another couple to make sure he'd be the one to be able to gift it to your grandma."

"Let me know how much I owe you and I'll split it with you."

Charlie blinks slowly. "You owe me a thousand dollars."

Leslie frowns. "You spent two grand?"

"I was prepared to pay more for it, but Frankie stopped me from going crazy."

"That's a *lot* of dough. I guess I shouldn't complain. Nan's worth it." Leslie picks up her wineglass and swirls the red liquid around. "Thanks for stopping him from getting carried away. He can be so darn stubborn."

"Hey, I'm *right* here, Les."

Watching the two siblings banter, I wonder what it would have been like if I'd had one.

"Why do I even bother trying to reason with you? You're my twin. We're too much alike." Leslie rolls her eyes. "So, Frankie . . . moving on. How did your dad's most recent date go? I've been dying to hear about it."

Charlie cocks his head to the side. "Date?"

"Uh-huh. My dad recently signed up for a senior dating app. I'd hoped it might help him leave the house and meet some nice mature women, but it hasn't *exactly* worked out that way."

"Meaning?"

"The first date he went on a couple weeks ago was a huge success."

"That doesn't sound bad," Charlie says.

"Wait for it." Leslie grins.

"It wasn't at first. But now they're out *all* the time. Three or sometimes even four times a week. Their relationship is moving too fast, if you ask me."

"And what did they do last night?" Charlie leans an elbow on the table.

"They went to an art gallery, then did another wine tasting and painting thing." I pull out my phone and find a photo of the latest masterpiece my father has created. "When I got home from Lake Wakahanra, I found this."

They take turns looking at the photo on my phone.

"It's interesting," Charlie says slowly.

"You can be blunt. It won't hurt my feelings. I think it looks like he's done some type of finger-painting activity. My dad is gifted in many things, but he's artistically challenged."

Leslie and Charlie burst out laughing. "It's not that bad, Frankie," she says.

"If you like it, it's yours. He won't miss it. We have three other canvases that are just as rough."

Her cheeks flush a shade of pink. "I'd love to, except I just remembered, I don't have any empty wall space left."

"That's what you get for buying all that crud from Hobby Land," Charlie says.

"It's not crud! It's all useful stuff."

"Oh really? What are you planning on doing with the inflatable peacock you were testing in the lobby the other day?"

"It's for the skating school's upcoming recital. The theme is jungle. We needed some animals for it.

"There aren't any peacocks in the jungle!" Charlie says.

"There are if you use your imagination," Leslie retorts.

It's my turn to laugh as I watch them go at it. For the first time since I left Dreams on Ice, I feel like my old self. A warm bubble rises up in my chest. I exhale. I've found some brilliant new friends and been given the gift of being able to skate pairs again.

Chapter Sixteen

A few weeks later, Charlie and I hold our opening pose on the ice. Our backs are facing away from one another, one knee bent, the other out to the side. The fast opening chords of our free-skate music play out over the speaker system from the classic Audrey Hepburn film *My Fair Lady*.

"Five, six, seven, eight . . ." I count off, patting my hand against my thigh.

Popping up from our opening stances, we grasp hands and perform a set of back crossovers diagonally across the ice. The element I worry about the most is the one that comes up first —the split twist.

I tap into the ice with my toe pick. Charlie pushes me up into the air. Holding my hands over my head, I rotate twice, but as I come down to land, I can tell Charlie's positioning is off. He catches me with a heavy thud and helps me find my footing on the ice. At least it wasn't a crash this time. I'll call that a victory.

We continue to push through, checking off each element as we perform it. The music changes one final time to "I Could've Danced All Night." We attack our footwork sequence, and thirty seconds later, hit our ending pose. The music fades. We bend over at our waists, breathing hard.

As exhausted as I am, every time we perform this program, I have chills. It's literally my dream come true. Charlie's done an amazing job putting the program together in such a short time. Who knew he had such a hidden talent for choreography.

"That twist was a hot mess. I'm still not pushing you far enough into the air," he says.

"It could also be that I'm picking in for the twist too far back. Don't blame yourself. It takes two to skate. When Gemma gets in, maybe she can watch it and give us her thoughts?" I pat his shoulder. "I still can't believe how much progress we've made. We almost have a *full* program."

"It is pretty amazing, isn't it?" He stands up straight. "Now all we need is to add in a few lifts and be able to make it through the program without being so winded."

"You and me both."

We head back out for one more run-through.

"How exhausted are you from doing our program twice?" Charlie asks me with a calculating look later that morning, after the last of our students have departed. We've taken off our skates and are stretching and warming up our muscles in the ballet studio.

I sit with my legs crossed on top of my purple yoga mat. "Not enough to skip out on this off-ice session, if that's what you're implying."

"No, it's nothing like that." Charlie dips his chin. "I was hoping we could start on lifts today. It wouldn't be anything too fancy. I just want us to start getting comfortable with the basics. I feel strong. I think I'm finally ready."

I regard him carefully. This is the moment I've been waiting for. We're two months ahead of where I thought we'd be. Up until this point, Charlie has been extra cautious with our skill progressions. Lifts are the last element we need.

I jump up and down like a puppy that's discovered a fresh set of tennis balls to play with. "Yes. Yes. Yes."

"You're sure?"

"Positive."

We unfold the foam panel mats normally stored in the corner and spread them out around us. Charlie removes his bulky outerwear and strips down to just a fitted black T-shirt and skating pants. His arms are sculpted, and the muscles of his chest ripple through the thin fabric. I can count six perfect little squares in his abs.

I gulp. The Charlie Welch I used to have a crush on is *fully* back. It's the first time I've gotten a look at what lies hidden underneath his fleece jacket. Even when we're ballroom dancing, he usually wears a loose long-sleeved shirt.

"If you don't feel safe at any point in time, tell me, and we'll stop immediately," he instructs me.

I clear my mind and focus back on the present. I can't afford to lose any focus here. "That goes for you too."

"Got it." His jaw tightens, and he rubs the back of his neck. "This is going to be the first time I've done any overhead lifts since my accident. If I have any doubts, I'll stop."

"Okay." We have to be one hundred percent committed to one another for this to work. I have full faith that Charlie won't let anything happen to me. I know we can do this. "I trust you," I whisper under my breath.

Charlie rolls his neck from side to side and loosens up the muscles in his arms, chest, and shoulders. "We'll take this nice and easy. I'm going to put my hands on your hips, lift you up, then put you back down. Just to get used to the motion, feel, and timing." I turn my back to him. His hands travel to my hips. "On your count."

"Three. Two. One. Ready. Go." I'm up and down in a matter of seconds. It was like a piece of silk flowing against my skin with how smooth and easily Charlie is able to move my body. My pulse increases, and adrenaline floods my body. There's nothing like the thrill of being up in the air.

"Easy peasy," I say. We high-five.

"Easy peasy?" He snorts.

I glance over my shoulder. "That's what my level one and two students always say to me."

"Mine say, 'Easy peasy, lemon squeezy' too. They have the funkiest expressions." He chuckles. "Let's do two more of these before we move on."

I move back into position. "Counting us down in three. Two. One. Ready. Go."

His hands grip my waist. Once again, it's as if I'm a marionette being suspended by a set of strings. I watch his face. It's relaxed, as if he could do this all day.

"Does it feel okay?" he asks, setting me down.

I flash a thumbs-up. "Everything was perfect."

For our next attempt, we mutually decide to go for a real lift. If everything goes according to plan, I'll be sitting on his hand, just like I used to in the Dreams on Ice finale.

"Do you still remember how to do this?" I tease.

"I think so." A glint of determination sparkles in his eyes.

"It'll be like riding a bike."

Charlie nods and takes a deep breath. I turn my back to him again. Our hands meet and fingers interlock. I count us down from three. He bends his knees and is in the process of lifting me past his face just as the door creaks open.

"Charlie, have you seen Frankie? I have some good news to share with her," Leslie's voice calls out, followed by the sound of glass hitting the ground and breaking. "What the Hades do you think you two are doing?"

My body fidgets. Lines appear on Charlie's face as he fights to stay calm. His arms quiver, but he doesn't let his sister's sudden appearance throw him off. He carefully places me back down on the ground before snapping his head in her direction. His eyes flash dangerously.

"You of all people know better than to raise your voice at me like that when I'm in the middle of a lift." His tone is clipped. "You can say whatever you want *after* my partner is back on the ground. Got it?"

My limbs have suddenly turned to lead. I'm frozen in place.

"Fine." Leslie's face is a deep-red. The muscles in her neck bulge. I wonder if this is what she looks like when she's itching to start a fight in a hockey game. "I'll ask you two again. What do you think you're doing?"

"What does it look like we're doing?" He crosses his arms. "Frankie and I were right in the middle of starting a lift when you *barged* in on us."

Has he not said anything to his sister, like he promised?

Leslie's eyes suddenly narrow. "Why?"

No, he hasn't. Uh-oh. This can't be good. My tongue remains glued to the roof of my mouth.

"Don't be dense. We're planning to skate together."

"Competitively?"

"Maybe? I don't know. We're leaving our options open."

"Do you know how foolish that sounds? Or the enormous risks you're taking? What happens if you fall again?"

"I'm *not* being foolish. Frankie and I have been working hard to build up to this. I'm sick and tired of being treated like I'm *damaged*. It's my decision. Not yours."

"Charlie, why do you have to be so darn selfish?!" Leslie punches the wall. A few tears leak down her cheeks. "Your decision affects everyone around you. Have you ever considered the physical and mental toll your accident has taken on me?"

Charlie stares at her blankly.

"You're not the only Welch who was broken." Leslie shakes her head, the tears flowing like a melting ice cube. "If you want to roll the dice and skate pairs again, fine. Like you said, it's *your* life. Just don't expect me to be there to pick up the pieces. You're on your own."

I find my voice and take a step toward my friend. "Leslie . . ."

As if she'd forgotten I was present, she snaps her head toward me and glares. "Don't. Speak. To. Me." She sprints out of the room.

"Why didn't she ever say anything to me about how she felt?" Charlie stands rooted in his spot. His eyes are wide, and his shoulders hunched. He looks so lost. "What should I do?"

"Leslie may be strong, but she's not a robot. She's human. Maybe she was too afraid to say anything to you." I place a hand under his chin and lift it. "Whatever the reason is, she needs you right now. Go find her and talk to her."

"Frankie . . ." His voice comes out strained.

"Go. I'm fine. We can touch base later. Besides, somebody needs to clean up the mess."

Charlie walks to the doorway and glances at me one more time, then disappears from sight.

I hope he and Leslie can work things out between them. I swallow hard. It's partly my fault she's so upset. Charlie is doing me a favor. I need to apologize to her once things have cooled down. I don't want to lose her friendship over this.

L ater that evening, I text Charlie.

> Frankie: Hey. Sorry I didn't get a chance to touch base with you before I left. It was crazy tonight without Leslie around. Half the teachers didn't know what to do, but we figured it all out eventually.

> Charlie: It's okay. I can only imagine how busy you guys were. I would've come in to help if I had known she wasn't going to show up. She's never done anything like this before.

> Frankie: She must really be hurting and angry.

> Charlie: I think so too.

> Frankie: Were you able to talk to her?

> Charlie: Sort of?

> Frankie: ???

It takes Charlie several minutes to send a reply.

> Charlie: She hopped into her car right after she left us. I left her apology messages on her phone until the mailbox was full. Then I spent a couple hours checking in with her friends, seeing if they know where she might've gone. I was worried about her.

Three dots blink as he continues to type.

> Charlie: Sorry, if my phone is lagging, I'm using the voice-to-text feature. It's slow.

I'd always wondered how Charlie was able to text without any problems.

Charlie: The good news is Leslie called Nan about an hour ago. She's at her hairstylist's place. She flat-out refuses to speak to me, but Nan promised to pass on the message that I'm here whenever she changes her mind.

Frankie: Oh, Charlie, I'm so sorry.

Charlie: She'll come around. She just needs time. We're both hardheaded. I just want to warn you, she might not be speaking to you either.

Frankie: That's what I figured. How are you doing?

Charlie: I'm tired and have a headache, but I think some sleep will cure it. If not, I'll text you in the morning.

Frankie: We can take tomorrow off if you'd like.

Charlie: I'd rather not. I need to stay busy.

Frankie: Okay, in that case, see you then. Good night.

Chapter Seventeen

A few days later, I stand inside the men's department of the Wardrobe Emporium with Gemma, who arrived in town three days ago. The soft hum of conversation fills the store. After spending over an hour combing through rack after rack of suits with my best friend, I pray that the traditional-cut one we've found for Dad will be to his liking. He's been as picky as a kid who hates eating vegetables.

The dressing room door opens and closes. Dad clears his throat.

"Mr. T, wow." Gemma lets out a wolf whistle. "Looking sharp."

"That's one approval down. Frankie?" He turns and strikes a pose. "What do you think? Will Suzy approve?"

"Navy-blue suits you, Dad. It brings out your eyes." My throat is dry. Leave it to my father to pick navy-blue. It must remind him of his military uniform. "I think she'll love it."

"How's the fit? Do you think it needs any alterations?" His hands brush over a few wrinkles in the pants.

"Spin around for me." He turns slowly, and I look over the alignment of the seams. "I think the fit is pretty good."

"Excellent." He smiles. "I'll just change and then we can get in line to check out. Can you believe this is the first suit I've bought since your middle school graduation, kiddo?" He walks back toward the fitting rooms.

I elbow Gemma. "Do you see what I mean? Dad's *really* serious about her. Should I be worried he'll be buying a ring next?"

Gemma shakes her head, and her blond ringlets bounce up and down. "Not yet. I think he's just happy to have a woman close to his age to spend time with. How often are they seeing one another?"

"Four to five times a week."

Gemma's eyes widen. "Seriously? What do they do?"

"I have no idea. He's tight-lipped about it. All I know is he gets a lot of enjoyment out of telling me not to wait up for him."

"You sound like the parent, not him." She laughs. "You were the one who wanted him to pick up a hobby and spend time out of the house."

"I did." I move my ponytail to my shoulder, combing my fingers through it. "It's not that I regret doing it either. It's just a lot for me to get used to."

"Have you told your father how you feel?"

"No. I don't want to run interference. I'm a grown adult and so is he. If Suzy makes him happy, I'm all for it. Besides, it's motivated him to work on his hip exercises. He's walking just as well as before his surgery."

Dad rejoins us. The suit blazer and slacks are draped over his arm. Gemma and I pause our conversation. I reach my hands out for the clothing. "Dad, I'll take care of paying for this."

He hesitates. "Are you sure?"

"Positive. It can be one of your Father's Day gifts."

He pecks me on the cheek. "Thank you, sweetie."

"I meant to ask earlier, what do you think we should bring to Suzy's place for dinner tonight?" I readjust the strap of my purse. "Wine? Dessert? A charcuterie board?"

"Honey, you don't need to bring anything. I'll pick up some flowers before we head over and say it's from all of us."

"Dad, I know we don't have to, but I want to as a hostess gift. This is our first time meeting, and I want to make a good first impression."

"That's thoughtful of you." He rubs his chin. "In that case, how about wine. Suzy-kins loves a good white, like Riesling."

Gemma steps in. "Mr. T, how about you and I head across the street and pick up a bottle while Frankie checks out? That way I can pick up some dinner too."

"That sounds great. Except you're coming with us tonight, Gem."

My body shakes with silent laughter. Gemma's face is comical. "I am?"

"Of course, you're part of the extended Tomlinson family."

I point to the register. "I'll meet you both across the street when I'm done."

Dad sticks out his arm for Gemma, who loops hers through it. "Have I told you my joke of the day yet?"

"No, Mr. T, I don't think you have."

"What do you call a pile of cats?"

"I'm not sure, Mr. T?"

"A meown-tain!"

She laughs. "Do you have any more?"

"Do I!"

I cover my mouth with my hand. Gemma's a good sport. I can't wait until she finally meets Charlie later this week. What will she make of him? What will he make of her?

My mouth drops open as the cool female voice on the phone's GPS directs us down a long gravel driveway.

"Is this a home or a castle?" Gemma sputters.

Dad half laughs, half coughs. "Suzy describes it as a cottage."

"Um, it looks more like a mansion to me," Gemma says.

Stepping out of the car, I'm instantly reminded of a medieval home I might find if I were in Germany. The structure is two stories tall and painted white, with exposed wooden beams. Arched windows let in plenty of natural light. The roof is sloped, with three chimneys. There's even a castle-like turret jutting out to the side.

We walk up to the front door. There's an intricately carved wooden figurine of a bear sitting on its haunches, wearing a doctor's stethoscope and holding a clipboard. "Huh. That's interesting."

Dad's lips twitch. "Suzy is a retired nurse." He knocks three times.

"It's open!" a singsong female voice calls out.

Dad opens the door to a lavishly decorated living room. The interior walls are white, mirroring the building's exterior. The floor is carpeted in a dark turquoise color, complementing the cherry tones of the built-in wooden bookcases on both sides of a gray stone fireplace. There's a long olive-green sofa, three hunter-green wingback chairs, a clear coffee table, and to my amusement, a knight's full suit of armor.

"It's like we're in an upscale boutique hotel," Gemma mutters.

"If you think this room is spectacular, wait until you see the rest of the house. It's done up beautifully. One of the hobbies Suzy picked up after she retired is interior design. It's fascinating going to antique markets and furniture shops with her. She knows so much, like how to tell a real piece of Sèvres porcelain from a . . ."

When did he learn all this? Was this what he did on dates with her?

"Rich, good timing! I was about to give you a call to see when you might be arriving." A woman with short silver hair greets Dad with a kiss on each cheek. She's elegantly dressed in a flowing floral top and black trousers cuffed at the ankle. "You look exceedingly dapper in that suit. You didn't have to get all dressed up for me, but I do appreciate it." She adjusts his tie.

Dad's chest swells. His cheeks turn a rosy-red. "These are for you." He holds out the things we brought.

She splays a hand on her chest. "Stunning." She sniffs the flowers and accepts the gift bag containing the bottle of wine. "You spoil me so. Thank you." Placing the items on the coffee table, she glances behind him. The corners of her mouth fold up. "You must be Frankie, lovely to meet you. Your father has spoken highly about you."

I step forward to offer the woman a handshake, but instead, she wraps her arms around me. My body stiffens, then relaxes. "I'm a hugger. It comes with the territory of being a mother and a grandmother." She laughs.

I hesitate, not sure how to reply.

"Suzy-kins, this is Gemma."

"Of course, you're welcome too! You're with Dreams on Ice, if I remember correctly, and Frankie's closest friend?" Suzy glances at Dad, who nods.

"Yes, ma'am, that's right." Gemma, too, receives a hug.

"Do I detect a hint of a Glaswegian accent?"

"Er, yes, you do."

"My late husband was from Fort Williams—in the Scottish Highlands, to be exact. We lived in Glencoe, Glasgow, and Aberdeen before moving to the States in the seventies."

"Did you now?"

It's nice to see the way Dad's friend—no, let's get real, his girlfriend—is going out of her way to make everyone feel at ease. She's a model hostess.

"You have a lovely home, Suzy. Thank you so much for inviting us to dinner tonight," I say.

Suzy leads us to the formal dining room. Floor-to-ceiling windows on three sides of the room look out over the shimmering blue water of Lake Wakahanra and the surrounding forest of pine trees. A speedboat zips through the water in the distance.

"I'm thrilled you could all come tonight. I'd hoped our families might be able to meet, but both my sons had to work this evening, and my daughter doesn't live in the area. So it'll just be my eldest grandson and possibly granddaughter dropping in on us today."

"We don't mind at all. I've been eager to meet your grandchildren." Dad rubs his hands together.

"Would you like any help in the kitchen, Suzy? Gemma and I would be happy to be put to work," I offer.

"Oh heavens, no. You're my guests this evening, and in any case, we have a housekeeper who runs the kitchen."

Suzy picks up the wine and turns the bottle over in her hands. "Good choice! I haven't heard of this winery, but the label is stunning. I love the watercolor detailing."

"Mr. Tomlinson mentioned you collect wine labels. We thought this one might be unique. It's a local special reserve. The liquor shop owner also mentioned that all their labels are created by hand," Gemma says.

Suzy's eyes dance. "That makes it all the more special."

We chat a little more about the home and learn it was a

passion project of her late husband. It has seven suites and a separate annex where her oldest son resides. Suzy promises that her grandson will give us a full tour of the cottage after dinner.

We sit down at the oak dining table with a charcuterie board and a few other appetizers to nibble on as the house-keeper prepares a roast for the main meal. Plates are passed around, and everyone begins to serve themselves.

"Suzy, I'd love to hear a little bit more about what made you decide to ask Dad out on the Golden Years app," I say.

A smile tugs at the corners of her lips. She glances at him. "After the holidays were over this past winter, I was hit with a case of seasonal depression. It happens every so often, but this time it was worse than normal." She blinks slowly. "One would think that after being widowed for twelve years, a person might become accustomed to the quiet and the soli-tude, but in truth, you never do. Normally, I try to keep busy to keep my mind off things, but this year, it wasn't working."

Dad's hand disappears under the table in Suzy's direction. He's fallen for her. It's all over his face. I've never seen him like this.

"My eldest grandchildren bought me a premium member-ship to the Golden Years app. They thought it might be the best way to get me out of my funk, and they were right. I had a hoot and a holler scrolling through different profiles, but it was Rich's cheeky photo that spoke to me. I loved that it was in black and white, and he was clutching a rose between his teeth."

I blanch. "I thought we had removed that one?"

"You did, but I added it back to my account after I saw how many more profile views it generated," Dad says.

Gemma high-fives him.

"I picked up the idea from the episode of *Cupid's Arrow* where the contestants were asked to participate in a vintage photoshoot."

"Zach won the challenge, didn't he?" Suzy lets out a sigh. "I'm so happy he ended up winning. Johnny was a nice young man, but he didn't have the same spark to his personality as Yvonne."

"You watch reality TV?" I ask.

Dad laughs. "Suzy-kins is just like our Gemma. She lives for them. Her DVR is full of not just *Cupid's Arrow*, but also travel shows, survival shows, and cooking shows. You name it, and Suzy probably watches it."

Gemma leans forward in her seat. "Have you heard the announcement about the next season of *Cupid's Arrow*?"

"Have I?!" Suzy exclaims. "I can't wait for Johnny to be in the hot seat. From the trailer that dropped this morning, his friends look like they'll be just as much fun as Selena and McKenzie were for Yvonne."

We debate the season over dinner. An hour and a half later, just as we're eating Dutch apple pie, the front door opens and closes. A man speaks in a soft, muffled tone to the housekeeper in the kitchen.

"About time my wayward grandson arrived." Suzy pats her mouth with a napkin and scoots her chair back. "Excuse me." She disappears into the kitchen.

Dad leans back in his seat and pushes his plate away. "I can't eat another bite. Would either of you two ladies care for my piece?"

"If you felt that way, Dad, why didn't you refuse it?" I tilt my head.

"I can't say no to that woman." He glances toward the kitchen with a faraway look in his eye.

Gemma reaches for the plate and offers to eat the remnants. I squeeze my knees together. My father is genuinely happy. I never thought I'd see him like this. Especially after all these years as a bachelor. "Dad, you really like her, don't you?"

"I do. When I'm with her, I'm a young and energetic man again. Not a seventy-something senior with a bad hip."

I stare at my plate. "I've always wondered . . . your first marriage . . ."

"You want to know why it broke down." Dad's shoulders slump. "The short answer is my ex-wife and I were both too young and inexperienced at life. I was eighteen and she was seventeen. We'd been neighbors growing up, and I'd always had a crush on her. The evening before I was about to ship out for my first deployment, I'd intended to ask her out on a date, but instead, I asked her to marry me. To my shock, she said yes."

Gemma and I hang on to his words. He's always been tight-lipped about the past. It's the first time I've ever heard this much of the story. I'd never realized he'd only just become an adult. When I was eighteen, I was focused on training. I would never have wanted to be tied down and married.

"The first two years of our marriage, I was gone more than I was home. We exchanged letters, but I can count on one hand the number of times we saw one another in person. Everything changed the day I received orders to return stateside. I learned I was to be based in Hawaii. Shirley was over the moon and jumped at the opportunity to live in an island paradise. We were finally able to move in together."

"That must have been awwwwwwwwwwwwwwwkward," I say.

"You called it, sweetie. We realized almost instantaneously that we had nothing in common. Adding to that, my wife found out the hard way that living on an island thousands of miles from the mainland is isolating. She grew to resent me for it. We fought constantly. She might have loved the idea of being a wife, but she didn't enjoy having a husband. So I did the only sensible thing. I offered her a way out and she took it."

Gemma frowns. "I'm sorry, Mr. T."

"Don't be. It was a valuable learning experience. I enjoyed being a bachelor. One of the most important lessons I learned was that I didn't have to conform to the norms of society. When I was ready to become a father, I had no qualms about taking the adoption route."

"And I'm all the more grateful for it." I walk over and hug him.

"You were the most perfect baby I'd ever laid eyes on." He sighs deeply. "I only wish I'd been able to take both you and your sister home. I've always wondered about the family that adopted her."

Gemma's fork clatters on the plate.

I drop my arms from around my father, taking two steps back. All the air leaves my lungs, and my chest grows tight. The walls are closing in around me. "I . . . I . . . I have a sister?"

He pales. "Frankie, you weren't supposed to find out this way. I tried to tell you when you were eighteen, but you didn't want to know anything about your adoption."

I don't have any words. All I can do is stare.

Suzy reenters the room. "Here he is. Everyone, meet my grandson, Charlie."

A familiar brown-haired man waves. "I'm sorry I'm lat—Frankie?"

My eyes widen and my vision goes fuzzy. I start to shake. It's all too much. I need air. I need to get away. "Excuse me." Without a clue as to where I'm going, I open the glass door by the kitchen and run straight toward the forest.

Chapter Eighteen

Tears trickle down my face as I pump my arms and legs. Question after question runs rampant through my mind. Is Dad keeping more information from me? How could he not have ever mentioned a sister? Why didn't he take both of us? All this time, I've had another biological family member. Did my sister find a good home? Or did she grow up all alone? Where is she now?

My sides begin to cramp. I can't run any longer. Slowing my pace, I sink down onto my hands and knees, breathing hard. Sharp, dried, tacky pine needles stick to my palms. A pinecone digs into my knee. It's eerily silent except for the soft hooting of an owl somewhere off in the distance. It smells like a mixture of vanilla and fresh butterscotch.

I glance up. The thick canopy of trees obscures the sky, matching my mood. Is my sister looking at the same sky? Is she older? Younger? Sitting down, I bring my knees to my chest and rest my forehead on them, rocking back and forth.

My throat constricts as I dry sob. I have a sister. Would we have been friends? Do we look alike or share any common interests? For years, I've tried to put on a strong front, never dwelling too much on who my birth parents might have been or the circumstances of the adoption.

Back then, I claimed I didn't care if I ever saw my official adoption agency records—I never wanted to hurt or offend my dad—but if I'm being honest, I've always been curious. I was afraid of what I might or might not find. I didn't want to be left with more questions that couldn't be answered. What was the point of learning the names of people who didn't want me?

I rub my hands against my forearms, shivering slightly. I was so hot when I was running, and now, I'm freezing. I replay Dad's confession in my head. His ashen face causes me to shiver harder.

I can't believe how badly I overreacted when I ran out of the house. I ruined dinner. Dad's probably freaking out. I hope he and Suzy aren't furious with me. At least Gemma is there to help defuse the situation.

I stand and wince. My body aches. I have no idea how much time has passed. I squint. The small amounts of light visible through the gaps in the dense forest scape have faded. I have a difficult time seeing what's in front of me.

It's like being inside a maze. Which direction did I come from? Every way I look appears the same. Maybe my phone can help me. I pat my pockets. They're flat and empty. Ugh. I put it in my purse before we sat down for dinner. How could I be so dumb as to blindly run into a forest?

I hold my head in my hands. Panicking is what got me into this mess in the first place. If I want to figure out a solution to the problem, I need to stay calm. I take a deep breath, hold it for ten seconds, then exhale.

"Okay, Frankie, you have two options," I say to myself. "One, you could stay put until help comes to you, or two, you could start moving and hope that if you walk in a straight line, it'll lead you out of the forest."

Neither one is particularly appealing. If I stay here, it could be a long cold night. I don't want to find out if there are bears, coyotes, mountain lions, wolves, or who knows what other beastly animals in these woods. By default, that leaves option two.

Sending a silent prayer that I'm doing the right thing, I take a guess and start walking. My feet crunch against the fallen leaves and pine needles. Progress is painfully slow as I keep my head directed toward the ground, watching for exposed tree roots.

Trying to keep my mood positive, I start softly singing "Wouldn't It Be Lovely" from *My Fair Lady* to myself.

I cross my arms toward my body, tucking my hands under my armpits. The chiffon sleeves of my blouse may have looked beautiful when I left the house, but they aren't practical for an evening in the mountains.

Suddenly, I hear Charlie's familiar voice yelling in the distance. "Fran-kie! Fran-kie! Can you hear me? Where are you?"

Relief floods my body. I cup my hands to my mouth. "Over here!"

"Stay where you are! I'm coming for you!" A series of twigs snap as Charlie moves through the underbrush.

I spin in a circle. "I can hear you, but I can't see you!"

"I'm coming! Keep talking!" His voice is closer.

"I thought you preferred solitude when you were out in nature," I say sarcastically.

"Not when one of my friends is lost."

"I *was* lost, but you've found me."

A beam of light flashes in my direction, temporarily blinding me. I avert my eyes. "Bright."

Charlie jogs toward me. "Frankie!" He's breathing heavily. "Thank goodness. You've had everyone so worried."

He tosses the flashlight onto the ground and quickly unzips his jacket. Draping it over my shoulders, he starts running his hands over my arms.

"I'm sorry. I just had to get out of there. I wasn't thinking. I was acting on instinct." The tears return as the reality of the situation fully sinks in. "Everyone is going to hate me. I ruined the evening."

"Shh . . . it's all right." He hugs me tightly to his body. It's like a human furnace. "You didn't ruin anything. I pinkie promise."

My lips tremble. I was so worried about myself, I've forgotten about the most important person in my life. "Is my father all right?"

"He was in shock, but he'll be fine with your friend Gemma and my nan. Try not to worry too much. All I want you to focus on right now is your own well-being." Charlie wipes the corners of my eyes with his thumbs. "Give me the honest truth—how are you doing?"

"I'm an emotional mess and I'm barely holding it together." My voice cracks.

"Okay." He rubs comforting circles on my back. "Okay," he repeats. I rest my head on his chest, listening to the rhythmic drum of his heart. "I'll tell you what . . . How about we get you warmed up in front of a fire and make s'mores? You don't have to talk about anything. Your only job would be to make sure that your marshmallow gets a nice golden-brown coating on the outside."

I tense. "I don't know if I can face everyone just yet."

"You won't have to. The firepit is away from the house. Making s'mores will buy us a little extra time for you to gather your composure. I'll tell your dad that I've found you, so he won't worry." He cups my cheeks and tilts my chin up. "I'm here to take care of you. If that means acting as your body-guard, I'll happily do it. I care about you, Frankie."

As I gaze into Charlie's intense eyes and perfectly lush rosy-red lips, I know I can't fool myself any longer. I've fallen hard and fast for the man who's just rescued me.

"You're staring at me," Charlie says with a hint of amusement as he pokes and prods the embers and kindling in the firepit.

I sit on a raised stone bench, a blanket draped over my shoulders. "I never realized you had so many outdoorsy skills. It took you about two seconds to start a fire. Where did you learn to do that?"

"From my grandad. We used to go camping together every weekend. He made sure Leslie and I learned the survival basics just in case we ever got stranded."

"Besides building a fire, those would be . . .?"

"Knowing how to erect a temporary shelter, sourcing and purifying water, identifying edible plants, and basic first-aid."

"He sounds like a smart man."

Charlie grins. "He was."

My throat constricts. "Do you think he would approve of your grandma dating my dad?"

"I think so. Nan has been alone for a long time. He was the light of her life, but from how excited she is when she talks about Rich—er, your father—I think he'd give Les and me a good kick in the pants for not signing her up for a dating app sooner."

"Dad's been the same. He glows around her." I stare at the intense violet, orange, and yellow hues of the growing flames. "It's just something that's hard to wrap my head around."

"You're telling me."

I exhale deeply. "That's love for you. You can't choose who you fall for. It just . . ."

"Happens?" Charlie says.

"Yeah."

"Just between us, I think your dad and Nan are serious. I can see them tying the knot in the near future."

"I think so too." I'm happy he didn't have any plans to do something like propose to her tonight. I don't want to think about me becoming Charlie's step-aunt. I'm not ready for any more huge surprises or changes. Finding out about Dad's past and that I have a sister has drained all the energy out of me and pushed my brain to the limit.

The fire crackles. My body soaks in the warmth.

"I haven't gotten to know your father too well yet, but he seems like a guy who likes to crack jokes. That's one trait he shares with Grandad. He was a practical joker. One of my earliest memories is hearing the sound of Nan and Grandad laughing." Charlie blinks slowly.

"Did you spend a lot of time with him?" I ask.

"I did. We had a close bond."

At the mention of Charlie's family, my chest grows heavy. Leslie is still angry with us. That's another mess I have to try and figure out how to fix. "Have things improved at all with your sister? It's been so awkward coaching with her. She still doesn't speak to me unless she has to. It's almost as if I don't exist."

Charlie lets out a deep sigh. He pokes the fire one more time before planting himself next to me. "No change on my end either. A part of me hoped she'd show up here. She knows how important tonight's dinner was to Nan. It's rare for Leslie to not follow through on a request from her."

"It makes me feel like I'm this terrible person. I never wanted to have to take sides between the two of you."

"Frankie, have you been blaming yourself for this the whole time?"

I don't answer him.

"Hey." Charlie scoots closer to me. "You haven't done *anything* wrong. I made the decision to return to the ice. I'm also the one who asked you to skate with me." He exhales deeply. "As usual, Leslie was right about everything she said. I've been a self-centered fool. Since the accident, the only person I've thought about was myself. I lost sight of how important Leslie, Nan, and the rest of my family were to my recovery."

I play with a stray piece of thread on the edge of the blanket. "Where do you go from here?"

"Once Les and I get past this latest roadblock, I'll have a meeting with Uncle Jack and tell him I'm stepping down. I shouldn't have been so afraid to tell him I never wanted the job in the first place. It should've gone to my sister. I hate everything about it. There's a ton of paperwork and it takes time away from doing what I love—coaching and skating with you."

I glance at him curiously through my lashes. My heart rate increases. "We do make a pretty amazing team."

"We do, but it's more than that." He stands, and picks up two long metal skewers and a bag of marshmallows.

"Thanks." I accept the skewer from his hand. Ripping open the bag of marshmallows, I seek out the largest and fluffiest one in the pack, trying to buy myself some time. My body is growing as warm as the fire.

"Ask me why," he says in a husky tone.

I continue to keep my head tipped down, staring at the marshmallows, which are all the same uniform size.

"Frankie, ask me why," he repeats.

I chew on my lip and slowly lift my chin. "Okay, I'll bite. Why?"

"Because I've come to see you as more than just a friend."

Could it be? Does he feel the same way about me? I laugh nervously. "Good one. I thought you'd be sick of me by now. We're together every single day of the week."

His brow furrows. "I could never grow sick of you."

We're moving into dangerous territory. The wings of a thousand-and-one fast-flying hummingbirds flutter in my stomach. My throat goes dry. "Charlie, once we leave the friend zone, there's no going back."

He licks his lips. "That's a risk I'm willing to take. The question is, are you?"

He's the man who brings me coffee bright and early in the morning. The man who puts a smile on my face after a tough practice. The man who literally searched for me in the forest because he was concerned. "I am," I whisper.

In two strides, Charlie closes the gap between us. He pops the skewers into the firepit. Sitting down on the bench, he pulls me onto his lap and slides the blanket off my shoulders. Staring directly into my eyes, he removes the small tendrils of brown hair covering my face. "Francesca," he whispers into my ear. "You have no idea how hard it is for me to resist you every time you're near me. I've wanted to do this for so long."

He leans his head toward me, and like a ballet dancer delicately balancing on the tips of his toes, he plants a series of soft, supple kisses up the exposed flesh of my neck. I catch the scents of whiskey and cinnamon, and feel the scratchy texture of the stubble on his cheek. I don't want him to stop.

It's as if my body is gathering speed, about to be propelled into the air to perform a quadruple jump. My heart pounds wildly in my chest. I can hear its steady thud, thud, thud pulsating against my ribs.

As Charlie traces the outline of my lips with his thumb, I shiver. His eyes meet mine. The vibrant green color is reminiscent of a field of four-leaf clovers. "You're not only my favorite person I've ever skated with, but you are also the most stunningly beautiful woman I've ever met."

Charlie is my human four-leafed clover. Most people could spend an entire lifetime searching and never find one. I'm the luckiest woman alive. I wrap my arms around his neck and close my eyes. We share an intimate yet gentle kiss. And finally, I know what being in a relationship feels like.

Chapter Nineteen

"We can stay out here as long as you'd like, but at some point, I'm going to have to get up and stir the fire, or else it'll be completely extinguished."

My head rests on Charlie's shoulder. I'm still sitting on his lap, his fingers playing with the ends of my hair. Our s'mores have long been demolished.

"When you move, I'll get up." I sigh. "I've stalled facing Dad long enough. At this point, I just want to get it over with."

"How are you going to approach the, uh, sister issue?" He releases me and I sit up.

"Like an adult."

A low throaty laugh escapes from him. "I'm glad your sense of humor is still intact."

I shoot him a tired grin. "I'm too drained to have any heavy conversations tonight. All I want is for Dad and me to be on the same page. I just wish I'd known about her sooner."

Charlie kisses the top of my head. "I love that you always try hard to see the positive side of things."

"I'm just thankful you're here. Gemma too."

"I'll be right by your side every step of the way. The thing about partners is we're always here to lift one another up."

After putting the fire out, Charlie and I walk hand in hand into the house. Gemma, Dad, and Suzy are all seated anxiously around the kitchen table. Gemma and Suzy speak in soft undertones.

I'm wracked with guilt when I see how haggard and old Dad appears. His forehead is creased with lines of worry. His eyes are bloodshot as he stares blankly into space, and he's hunched over in defeat.

"Daddy?" I drop Charlie's hand and run to him, kneeling by his side.

"Frankie?" He slowly cranes his neck to the right.

"I'm sorry," we both say in unison.

I cry as I embrace him in a fierce hug. I've lost count of just how many tears I've shed. At this point, I'm shocked my body still has any waterworks left to produce.

"Sweetie, I promise I never meant to hurt you," he whispers into my ear.

"I know everything you've ever done for me has been out of love. I just went into shock. My body shut down. I'm so sorry for running away."

"If I were in your position, there's a very strong probability I might have done the same thing. I'm not good with surprises." He kisses me. "We'll have a long chat later."

I nod and stand. My brain has turned to mush. I'm exhausted and all I want to do is crawl into bed and sleep.

Gemma doesn't wait another moment to check on me. "Still in one piece?"

"Mostly."

Suzy reappears, having made herself scarce before. "Charlie, thank you for finding Frankie and taking care of her."

"Of course, Nan."

She positions herself between my father and me. "It's

getting late, and I think based on how tonight has gone, if everyone is amenable to it, you should all spend the night." Dad opens his mouth to argue. "Rich, it's not an inconvenience at all. There are more than enough spare suites that are never used in the main house to accommodate everyone, plus the annex."

His cheeks color pink. "Suzy-kins, raising a daughter, I learned that the lady of the house is the boss. Whatever she says goes."

Gemma and I nod. I have no fight left in me.

"Excellent. Then there's only one other issue to take care of. We skipped out on the introductions earlier. Rich, this is Charlie. Charlie, meet Rich Tomlinson, his daughter Frankie, whom you already seem to know, and her friend Gemma."

Charlie and I exchange nervous glances. "We work and skate together at the rink," he says, his neck, cheeks, and ears all flushing.

"You're Mr. Blanks?" Dad coughs.

Gemma throws her head back and roars with laughter at the ridiculousness of it all.

I cover my face with my hands. Charlie looks on in confusion, and Suzy shrugs. I'll never be able to live this down. "I'll tell you later," I murmur.

It's past midnight, and despite my exhaustion, I can't quiet my thoughts as I lie in bed next to Gemma.

"Frankie"—my half-asleep friend groans—"you're shaking the bed."

"Sorry, I just can't get comfortable."

Rolling over, Gemma repositions so she faces me. "Talk to me. What's eating at you? Your long-lost sister?"

"Earlier it was, but now it's my biological parents." I turn from my back to my right side. "When I was younger, every so often, I'd go through these periods where I'd feel like I'd been abandoned. I'd try to tell myself that maybe they were just young and dumb and couldn't care for a child. Or that they'd given me up for my own good."

I fidget. "But now that I know there were two of us, everything's changed. What if I take a look at the adoption records and find out my sister is my twin? What if our parents surrendered us to child services because we were both accidents? What if I have other siblings besides her and my biological parents kept them and not us? What if—"

"You're going to rip yourself to bits if you keep thinking like this, Frankie." Gemma pulls the covers back. She sits up cross-legged on the bed, giving me her full attention. "You're not going to start in on all these what-if questions. I forbid it." She clears her throat. "Repeat after me . . . I am *not* an unfortunate accident."

"Gemma," I whine.

She gives me a hard stare. "Frankie. Come on, humor me. Repeat after me."

"Fine." I sit up. "I am *not* an unfortunate accident."

Gemma nods. "I am exactly where I am supposed to be."

"I am exactly where I am supposed to be."

"I have a family and friends who love me no matter what. Nothing I learn will change that."

I repeat Gemma's words.

"Feel any better?"

"Not really." I pull my knees to my body.

"Anytime those negative thoughts start to resurface, promise me you'll start repeating what I just said to you. Full stop."

"I'll try," I say.

Gemma gives me another glare.

"Fine. I promise."

"Better." She takes ahold of my hands. "Now, here's what's going to happen next. I cleared the rest of this week's schedule. In the morning, after you've had a shower and coffee, you and Mr. T will go off and have a private chat while I get to know your boyfriend a little better. When we get back, you can go for a walk with one or both of us and we'll help you sort out your thoughts."

I inhale sharply. "Charlie's not my boyfriend." At least not yet. We've only just admitted we have feelings for one another.

"You can call it whatever you want. You can't fool your bestie. The puppy-dog looks you two were giving each other say otherwise."

"Gemma . . ."

"After you ran out of here, do you know what your man did? He filled a glass of water and made sure your dad was taken care of first. He said that as much as he wanted to rush off and find you, you once told him your priority would always be your father. He wanted to make sure that when he found you, he'd be able to look you squarely in the eyes and tell you your dad was in good hands."

I let the words soak in. Charlie really said and did that? He remembered the conversation we had about my father. My heart swells.

"If that isn't some form of love, I don't know what is. You better not do anything to muck this up, because a bloke like that doesn't come around often. *My* best friend deserves nothing but the best."

"Gem, have I ever told you that you're one of my favorite humans?" I hug her.

"Likewise. Now, do you think you'll be able to get a few hours of rest?"

I fight off a yawn. "Maybe?"

We both lie down. I close my eyes. Thinking about Charlie helps calm me.

"If you can't sleep, try listening to an audiobook, like you used to do on tour. Nora Bennet's new book, *The Scandal of the Season*, is brilliant," Gemma suggests, but I barely hear her. My breathing has evened out, and I've fully surrendered to the world of sleep.

Everyone sleeps in late the next morning. It's after one p.m. when Dad and I finally sit down for our much-anticipated talk in the cottage's sunroom. The glass doors are propped open, and a gentle breeze tickles my face. Mature pine trees provide a barrier of natural shade. A symphony of birds chirps.

"From here, Lake Wakahanra looks like something you'd see on a tourist postcard," I say.

Dad agrees.

I feel like a speed skater waiting for the starting gun to fire. It's the first words we've exchanged in the ten minutes since Gemma brought us tea. Charlie volunteered to take her on a tour of the area, promising he'd drop her off at our apartment in time for dinner.

I reach for the teapot and pour myself a cup with trembling hands. "Would you like one too?" Dad shakes his head, stands, and walks outside.

Gemma said drinking tea would help calm my nerves, but all I've managed to do is spill half of it. I place the cup on the side table and join Dad outside.

He leans against the iron railing enclosing the garden, staring out at the pathway leading to the lake. "What do you want to know first?" he asks.

I've spent all morning thinking about it. "Were you ever told why I was put up for adoption? Why didn't you take both my sister and me? What do you know about her?"

Dad takes several deep breaths. "As you know, I left the Navy for civilian life when I was forty-seven years old. I'd always wanted to be a father, but I knew by that point in my life that it wouldn't happen the traditional way. So I decided to look into adoption."

I know this part of the story well. Dad was told that even with his stellar character references, as a single male, it would be challenging for him to prove to the adoption agency that he was a suitable candidate to raise a child. He spent two years as a foster parent to gain experience caring for children before approaching any agencies to strengthen his case.

"I was matched with you by the adoption agency about seven months after I'd first filed my paperwork. At the time, you were just shy of seven months old. I drove from Grizzly Springs to Los Angeles to meet you. It was love at first sight." Dad smiles widely. "I'd never seen such an angelic baby. I took you in my arms and I just knew we were meant to be together. I thought it was especially fitting that you'd been born right when I started looking for you."

I take a step closer to him. He kisses my cheek.

"It took about three months to finalize the paperwork before I was able to bring you home. A week before that big day, I received a call from your case agent. She informed me you had a full-blooded older sister. The family that had wanted to adopt her had withdrawn their application. She wanted to see if it might be a possibility to try and keep both siblings together."

I hang on to his every word. My sister is older. I have a big sister.

Dad's voice suddenly grows hoarse. "I agonized over the decision. I wanted more than anything to be able to say yes to the case worker, but at the time, I didn't think I could handle more than one child. That week turned into one of the longest of my life. I didn't sleep. I didn't eat. All I could think about was that if fate decided to keep you and your sister together, I didn't want to be responsible for breaking you two up."

He runs a hand through his hair. "When I finally managed to phone the agency back six days later, I was told they'd found another family for her in Seattle. I urged them to let me know if anything changed, but that was the last I heard about her."

I exhale deeply. My pulse is racing. Dad was only given a couple of days to figure things out. If I were in the same situation, would I have been ready to take on two children instead of one? It would've come as a shock, that's for certain. I don't know what I would've done.

"Dad, what happened next?"

"I brought you home and you legally became my daughter, Francesca Tomlinson." His eyes glisten with moisture.

"And my biological parents?"

"I'm afraid I don't know much. Your adoption was a closed one. All I can tell you is that you were born in the city of Aliso Viejo in Southern California."

A closed adoption means my biological parents didn't want any further contact with me. The records are sealed and information about their identities is withheld. I'll never know who they were.

Dad has always been open to discussing my adoption, but I've never had the courage to ask. After all these years, I finally have my answer. It's as if I've taken a sucker punch to the gut. There *aren't* any answers. My case is a cold one. There are no more clues to uncover.

. . .

"You can look over your official file anytime. It's in the fireproof safe," Dad tells me in a low tone.

My throat constricts. "Dad, I'd only be interested in maybe finding my sister. As far as I'm concerned, the only person worthy of the title of parent is you. What I really want right now is for you to just hold me." I bury my head in the stiff white cotton of his dress shirt and cry softly. "You're all I need. I love you so much."

Chapter Twenty

Monday, Charlie and I are back at the rink at four in the morning. I need the normalcy to stay sane. The ice is my refuge, the sole place where I can escape the outside world and pretend I'm living in a little bubble.

"Why do you two insist on keeping such insanely early hours? Charlie's family owns the rink! Isn't there a way he can arrange it so it opens late or closes early? It can't be all that difficult to get private ice time at a more *reasonable* hour," Gemma murmurs.

"Gem, it *isn't* that easy. We can't just push aside our students, the skating academy, the curling club, the hockey league, and all the other groups that pay for ice time."

"I know. I'm just complaining. It's early and I'm grumpy." She hides a yawn with her hand. "You know I avoid waking up before eight unless I have a good reason to. I kissed any practices before nine goodbye when I turned pro." Gemma follows me out of the lobby and onto the ice. "You used to be like me. *Not* a morning person."

We skate a few laps around the ice. "Spending time around Charlie has changed me."

"I can see that."

"I didn't get a chance to ask you yesterday, but how did the two of you get on?"

"He was nervous around me at first, and kept forgetting my name, but once I got him started on his favorite topic, which is you, the conversation started flowing."

Sounds like Charlie. I'm glad he and Gemma were able to find common ground. I knew she would be able to crack the code on him. "What did you end up doing?"

"We spent most of the time walking through the Sequoia Valley farmers' market. I told him all your darkest secrets."

My face pales. "Gemma! I have to skate with the man! What did you tell him?"

"Relax. It wasn't anything that bad." She giggles. "I only mentioned things like how you have a ridiculous magnet collection and how you always have to have your lucky stuffed Peter Rabbit in your skating bag."

I breathe a little easier. Those are both things Charlie already knows about me. He saw my poor beat-up stuffed toy during our first week as partners and wondered why it lives in my bag. The explanation is easy. It's one of the first gifts Dad gave me. It's my way of always carrying a piece of him wherever I am. Especially when I was on the road.

"Thank you? I think."

"He struck me as a genuinely good bloke. He passed the best-friend test with flying colors. He knows if he doesn't treat you well, he'll have to answer to me." She makes a show of rolling up her jacket sleeves and flexing her arm muscles.

A weight has been lifted off my shoulders. I know I don't need her approval, but it means a lot to me. "Good to know."

"I always have your back, bestie."

We skate over to the boards. I do some light stretching, and Gemma ties her hair into a low ponytail.

"Have you set the date for when you're going to take the

test? I've seen the videos you've sent me. You look like you'd pass it with flying colors."

"No. We're almost there, but still not at full strength yet. Our target is to be ready in three or four months. We need some more conditioning and a few more elements. We just started off-ice lifts last week."

"I hate seeing you stuck having to wait so long. Have you thought about asking Fernando if he could partner with you? You two could rework one of the show programs and knock the test out of the way in a weekend. I'm sure Charlie would understand. It was kind of him to get the ball rolling, but I thought by now he might be a little further along."

I've never considered having my Dreams on Ice partner skate with me. If Gemma had suggested the idea to me several months ago, I would've jumped at the opportunity, but the status quo has changed. Fernando is a fantastic skater and brilliant partner, but he isn't Charlie. We're in this together. I'm willing to wait as long as it takes for him to be ready.

"I appreciate the suggestion, Gem, but it's a hard pass from me. Remember, I've taken a few breaks, but never really stopped skating pairs. Charlie, on the other hand, had to start from scratch. I'm so proud of him for how far he's come in such a short time. He's the only person I'm willing to take this journey with."

"Of course, I respect that. I won't bring it up again."

Charlie joins us on the ice. "Good morning, ladies. What's up first on the agenda today?"

"I thought we could do a run-through of the program for Gemma."

He nods. "Okay let's get to work."

"You and Charlie didn't say much to one another today. Are you two normally so focused?" Gemma asks as we enter the Sequoia Valley Hobby Land.

"No. Usually we spend the hour bantering. I think we were just nervous. You're the first person we've ever skated the program in front of."

I downplay my concern. Something about Charlie did indeed feel off today. He was tense, and nothing I said or did could lighten his mood. Something's wearing on him. I wish he'd share with me what it is.

"I'm honored." Gemma grins.

We walk past the displays of clearance Easter baskets, bunnies, and plastic eggs and head to the floral department.

Gemma fingers the waxy petals of a yellow gladiola. "These are artificial? They all look so real." There are flowers of every shape and size in every color imaginable.

"Yup. A friend . . ." I hesitate. "A friend from the rink introduced me to them."

I remember Leslie gushing about the store the very first time we came. *A lot of people don't know it, but Hobby Land does a lot to support local artisans. Take the floral department, for instance. All the silk flowers they sell are handmade. And those paintings hanging behind the register? Those were all done by people who live here.*

It's too bad Leslie is still mad at me. I really could've used her help shopping today.

"What do you think?" I ask, picking up a bouquet of blue and purple hydrangeas.

Gemma leans forward and turns them over in her hand. "Do you have a picture of the costume?"

Reaching into my purse, I retrieve my phone, unlock the screen, and hand the device to her.

She lets out a low whistle. "I'd forgotten how stunning that dress is. Who made it, again?"

"I'm not sure. It was a gift from Dad. You'd have to ask him."

Gemma stares at the phone a moment longer and passes it back to me. "If you're going to go through the trouble of making a fascinator to go with the dress, it should match. Or at the very least be black and white." Her attention goes to the selection of white flowers at the end of the aisle. "These would be perfect for my older sister's wedding! I have to send her a picture and see if she wants me to pick these up for her."

The excitement I felt a few minutes before disappears, replaced by sadness. I carefully return the bouquet back to its place. "I wonder what my sister would like."

Gemma slaps her hand over her mouth. "Frankie, I'm sorry. I didn't think about what I was saying just now."

"It's fine. Go call your sister."

"Frankie."

"Really, Gem. I'm okay. I'll be outside. I need some air."

It's silly. I shouldn't be triggered by Gemma mentioning her own sister. But my stomach has been twisted in knots since I've found out about mine. The door on finding out anything about my biological parents is closed, but not the door to my sister. There are so many unknowns about her I'm dying to uncover.

Without paying attention to where I'm going, I find myself walking into the drugstore next to Hobby Land. My thoughts turn to the suggestion Dad made last night. *I've done a little research. If you ever decided to try searching for your sister, your best option would be to use one of those ancestry sites. The testing kit would take a sample of your DNA and run it through their database. It looks like there's been a decent number of adoptees who've had some success. The kits are even sold at the drugstore.*

"Can I help you?" a worker in a blue vest asks.

I'm on the fence about using a kit, but it wouldn't hurt to have one. "Do you have any family ancestry kits?"

A few minutes later, I shove the brown bag with my purchase into my purse as my phone rings.

"Hello?"

"Frankie, where are you? I thought you were just outside."

"I'm coming right now."

"I have some bad news. I'm going to have to cut my trip short." Gemma groans. "DOI just called. Vivienne's been injured and they need me to fly back to Phoenix in the morning."

"I understand, Gem. There isn't much you can do when someone gets hurt. I'll be right there."

Gemma envelopes me in a tight hug the following day at Fresno Yosemite International Airport. "Don't let another six-plus months slip by without my seeing you." We release one another, and she picks up her tote and rolling bag. "Charlie, I'm counting on you to take care of my bestie."

He nods solemnly. "I will."

Gemma waves one final farewell and joins the security line. My heart is heavy, but I'm thankful I was able to spend a little time with her before she had to leave. Some time is better than none at all. "Thanks for driving," I tell Charlie. "It gave Gemma and me a little extra time together."

"Sure."

We walk side by side at a slow, even pace, exiting the airport. As we reach the curb, we wait for the signal to change. A steady stream of cars drives by searching for an empty space by the airport's doors to drop off and pick up passengers. Luggage wheels clatter against the sidewalk.

"You're awfully quiet," I finally say.

"Just thinking."

"About?" I prompt.

"About us."

The hum of an airplane's motor roars to life.

"Our skating? Or us off the ice?"

I expected him to smile or at least give some type of reaction, but instead, he remains stoic.

"Skating."

The signal changes from red to green. I start to cross, but Charlie stays rooted in place. "If you've changed your mind about skating with me, I'd be more than happy to take a back seat and become your coach instead."

I freeze. The hairs on the back of my neck perk up. "Excuse me?" I step back onto the curb.

"I'm holding you back." He becomes interested in the ground. "I take a slow and cautious approach to skating. Skills don't come back to me as quickly as they should. Sometimes I have flashbacks, and it takes me time to process and push through them."

The strained sound of his voice almost breaks me. Did he overhear my conversation with Gemma?

He kicks a stray pebble. "I want to be fair to you. If you were to skate with your former show partner, you could pass your test tomorrow. Or if you want, I still have some connections. I could find you someone who'd be willing to—"

I grab his hand and tilt his chin up with my other one. "The only person I'm willing to skate with is you."

"You don't have to pretend with me." He looks away.

"I'm not. I meant what I said to Gemma. You are worth waiting for. *You* are my forever partner. You're stuck with me whether you like it or not." I rise up onto the tips of my toes and peck him on the cheek. His attention returns to me. "If it takes us a little longer to get from point A to point B, so be it.

I've waited eight years to take this test. A few more months won't make any difference to me."

Charlie hesitates. "You're sure."

"Positive."

The signal changes again. We cross the street.

"Do you realize you're holding my hand in a crossover grip?" he says in a lighter tone.

I smile, happy to see him back to the Charlie I've fallen for. "That's what you get when you're dating a figure skater."

Reaching the car, we climb inside. Charlie enters Sequoia Valley into the map app on his phone. "Ugh. It's rush hour. It's going to take us three-and-a-half hours to get back."

I drum my fingers against the armrest of the passenger door. My attention goes to the bumper-to-bumper cars inching along the elevated section of the interstate leading out of Fresno. My body is stiff from the two-hour journey to the airport. I don't fancy sitting another three hours in the car. A flashing billboard catches my attention.

For one night only, come and experience an unforgettable game of exhibition baseball between your hometown Fresno Flying Squirrels and the Scottsdale Sloths. Whether you're a baseball fan or not, you're guaranteed to laugh and be entertained! Tickets are still available!

I read the date and the time. The game is in an hour. The wheels begin to spin in my mind. It could be the perfect opportunity for a date night while we wait out the traffic. "Charlie, how do you feel about baseball?"

He frowns at his phone, still trying to find an alternate route. "When it's on TV, I don't mind if it's on in the background. I've never been to a live game before."

I snort. He doesn't even own a TV. I'm not the biggest fan of baseball either, but with a guarantee to be entertained, what have we got to lose? I open the internet browser on my phone and type in the website for the Fresno

Flying Squirrels. Tickets are only ten dollars for lower-box seats. I'm sold.

I glance at Charlie. "Do you trust me?"

"That's a loaded question."

I huff, pretending to be insulted.

He chuckles. "Yes, I trust you."

I add two tickets to my shopping cart and hit the Buy Now button. "Tonight, we're going to be doing something a little bit different."

"I'm afraid to ask what you have in mind."

A female singer belts out the last line of the national anthem, and the crowd of seven thousand fans cheers wildly before resuming their seats. The air smells of buttery popcorn, sunscreen, and grass. The sky is still blue, with hints of orange, and the stadium lights have just clicked on.

"And now, please give a warm welcome tonight to our visiting team, the Scottsdale Sloths. Playing left field and battle leadoff, number fifty-six Jose Alcano. Playing . . ."

"Is there a reason the players are walking in slow motion to their starting spots?" Charlie asks, replacing his hat on his head.

"I think they're imitating sloths."

He frowns. "Their uniforms are also very . . . green."

"This is an exhibition team. So what we see tonight is different than your typical baseball game." I almost sound like an expert thanks to a little help from my friend Google.

"And by that you mean?"

I smirk. "You'll just have to wait and see."

The public address announcer's voice rises in excitement and volume. "And now for your hometown Flying Squirrels, batting leadoff, second baseman, number five, Matt McClure.

A man standing in the on-deck circle taps his bat on the ground to slip the donut protector off the handle, walks toward home plate, and steps into the batter's box.

Everything, at first, appears to be business as usual. The umpire crouches down. The catcher flashes the pitcher a set of signs. Nodding, the pitcher waits a moment, then suddenly takes a knee, and using his glove like a microphone, starts belting out "Love Shack."

The other seven players on the field, the catcher, and even the umpire begin performing a line dance. The batter remains focused, knees bent, trying to maintain his composure, but failing. His body is shaking with laughter.

Charlie sits forward in his seat with wide eyes. "What in the world?"

Around the stadium, the crowd bursts out with resounding laughter, singing and clapping along to the well-known tune. Finally, twenty seconds later, a pitch is thrown.

"What just happened?" Charlie turns to me.

"The Scottsdale Sloths are an exhibition baseball team that plays by their own rules. Think Broadway meets baseball."

Another pitch is thrown. The batter swings and hits a foul. Fans sitting in the stands in left field cheer as a little boy about ten years old catches the ball and holds up his prize.

"You're out!" the umpire yells. Dejected, the batter returns to the dugout.

"I guess that's an out." I laugh. Whipping out my phone, I type in "Sloths' baseball rules." "It says here that if a fan catches the ball, it counts as an out." I keep scrolling through the page. "Huh . . . the team that scores the most runs in an inning also gets an extra point. At the end of an hour and a half, whichever team has the most points wins."

"Baseball with a time limit, I can get behind."

"I'm glad." I lean over and kiss Charlie.

"Can I see those rules?"

I pass him my phone. "While you do that, I'll be right back. I'm going to pick up some ice cream. I saw some being served inside a hat and it looked like a cute souvenir."

"As long as it's not a magnet."

I ignore him. Of course I'm going to buy a magnet. It's one of the only affordable things the teams sell. And this is our first real date as a couple. I want to remember tonight forever.

The teams manage to play a total of four innings before they reach the time limit. The Flying Squirrels win ten points to eight.

As we stand and stretch, Charlie asks, "Is there anything else you want before we head out? Another jacket? Pennant? More nacho steak fries?"

I bend over to retrieve two large plastic bags of merchandise and my giant stuffed sloth. "No," I say matter-of-factly, embarrassed I couldn't stop picking up stuff in the shop. Everything was so cute. "Here, this one is yours."

"My inflatable sloth costume. This has to be the best work purchase I've ever made." He grins. "The kids are going to love this. I have it all planned. For the summer showcase, we'll skate to 'I Like to Move It' and you can—"

"I am *not* wearing that. It's too bulky."

Charlie clutches the bag to his chest. "This is *mine*. You can dress like a monkey or a lemur or some other elegant animal."

I wipe my forehead in mock relief. "At least it's better than Leslie's peacock."

We share a laugh as we join the lines of people shuffling

toward the stadium exits. "What was your favorite part of the game?"

"The Rockettes-style kick line after the home run." Charlie glances over his shoulder at me. "And yours?"

"The relief pitcher's Michael Jackson 'Thriller' dance."

"Oh, before I forget, I still have your phone." He reaches into the front pocket of his jeans and hands it to me.

"Thanks." I frown at the smudge marks coating the screen. As I try and wipe it clear of fingerprints with my T-shirt, it glows to life. Three missed calls. It's probably another spam bot. I get so many calls asking if I want my car's warranty extended.

"Do you remember where we parked? I should've taken a picture," Charlie says.

"Um, yeah . . . we were on Kern Street," I reply, half paying attention, trying to open the voicemails. "Ugh, the signal is spotty."

"You'll have to lead us there," he says in a resigned tone.

"I'm sorry. Of course." I stow my phone into my pocket. "Do you need me to get us on the freeway too?"

"If I have the GPS voice talking to me, I can manage."

I lace my fingers through his and rest my head against his arm as we walk to the car. It's firm, but still makes a decent pillow. "Did you have fun tonight?" I ask.

"I did. It was the perfect escape. You've set the bar high. I don't know if I can top this for our next date."

"You'll come up with something clever."

We reach Charlie's car. He clicks the fob to unlock the doors. "Do you want your bags in the back seat?"

"No, I'll just put them by my feet."

He nods and places his own stuff in the back. "Remind me when we get home that these are back here."

"I'll put the reminder in my phone now."

Opening the passenger door, I slide inside and unlock the

screen. The glowing red number three reminds me about the voicemails. I tap the button and hold it to my ear. A robotic voice says, "You have three unopened messages. First message." Then my father's voice comes on. "Frankie, it's Dad . . ." I press the phone closer to my ear. The rest of the message is garbled and cuts off.

Okay. That's weird. Why would Dad be reaching out to me? As far as I know, he and Suzy were supposed to be home tonight having a James Bond movie marathon.

"Second message. Fran . . . kie . . . " It's Dad's voice again, sounding even worse than before.

My heart lurches. What's going on? I tap the final message, my hands shaking badly. "Frankie, this is Suzy. I'm over at your apartment. Your father has a high fever. I'm taking him to urgent care. Please call me when you can."

I grip the edge of my seat. My pulse pounds erratically like a horse galloping full speed ahead. I take shallow breaths, trying to keep my mind from jumping to the worst possible conclusion.

Charlie climbs into the driver's seat and closes the door. "Okay. Let's see. Maps. Sequoia Valley directions."

His voice startles me. I drop my phone, then scramble to find it inside the bag of merch. I lean forward, but the seat belt holds me firmly in place.

"Sloth got your phone?" he jokes. But the words die on his lips.

It's happening again. I shake my head and start to cry.

Racing around the car, Charlie is by my side in an instant. "Frankie? What happened?" He removes my seat belt and takes me into his arms.

"Something's wrong with Dad."

Chapter Twenty-One

The memory of Charlie's words still rattles around in my brain. *"I spoke to Nan. They're at the Grizzly Springs Hospital. Your father was admitted for observation. They're running tests now."* It's as if someone has taken a wire brush to my scalp and rubbed it raw. My head just hurts.

"We'll be there in five minutes."

Everything Charlie says goes in one ear and out the other. All I can do is nod and stare out the window. There're a few lights on this stretch of roadway. The inky blackness gives me the impression of being in a black hole, a force so strong that even light can't escape.

Dad was alone when he needed me most. Again. The reason I moved here was to be closer to him in case anything ever happened. Was he sick before I left for Fresno? Why didn't I notice anything?

The turn indicator clicks, and Charlie enters the hospital parking lot. He parks, turns off the engine, and for a few moments, we sit in silence. "Frankie, I know you may not feel like talking to me right now, but remember, no matter what, your father is receiving the best possible care. You won't be left alone in all this. I'll be right beside you the entire time."

I manage a feeble bob of my head.

We get out of the truck. I lean heavily on Charlie's arm as he escorts me inside. Suzy is the only person in the waiting area, looking well put together in a green floral top and jeans. She's flipping through a quilting magazine.

"Nan," Charlie calls out softly.

Suzy glances up, closes the magazine, and stands. She removes her reading glasses and hugs us. "Charlie, Frankie. You made good time. I'll let the receptionist know you're here. Since I'm not family, unfortunately, they weren't able to disclose any details of Rich's condition to me."

Around us, the walls are a stark white. Three televisions are turned on and muted. Black-and-white captions flash across the screens. A dozen or so brown-and-white chairs with abstract circular patterns are set in a horseshoe pattern. Magazines are scattered across the empty seats. It's such a cold, sterile environment. I shiver. Charlie keeps hold of my hand and draws circles over the top of it.

Soon, Suzy rejoins us. "How was he when you found him?" I ask, my voice hoarse.

She looks me directly in the eye. "He was feverish and confused. His pupils were dilated, and I could tell he was in a lot of pain. Although I don't think it's anything life-threatening, I still thought it was better to take him to urgent care just to err on the safe side."

"Nan was a nurse for over thirty years. She'd know right away if it were something like a heart attack," Charlie says, trying his best to comfort me.

My body stiffens. What if Suzy is wrong because she's out of practice? It could be a heart attack for all we know. Or something that's equally as bad.

"Charlie, let's leave any diagnosing to the medical professionals," she says carefully. She approaches me with slow steps and grips my other hand.

The automated doors leading to the exam rooms open with a whoosh. A doctor in blue scrubs and a white lab coat exits, carrying a clipboard. "Francesca Tomlinson?" he reads out.

"Here!" I shout.

"Hi, I'm Dr. Rudd. I've overseeing your father's case since he was admitted." He eyes Suzy and Charlie. "Would you care to chat somewhere more private?"

"No, they're extended family."

He nods, reviewing the chicken scratch on the clipboard. "Your father, in layman's terms, is presenting with a case of shingles."

Suzy winces. "Poor Rich."

Dr. Rudd continues. "Shingles is an illness caused by the same virus as chicken pox. It can manifest in anyone, at any age, although it's more common in adults than children."

"Shingles . . . is that serious?" I ask. "I know chicken pox in adults can be complicated."

"In your father's case, yes, it can be. As a geriatric patient, Mr. Tomlinson is at greater risk of suffering complications from the illness." Dr. Rudd hesitates. "I admitted him due to his fever and level of pain, but I'm confident it's been caught early enough that he'll make a full recovery. In any case, I've started him on some anti-viral medication. I'd like to keep him here for a few more days before releasing him to your care. The time for recovery ranges from two to six weeks."

"I work with a lot of children. Should I be worried about any exposure they might have had? Is it contagious?"

"The virus can be passed around like any other illness, but the chances of it turning into shingles are low. Generally, shingles is triggered by the onset of a stress-inducing incident or anxiety."

My body grows weak. Charlie is the only thing keeping me upright. My sister. The adoption.

"Thank you, Doctor," Suzy says.

"Visiting hours are over for the evening. I'd recommend you go home and get some rest. The nurses will call you with any changes. Just be sure to confirm your contact information before you leave."

"Thanks," I manage. My head aches. My pulse is too loud for my own ears.

Dr. Rudd leaves and goes to exchange a few words with the nurses at the front desk.

"Charlie, here's some cash. Get Frankie a sports drink from the vending machine," Suzy instructs him. "She's in shock and could use some electrolytes. We'll just be sitting here."

"On it." He disappears down the hall.

Suzy guides me into a chair. "Shingles is manageable. Rich will recover. He's also got a strong support system. As do you."

Her words are hollow. I understood what both the doctor and Suzy are trying to tell me, but it doesn't help ease any of my guilt. It's like a colony of termites is slowly eating away my skin from the inside out. I feel raw and exposed. How can anyone stand to be near me? "This is all my fault." I bury my face in my hands.

"Frankie, this is *not* your fault. Rich would be the first person to say that you didn't cause him to become ill."

I shake my head and clench my fists. "I wasn't there when he needed me. It *is* my fault. I should've noticed something was off this morning. I should've had my phone on me."

"None of us is perfect. You can't have your phone on you twenty-four-seven." Suzy drapes her arm around my shoulders. "Rich is an adult. He knew to call me when he couldn't reach you."

My head shoots up. "But it's my *job* to take care of him. I promised I would after the last time."

"Oh, Frankie, you can't do everything, as much as you may want to. We all need somebody to take care of us. Even you. I'll keep repeating it over and over—you and Rich aren't alone anymore. You have me and Charlie. We're your extended support system. Even if your father and I decide to no longer date, I'll still be there for you two."

My body shakes and I start to cry. Suzy's words hit home. I know she means every word she says. I've never had a mother or a grandmother before, but in Suzy's arms, I know I'm safe from the world. I know that everything will eventually be all right.

"It's been an emotional last couple of days for you both. What you need is a good night's sleep."

Charlie shuffles back to the waiting area. "Nan, I'm sorry I took so long. I couldn't decide what flavor to get so I bought one of everything in the machine."

Suzy releases me. I look up. Charlie's arms are laden with about eight or nine different colored bottles. I wipe my eyes on my sleeve and fan myself, drying the tears. "I'll take the yellow one." I sniffle.

Charlie untwists the top and hands it to me. The icy cold bottle is refreshing against my hot skin. I take a long drink, not realizing how thirsty I am until three-quarters of the bottle has disappeared.

"Charlie, take her home and make sure she goes straight to bed."

"Yes, ma'am."

I open my mouth to protest.

Charlie places a hand on my shoulder. "Never argue with Nan. She's the head of the family."

"That's right. We grandmothers have awesome powers."

I sigh deeply, too tired to argue with either one. "Fine."

"Charlie, I appreciate everything you've done today, but I promise, I can make it from here." I retrieve my keys from my purse and step out of the car. "I don't want to keep you any longer. You're probably as exhausted as me, and I don't have to drive another half hour to Sequoia Valley."

"I told Nan that I'd tuck you in. Once you're in bed, I'll leave."

"You are so stubborn," I grumble as he escorts me to the door.

"You can blame my mom's side of the family."

With a click, the deadbolt unlatches, and we walk inside. If it had been any other time, I would've ensured our apartment had been cleaned from top to bottom before inviting a guest inside. I cringe at the idea of making a bad first impression on Charlie.

I tap the switch, flooding the kitchen and living room with light. It's just as bad as I'd thought. There are dishes in the sink, a takeout container on the counter, blankets and pillows on the floor. "Sorry for the mess."

Charlie enters behind me and closes the door. "You've seen my office. Compared to that, this place looks spotless."

I set my keys on the kitchen island and start toward the sink, rolling up my sleeves to my elbow.

"What are you doing?" He raises an eyebrow.

"The dishes?" I pinch my lips together. "If there's one thing I can't stand, it's a sink full of dishes. It's an invitation for creepy crawly things to invade the kitchen."

Charlie moves beside me and rolls up his own sleeves. "Go change and get ready for bed. Leave the dishes to me."

"Charlie, no."

"Look, the sooner you do as I say, the sooner I'll be out of your hair." He gently nudges me with his hip. "Let me do this for you. You're dead on your feet."

As soon as he says that, my limbs take on extra weight. Words have magical powers. I glance toward the hallway with the bathroom, then back to the kitchen. He's already added the orange dish soap to the sponge by the sink.

"Go."

He starts to whistle a tune from our *My Fair Lady* program and dances in place as he scrubs the plates and silverware. Grabbing a set of pajamas, I make my way to the bathroom. Being able to change, wash my face, and brush my teeth gives me a little sense of normalcy.

When I return to the living room, I find Charlie sitting on the couch, flipping through a photo album Gemma and I have been working on putting together.

Hearing me approach, he looks up, a sheepish expression on his face. "I hope you don't mind. This was just sitting here, and I was curious."

"It's fine."

"Are all these from Dreams on Ice?"

"Yeah, from my last week."

I pull my hair loose and shake it free, massaging my tender scalp. "Mmm . . . much better."

Charlie closes the album, places it on the coffee table, and watches me. "Your hair looks beautiful when it's down. I never noticed you had purple streaks in it, or that it was so long. When I see you, it's always up in a bun."

"That's my signature look. If it's down, it gets in the way." He pats the couch, and I sit next to him, scooting into his arms, resting on his shoulder. All I want is to be held by him and for this living nightmare to be over.

"It smells like strawberries too." He plays with the ends.

For a long while, we sit there, both content. I finally allow my body to relax. "You're the perfect pillow. Now all I need is a massage."

"As the lady wishes," he says softly. "Where do you carry most of your stress? In the neck? Shoulders?"

"Neck."

He repositions himself and begins to knead the tender area between my neck and shoulders.

"That feels so good. You have the magic touch." I feel like I'm a happy bear who's just scratched a bothersome itch by rubbing my back against a tree. Now I'm ready to have a long hibernation.

"You have so many knots here. It's no wonder your back is always bothering you."

"I should have you massage me before every practice. Your hands are so much better than a foam roller." I yawn. My eyes are growing heavy.

"If you ask, I'd be happy to. But for now, bed. Is your room down the hall? I'll carry you if you can't walk."

I don't respond. I'm already mostly asleep. Charlie grabs the nearest blanket, kisses the top of my head, and drapes it over me.

As he turns the light off, I barely hear him whisper, "Sweet dreams, fair princess."

Chapter Twenty-Two

"Hello, Ms. Tomlinson? This is Dr. Rudd. How are you doing?"

I deposit my keys on the kitchen island, holding the phone to my ear with my shoulder. "I'm doing well. Thanks for asking. Is everything all right with my father?"

It's been two days since he was admitted to the hospital, and I've been eager for another update.

"He's doing just fine now, but I thought I'd phone you to let you know that during the night, he experienced a slight fever. I'd initially planned to release him tomorrow, but I'd like him to stay in our care a little longer."

"Oh." My stomach drops. "Okay."

"There was one other topic I'd like to discuss if you have a moment."

I walk over to the couch and sit down. "I have time."

"Great. It involves Mr. Tomlinson's home care."

"Oh, sure."

"Based on my evaluation of him this morning, I'm projecting that he'll be released to you sometime later this week. Once home, you can expect that he'll spend the majority of the first few weeks on bed rest and will require extra assistance with everyday tasks such as bathing. Are you with me so far?"

Dad is *not* going to like this. Bedrest the first time around was hard on both of us. But it's a necessary evil we'll have to deal with. "Yes."

"Good. For my records, I just needed you to go ahead and confirm with me that you'll be able to provide the care for your father. Or that you're planning to hire a visiting nurse."

I won't let anything stand in the way. We can't afford a nurse, but I can at least make sure I'm here around the clock to do what needs to be done. "Everything's been taken care of."

"Fantastic, I'll make a note in his chart."

After I get off the phone with the doctor, I send a text to Charlie. There's too much that needs to be done today to prep for Dad's homecoming, like laundry and grocery shopping. It's going to take me all day to get my chores done.

Frankie: I won't be coming to the rink today.

Charlie: No problem. Take all the time you need.

Frankie: *thumbs-up emoji*

Charlie: Is there any update on your dad?

Frankie: The doctor said he's on the road to recovery.

Charlie: That's good news!

Frankie: Yeah, it is.

Charlie: I'm only a text away if you need anything.

Two days later, Charlie texts me. I lie on the couch in the fetal position, not having the energy or interest to do anything. But if I don't text him back, he'll come over. And I'd rather be alone right now.

> Charlie: Hey, Frankie, I heard from Nan that you spent all day at the hospital yesterday. I'm sorry to hear about your dad's secondary infection. Is there anything I can do to help?

> Frankie: No. It's a waiting game.

> Charlie: I'll talk to Jack and let him know you need a couple more days off.

> Frankie: Thanks.

I set my phone down, hoping that's the end of it, but it chimes again.

> Charlie: Do you need me to bring you food? Coffee?

> Frankie: No. I'm fine.

> Charlie: Okay, if you change your mind, let me know.

> Frankie: *Thumbs-up emoji*

Setting the device on the table, I continue sitting in the dark. This is all karma. The universe is paying me back for going out. I should've been at home.

A text alert goes off the next morning as I'm getting ready to make the drive to the hospital.

Charlie: Good morning, Frankie.

Frankie: Hi.

Charlie: I know you still have a lot going on, but how about I swing by and take you out for lunch?

I frown. He means well, but I'll be at the hospital all day until I'm forced out.

Frankie: Thanks, but no.

Charlie: Even a piece of cake from Millie's?

Frankie: Not interested.

I puff my cheeks out. Doesn't he get it? I don't want to be bothered. I just want Dad to get well. Nothing else matters right now. There's only one way to get Charlie to leave me alone. As much as it hurts, I know what I have to do.

Frankie: Charlie, I'm also sorry to tell you this over a text, but I've decided to scrap any plans to take my senior test. I appreciate you putting up with me the last few months, but I'm done.

There. It's sent.

Charlie: Frankie, you don't mean that.
You're not thinking straight. You've been
under a lot of stress.

Frankie: You're wrong. It's never been
clearer to me that I've had my priorities
wrong all along.

"It's over, Charlie," I mumble to the empty living room.

Charlie: Can I come over so we can talk
about this in person?

Frankie: I'd rather you didn't. I won't
change my mind.

Charlie: But Frankie . . .

Frankie: No. I'm done.

Another day has passed. Once again, I'm sitting on the couch with my knees curled up against my chest. The TV is on, the only source of light in the darkened room. My phone chimes, but I'm tired of answering it.

It'll be Charlie. He's been messaging me since I decided to call things off with him yesterday. I don't want to speak to anyone. I'm out of energy.

Suddenly, there's a pounding sound on the door. "Francesca, open this door right now! Or else!" Leslie shouts.

I continue to stare at the screen. Leslie can do what she wants. I don't care.

"Leslie, you promised you wouldn't yell," Charlie grumbles.

"No, I promised I wouldn't give her a hard time. There's a difference." She pounds again. "Fran-ces-ca."

I don't move. The door creaks open. The lights flicker on. I blink a few times, feeling like a bat venturing out of its cave during the day.

"How did you do that?" Leslie asks her brother.

"It was unlocked," Charlie says.

"For goodness' sake, this has to end now." She marches in front of the TV and turns it off, standing with her arms crossed.

"I was watching that," I say in a weak monotone voice. In reality, I don't even know what was on. Or what time of day it is.

"As the level ones might say, too bad, so sad." Leslie sticks out her tongue. "When did you last eat? Shower?"

"I don't know. I think I grabbed something at the hospital."

Leslie and Charlie exchange twin looks of concern. "We're under Nan's orders," she says. "You're coming home with us. You've reached the point where you can't be trusted to be left on your own any longer."

"I'm not going anywhere."

"We can do this the easy way or the hard way." Leslie rolls her eyes. "My baby bro is stronger than you and won't have a problem carrying you to the car like a child." Her eyes flash like a bird of prey ready to attack. "Make your choice."

There's a rustling sound. Charlie sits down on the opposite side of the couch and slowly peels back the lid from a container of food. The second the scent of the omelet hits my nostrils, my stomach grumbles.

"How about Frankie eats first, then we talk." He slides the container and some cutlery in my direction. Reaching into the bag once more, he also pulls out a metal thermos and shakes it.

Ice cubes rattle around inside it. "One iced coffee, just the way you like it."

So bribery is their game. Until now, I haven't realized just how hungry I am. I can't resist it any longer. I have to eat. "Do you two always use a good cop, bad cop routine?"

"Yes," Charlie says at the same time Leslie answers, "No."

He places the container in my hands. "Eat," he commands. Taking hold of the takeout container, I do.

"Where's Charlie?" I ask as I dry the tips of my hair, damp from the shower.

"I sent him to the grocery store so we could talk alone for a couple minutes. Speaking of which, your kitchen is woefully empty. What have you been eating this last week?"

"Hospital food."

Leslie grimaces. "That's like eating cardboard. It doesn't have any flavor."

Food, coffee, and a shower are just what I needed to feel a little more like myself and give me some energy. "It's not the greatest, but it's convenient."

Leslie sighs. "Look, before we go any further, I'm really sorry for acting like a first-class jerk to you. You didn't deserve it. I was being petty because I was mad at my brother for keeping his skating from me. I should never have lashed out at you. I know Charlie's a grown man and he's more than capable of making his own decisions, but it still upset me."

I shift my weight from one foot to another. I'll accept Leslie's apology in the long run, but my emotions are still a tangled mess right now. I don't trust myself to speak. Instead, I nod.

"You're one hundred percent justified if you don't want to be friends with me anymore. I just want you to know that no matter what you decide, I'm not going anywhere. I'm here to offer you my support." Leslie touches my forearm. "Nan and Charlie brought me up to speed with what's been going on with your dad. I've been in your shoes before. I know exactly the physical and emotional toll being a caregiver can take on a person. Charlie's accident changed me in ways I never expected."

My eyes widen. I've forgotten Leslie was the main person who helped Charlie with his recovery.

"For two years, nobody could give us an answer as to why he wasn't getting better. It was a stream of never-ending tests and experimental treatments. All I could do was sit helplessly on the sidelines. I felt like a failure as I watched his mental health deteriorate."

"That's *exactly* how I feel about my dad. Like I've failed him." My legs quiver and I sink down onto the couch.

"I was able to get past it with assistance from Nan." Leslie's cheeks flush. "She helped me to understand that I hadn't failed Charlie. Instead, I had a fear of failing him."

That can't be true for me too. Can it?

"As caretakers, we think there isn't anyone else out there who can do our job. We push people away because we don't want to risk having someone from the outside messing things up. What ends up happening is a recipe for self-destruction." Leslie blinks slowly. "Take it from someone who's been where you are—it's *okay* to ask for help. You *don't* have to do things alone. We need somebody to take care of us too."

"I don't know if I can. I'm used to being on my own." I study the ground.

"Accepting help is tough. But I promise, if you decide to give it a shot, you'll find that not only will things get a lot easier, but you'll be a lot happier too."

"Thanks for sharing that with me, Leslie."

"Of course."

"I'm back!" Charlie calls out, entering the apartment and heading straight to the kitchen.

"We're in the living room," Leslie replies.

A moment later, he joins us. "I picked up mostly frozen foods, since they'll keep longer. Frankie, um . . . hi. You look, er . . . wet."

Leslie face-palms. "That's *not* something you say to your girlfriend."

I crack a smile for the first time in several days. I've missed him.

"Are you ready to go?" Charlie asks.

"Go where?" I look at the siblings in confusion.

"To Nan's?" He turns to Leslie. "I'm guessing you didn't tell her everything?"

"No. You were supposed to take longer at the store."

"Tell me what?"

Charlie walks around the couch and sits on its arm. "Your dad is supposed to be released from the hospital tomorrow, right?"

"Uh-huh."

"Well, Nan wanted to see if you might be open to having him stay at the cottage while he recovers."

I stare at Charlie. My brain is slow to process what he's saying.

"Nan's invitation extends to *both* you and him," Leslie adds quickly. "She thought that instead of having us take turns coming over to your place, we could have everyone stay in one location."

Suzy, Leslie, and Charlie are willing to help care for Dad? The doctor mentioned it could take several weeks for him to recover. If I'm being honest with myself, I'm already feeling pretty run down, and Dad isn't even home yet.

My thoughts turn to Leslie and our earlier conversation.

My decision has to be about what's best for Dad, and it's going to be having Suzy near him. Her nursing background and the love she has for him are better than any sort of medicine.

"Dad can stay at the cottage for however long he needs, but not me. I'll stay a day or two while he settles in, but I need some space."

Leslie's eyes narrow. "Frankie, can you clear something up for me?"

"Sure."

"This is a one-bedroom apartment, is it not?"

"Yes," I answer slowly, wondering where she's going with this.

"Where do you sleep?"

"In here."

Charlie scratches his head. "I don't get it."

"The couch." I pick up a pillow and clutch it to my chest. "It folds out into a bed."

His jaw clenches. "You've been sleeping on the couch since you moved here?"

I try playing it off. "It's not that bad. After Dad broke his hip earlier this year, we had to find a place that had step-free access to everything."

"Where was he living before?"

"In a split-level place."

"And you couldn't get a place with two bedrooms?" Leslie questions.

"The rent would be more than we could afford." My face burns hot, like lava. I decide to be completely open with them. "Dad's veteran's insurance took care of most of the medical bills, but it didn't fully cover everything. While I was finishing my Dreams on Ice contract, he needed access to care. We didn't have anyone else to help. A professional facility seemed like the perfect answer at the time. After I paid off the bills for that, the remainder of the lease on Dad's old place, and put down a security deposit for this place, I didn't have much money left. This was the best option."

"Doesn't your father receive a pension of any sort? Social security?" Leslie asks.

"Yes, but it still doesn't go as far as you think. Grizzly Springs is an expensive place to live. With my limited hours at the rink and his fixed income, we just manage to break even every month. Trust me, we're doing better since I've started helping Charlie out."

"Why didn't you say anything to us? To Jack? We would've found you more hours," Charlie says, his voice cracking.

"I don't know," I admit. "Jack said when he hired me that he didn't have any full-time openings. I took the only job that was available. My original plan was to find a second job, but then you and I started to train together, and I didn't think I could physically handle much more."

The twins wear identical looks of frustration on their faces.

Leslie speaks first. "When your dad starts to recover and you're back at the rink coaching again, come talk to me. If you're still interested in full-time hours, they're yours."

Charlie clears his throat. "Don't forget, you also still have an open offer to become my full-time coaching partner. As a private coach, we set our own rates and earn more than double what the skating academy pays."

A full-time gig? And at the rink? How can I say no to that? "Thank you." A rush of gratitude fills my body. "I don't know what to say."

Charlie crosses his arms. "Like my sister said, we can figure everything out later. Right now, we have a more important matter to settle—where you're going to stay."

"I'll sleep in Dad's bed."

"No," they both answer at the same time.

"Everybody's worried about you. We don't want you to be on your own right now. If you still don't want to stay at the cottage, your options are my place or Charlie's," Leslie says.

I slouch against the back of the couch. "Whose place is closer to the cottage?"

"Mine." Charlie raises his hand. "You'd get your own room too."

"How big is Leslie's place?" I furrow my brow.

"Two bedrooms. But keep in mind my sister uses her second one as a craft studio."

"Oh." Knowing how much stuff Leslie has at the rink, I'm sure her second bedroom is packed just as full. Or worse. I don't want her to have to go to any extra trouble of clearing it out for me. Who knows if there's even a bed in there. "I guess it'll be your place, Mr. C."

"You won't regret it." He grins.

Charlie and Leslie are becoming the family I never had. What would I do without them?

Chapter Twenty-Three

After dinner with Suzy, Charlie and I make the fifteen-minute drive to his place. "You live in a cabin? I just assumed it would be an apartment," I murmur as he drives down a long private-access road leading to a rustic cabin with large glass windows and a wraparound deck.

"You never asked."

Much like the cottage, Charlie's cabin is nestled among a thick patch of woods and vegetation. Towering pine trees surround the property on three sides.

"I'd never know we were only a few minutes outside of town based on the location. It looks and feels like we're back at King's Summit."

"That's one of the main things that made me fall in love with the property. It's a little bit like Nan's place, but not as grand."

Next to the front door, I notice a carved wooden statue of a grizzly bear standing upright, holding a pair of figure skates. Charlie must've gotten it from the same place as Suzy. It looks like it was created by the same company.

"We're entering through the back door. It's closer to the carport. I never use the front."

I wipe my feet on a mat as Charlie turns his key in the lock and lets us into the kitchen. I see wooden cabinets painted a forest-green. There are high-end stainless-steel appliances and a medium-sized white marble island. A few fake flowering plants on the windowsill add a touch of color to the space. How is Charlie able to keep his kitchen spotless when his office is a disaster?

Skirting around the island, we step into the main living area of the cabin. The wall opposite the kitchen is made from red bricks and holds a black wood-burning stove. The top half of the remaining two walls are painted white, and the bottom half contain exposed wood.

The center of the room has an amber-brown couch and matching oversized chair with a red-and-black plaid blanket draped over it. I smile as I notice the mahogany coffee table is covered with stacks of mail, books, binders, and other assorted items. The dining table and four chairs are also covered in piles of random objects. Here's the proof that this is Charlie's place.

"I know you don't have a TV, but what do you do for entertainment when you're not at the rink?"

"Woodworking. My grandad taught me when I was a boy."

I absorb the information. "Do you make birdhouses? Or are you more advanced and you make things like furniture?"

Charlie lets out a raspy laugh. "Neither. I carve figurines."

"Can I see?"

"I don't know. They aren't very good." He studies the carpet.

"Anything you made is going to be ten times better than anything I ever could've come up with. I can draw, I can paint, but I have no talent for anything that's three-dimensional."

"Follow me."

We enter one of the three darkened rooms off the living room. He clicks the light on, illuminating a set of tools hanging from a pegboard attached to the wall. Stacked neatly on top of a workbench are more bear figurines. There's one that's sleeping, and another bear sticking its paw into a jar of honey.

Picking up the closest carving, a rabbit, I run my fingers along the ridges of its ears, across its back, to the tip of its fluffy tail. It's so lifelike. "These are amazing!" My eyes flicker to Charlie, who's leaning against the door frame. "You made *all* of these?"

He nods.

"And the bear with the ice skates? And the one at Suzy's?"

He bobs his head up and down again. "When I was recovering from the accident, woodworking was one of the few activities I could manage. I had a lot of time to perfect my skills. I started with small projects like my kitchen cabinets and worked my way up to things that were more intricate, like figurines."

I bet if I asked him, I'd find out that every wood element in this cabin came from his own two hands. Just as I'm beginning to get a feel for who Charlie is, he manages to continue surprising me.

"Do you do commissions?"

"My work isn't for sale. It's all for fun."

My face falls. I carefully replace the rabbit on the worktop. "Oh."

He steps in closer to me. "But for the woman I'm dating, I just *might* be willing to create something special." He brushes a few stray pieces of hair from my forehead. "What would you have me carve for you? An elegant swan? A delicate ice skater?"

I shiver as his touch sets my body aflame. All my exhaustion is replaced by rapid energy. I could bound across a grassy savannah with the speed of the fastest cheetah. My arms reach around his neck. "If I could only pick one animal, it would be a koala bear."

"A koala?" He blinks in confusion.

"That's your spirit animal. They're usually gentle and focused on their biggest needs—eating and sleeping—but they can also be grumpy when they feel threatened or stressed."

"So they're the animal version of me?" He nuzzles my nose with his.

"Yes."

"I'll take that as a compliment."

He brushes his lips against mine in a kiss. They're soft and warm, like the smooth chocolate outer layer of a peanut butter cup. With each bite I take, I'm treated to a new and exciting flavor. Individually, the chocolate and peanut butter are delicious, but together, they're the perfect melding of flavors, just like Charlie's kisses.

Eventually, when we break apart, he shows me into his guest bedroom. As soon as I climb under the covers and my head touches the pillow, I fall into a deep sleep. My dreams that night are vivid. I experience exactly what it's like to skate with Charlie under thousands of glittering stars, to the theme music of *Beauty and the Beast.*

"Welcome home, Daddy," I say, kissing the top of my father's head two days later. He's propped up in a recliner in one of the ground-floor suites at Suzy's cottage, working on a new crossword book.

A small tear escapes down my cheek.

"Frankie, what's wrong?"

"Nothing." I wipe my face dry. "I'm just so happy to see you."

Although Dad's spirits were high when he was discharged, he still needed Charlie's help getting into and out of the car. Every movement he took was slow and deliberate. Later, he confessed to us that he was still experiencing some bouts of nerve pain. It hit home to see him looking so fragile and vulnerable.

"You've seen me at the hospital nearly every day. I haven't changed. I'm just as handsome as I was before."

I giggle. I know he's on the road to recovery when he starts cracking jokes again.

"Remember, you can't keep a navy man down. We're built to last."

"I'm glad." We hug. The sharp hairs of his beard tickle my cheek. As we break apart, I ask, "Are you sure you don't mind staying at the cottage? It was Suzy's plan. I can take you home if you'd prefer."

"No, sweetie." He pats my hand. "The cottage is perfect. I can't think of another place I'd rather be right now. Other than near you, of course."

"Suzy has it all arranged. She, Charlie, Leslie, and I are going to take turns helping you out whenever you—"

He holds up his hand. "About that." A glint of determination fills his eyes.

"Dad?"

"Suzy-kins and I spoke about it at the hospital yesterday. As kind as you kids were to offer, I don't want, nor do I need, you three to play nursemaid to me."

"But the doctor said—"

"Honey, I know what the doctor said. I was there." He squeezes my hand. "I'm feeling much, much better than I was last week. I'll be back in fighting form before you know it. I only need one person to take care of me, and that's Suzy."

My stomach lurches. "Suzy? Not me?"

"Suzy," he repeats. "I promise, I'm not replacing you with her. Our bond is special. You are my daughter. My baby girl. It's just that unlike you, my little princess, Suzy is retired. She won't be interrupting her life to take care of me."

"But Dad, it's my job to take care of you. You wouldn't be inconveniencing me at all."

"Really?" He raises an eyebrow. "Because a little birdy mentioned to me that you'd decided to give up on your senior pairs test. *And* that you were taking extended leave from your *actual* job."

I clamp my mouth shut. Who spilled the beans? Was it Charlie or Leslie? I can't believe they went behind my back.

"I didn't raise you to be a woman who quit when things got tough. I raised you to be a young woman who would do anything to chase her dreams. Nothing would make me happier than to see you finish what you started all those years ago."

I rub my forearms and breathe deeply. I've lost this battle. "You're really enjoying guilting me into this."

"Darn right, I am. It's always worked like a charm with you."

"Does Suzy make you happy?"

"She does." His eyes twinkle. "When I'm spending time with her, the years melt away and I'm a young man again." He fights a yawn. "The funny thing about life is that nothing stays the same forever. In any case, if Suzy and I decide to marry down the line, remember—You won't be losing me; you'll be gaining a family."

I'd never thought about it from that angle before. A family is so much more than just a set of people who happen to be related to one another. A family is a collection of people who love and support one another through the good times and the bad times. Through life's ups and downs. The highs and lows. I have Dad, but I also have my extended family—Charlie, Leslie, and Suzy.

Dad and I chat a little longer before he falls asleep. Tiptoeing out of his room, I feel lighter and more hopeful for the first time in several days.

Chapter Twenty-Four

It takes Dad upward of four weeks to fully recover. In that
time, his relationship with Suzy continues to blossom.
And it's a surprise to no one when they announce he'll be
moving to the cottage on a full-time basis.

No matter how prepared I am, the change is still startling.
Our apartment is too quiet and empty. The environment is
almost sterile. I've always wondered how it might be to live on
my own. And now I know, I hate it. Without Dad here, the
apartment is just four walls. It's only a place I sleep and shower
in. It doesn't have a heart, like the cottage or Charlie's cabin.

I discuss the situation with Alyssa and Leslie as I sit in a
chair at the Mane Event, having my hair touched up. The
more time I spend here, the more Alyssa is becoming a confi-
dante and makeshift therapist. "Charlie keeps hinting that I
should seriously consider officially moving in with him."

"And what reasons is he giving you?" Alyssa asks.

I count on my hand. "He says I won't have to pay rent, it's
a short commute to the rink, and we could carpool together."

"Those sounds reasonable to me." Alyssa massages the
shampoo into my scalp. "What's stopping you?"

"We've only been officially dating for two months. It feels too soon. What if spending all our time together in the same house is too much for us to handle? We might drive one another crazy."

"I hate to point out the obvious, but you two *already* spend *all* your time in one another's company." Leslie laughs. "You train together. You coach together. You eat every meal together. Even your days off are spent together. If he hasn't driven you crazy yet, you'll be just fine."

"Let me ask you this," Alyssa says. "When are the two of you apart?"

I think long and hard. "When we're asleep?"

"I rest my case," Leslie says sarcastically.

"Do you think I'll be able to cope with Charlie's messiness? I'm a neat freak."

"Now you're nitpicking. I'm sure you two will figure out a middle ground. But if it really bothers you that much, when Charlie and I lived together, our agreement was that the communal areas needed to stay clutter free. All his stuff was kept in his room; that way the mess was contained to a single area."

"That's a great idea! I'm going to try that with my husband," Alyssa says thoughtfully.

"When my boyfriend is home, I use the same trick. I hate it when he dumps his hockey gear in the hallway."

Alyssa repositions my chair so it's upright. I face Leslie. "How long have you and Ron been together, again?"

"We're coming up on four years." She smiles.

Alyssa looks at me. "Has Les ever told you how they met?"

"No." It's rare Leslie ever mentions much about Ron. I've put together a few bits and pieces of information about him. I know he plays hockey professionally, and that he's on the road most of the year. When he's home, Leslie disappears for days at a time, spending every available moment with him.

"It was romantic. We both played on the second line on the Sequoia Valley adult hockey team. One game, I took a hard body check that really rattled me, and Ron jumped right off the bench and defended my honor."

That's not exactly my idea of romance, but to each their own. I wonder what type of person he is. Is he ultra-outgoing like Leslie? Or more closed off?

As if reading my thoughts, she adds, "The next time he's in town, I'll introduce you to him. You'll be the first person outside the family and Alyssa to meet him. Ron keeps a low profile. He's painfully shy, which is ironic given his profession."

I can see it. As a pro hockey player, he's probably inundated with fans and the spotlight. When he's home, he probably just wants to be himself.

"What colors were you thinking about adding today? When I texted, you said something about pink?" Alyssa asks.

"Yes, I'm taking my skating test next week, and I was hoping you could color the ends of my hair to match the color of my dress. That way, when I perform, the judges won't be able to tell my hair isn't 'normal'"—I make air quotes—"but when it's down, it'll be a fun surprise."

"That sounds great. Show me the exact shade, I'll try to re-create it."

I get up from the chair and walk over to my purse.

"What about you, Les?" Alyssa questions.

Leslie's face lights up with a wide jack-o-lantern smile. "I've been inspired recently by all the Halloween merchandise that's starting to pop up in the stores. I want a dark purple with white and orange streaks. There isn't a way you can dye shapes in my hair, is there? It would be next level if I could have silhouettes of ghosts, pumpkins, and bats in my hair."

"Sometimes I think you like coming up with the most complicated styling options possible just to test me." Alyssa sighs. "I can't make any promises, but we'll experiment with some stencils."

Leslie fist-pumps.

"Well done, everyone. You've all officially passed into the intermediate-level adult ballroom class." Excited chatter breaks out around the room at Madame Miller's announcement. "You've learned the mambo and the jitterbug for social dances. And we've also covered the waltz, foxtrot, cha-cha, and a little bit of the quickstep. Today, we have just enough time to start on the rumba. It's a very sensual dance from eastern Cuba."

Madame Miller walks out into the center of the floor. She asks the couple closest to her to come out and act as her demonstrators.

"In this Latin dance, one of the most recognizable features is the active hip movements. The difficulty lies in making the motion subtle while keeping your torsos upright."

"It looks to me like we're about to get a good ab workout with all the side-to-side movements," I whisper to Charlie.

"You will also take note of the arms in the rumba. The best way I can describe it is to pretend as if you're throwing a Frisbee. Picture that Frisbee directly in front of your face. When you initiate a throw, you start with your back, shoulder, upper arm, elbow, lower arm, wrist, and then release the fingers when you finally let go."

"I was afraid she was going to say pretend you're throwing your partner," Charlie whispers.

"You would never throw your partner in ballroom," I say with mock horror.

Madame Miller claps her hands together. "Now if you

would all line up. We'll learn the box step, arms, then try putting it to music. It goes like this . . ."

The six couples in the room turn and face the mirror. Walking through the motions, we work on them on an individual basis, then we're instructed to try it with our partner.

"I like the rumba—it's a nice slow-and-easy pace." Charlie offers his arm to me.

The music clicks on. I try my best to stay on the balls of my feet as I imitate the movements Madame Miller demonstrated.

"Well done, Frankie," she says, correcting us while perusing the room. "Close your ribs a little more. Charles, no slouching. Lift from your back. Extend your chest out. Better."

Charlie waits for her to move on, then whispers to me, "So, I've been wanting to ask you if you've given any thought about what's going to happen after you pass your test?"

"*If* I pass—"

"It's not an *if* any longer," he interjects. "It's a *when*. You're more than ready."

"Don't blame me for not wanting to jinx myself, but no, I haven't thought about anything else." And that's the truth.

"Well, I'm so confident you'll pass; I didn't think it would hurt to look into what it would take for us to qualify for nationals."

My curiosity overrules my head. "And?"

"It's all pretty straightforward. We'd sign up to compete at regionals. Place in the top three to get to sectionals. Repeat a top-three finish there, and boom, nationals, here we come."

I snort. He makes it sound so easy, but it's not. "Charlie, that's asking a lot. A top-three finish? We've never competed together before."

"Here's the best part." His smile widens. "Last season at regionals, the pairs field consisted of three teams. At sectionals, there were only five teams. All we'd have to do is layer in a little more difficulty and skate a clean program."

We'd also need to come up with a short program, and costumes for that, and clear our schedules. It's not exactly as easy as he's making it out to be, but it's doable. "I'll think about it, but I don't want you to bring it up again until after Wednesday. This week, I want to stay focused on the test."

He kisses me on the cheek. "I can respect that."

The music pauses. "Wonderful. Who's feeling adventurous?" Madame Miller asks.

A few meek hands rise into the air.

"The dance floor is open. Take the last few minutes to freestyle. Try out the rumba, cha-cha, mambo, whatever dance captures your fancy. You've all earned it."

"What do you say, Mr. C?" I poke his firm chest. "Shall we try some freestyle?"

"I'd like to keep practicing the rumba." Charlie presents his arm to me just like he does when we're on the ice.

Holding out my long swishy skirt, I sweep out onto the floor, take his hand, and we dance.

"I'm skipping the gym tomorrow." I laugh, gripping my stomach. "Ow. Abs."

"You're that sore?" Charlie teases, opening the door to the cabin.

I poke him in the ribs and walk past him inside. "At least I know I was doing the rumba correctly."

"And I wasn't?" He closes the door.

"Are you sore?"

"No."

"There's your answer." I slip off my shoes and sit on his couch.

"Maybe my abs are just too well-conditioned for me to notice." He removes his jacket and pulls up the hem of his shirt to reveal a chiseled set of perfectly square lower muscles that disappear into the waistband of his sweats. He pokes them. The skin around them doesn't move. It's tight and firm.

I lick my lips. I've always found Charlie attractive, but in peak physical form, he's even more handsome. Here is a man who has spent the last five and a half months working out hard in the gym and eating clean so he can skate with me. Me!

My eyes travel up. I spy veins and sculpted muscles in his forearms, biceps, and triceps. I know exactly how powerful and strong they are. When he lifts me over his head, it's easy. Suspended in the air, I'm like a bird in flight, able to extend her wings and effortlessly glide through the skies. He lets go of his shirt, oblivious to my staring. I quickly averted my gaze.

He steps into the kitchen and opens a cabinet, pulling out a glass. "Water?"

"No, thanks. I'm good."

"You sure? Your throat sounds like it's dry."

"Um, okay. I'll have some."

He returns a moment later with the water and sits down.

"Thanks." I drink from the glass, set it on the table, then stretch my legs across his lap. "Did I tell you I mailed my ancestry test kit today?"

"No." He places his own glass on the table. "I didn't notice you moved it from the kitchen table. It's been there for a few weeks. What made you decide to finally pull the trigger?"

"I want closure. I'm tired of not having any answers. My sister is always lingering in the back of my mind." Charlie wraps his arms around me. I take my favorite position and rest my head in the spot between his shoulder and pec. "If the test comes back with nothing, fine. I'll know it wasn't meant to be, but it isn't for lack of trying. However, if there *is* a match, then I'd like to reach out to her just to let her know if she ever wants to establish contact, I'm here."

"I'm so proud of you. It couldn't have been easy to reach that decision." He kisses my cheek.

"It wasn't, but I'm glad I did it." I snuggle further into Charlie, thinking about the coming days ahead.

Chapter Twenty-Five

"Do you guys need some more time to warm up?" Leslie shouts from her perch behind the boards, near the middle of the ice. She's in a thick parka, leg warmers, and hockey skates.

"I think we're good," Charlie replies.

The glowing red numbers of the clock on the rink's scoreboard show the time as 4:12 in the morning.

"This is just like another run-through," Charlie says, putting his hands on my shoulders. "Remember, there's no pressure. I cleared our lessons for today. The rink is ours until ten. We can take as long as we need to do this. Got it?"

I don't speak, giving him a customary fist bump with shaky hands. Every muscle in my body hums with adrenaline. I pound my legs with my hands, hoping to relieve some of the hollowness. He may not think there's any pressure, but he's already passed his senior test. I haven't.

The last six months of preparation has all led to this moment. I haven't had to skate a long program under pressure in years. I'd forgotten about all the nerves that come with it. I wish I had my Peter Rabbit with me instead of in my locker. I never skate without it. I consider getting it, but at the last minute decide against it. One time shouldn't matter.

I unzip my jacket. My dress is cherry-blossom-pink, with a square neckline and chiffon skirt. Although the silhouette is simple, it's adorned with hundreds of shimmering silver Swarovski crystals. I touch the top of my head. The pink fascinator I made is still firmly in place. Charlie's costume is a black tailcoat, white shirt, black tie, and black trousers. He appears every inch the upper-class gentleman from *My Fair Lady*.

After checking the laces on my skate boots are tied securely one final time, I take hold of Charlie's hand, and we glide out to the center of the ice. From our starting position, I give Leslie a thumbs-up.

She holds up her phone to her watch to record the time and date stamps. "This is Francesca Tomlinson from the Sequoia Valley Figure Skating Club testing Senior Pairs Free Skate."

We kneel down on the ice. My pulse pounds relentlessly against my ribs, and my muscles quiver. My breathing is faster than normal.

"Don't forget to smile. This is your moment to shine," Charlie whispers.

The opening notes of our music fill the rink. I lace my fingers through his as we stand and start across the ice diagonally. Our first test is the split double twist. Facing backward, I place my toe pick into the ice as Charlie's arms push me up. He catches me cleanly coming down. A smile crosses my face. One element down, a couple more to go.

Next, we set up for our first of two side-by-side jumps on the opposite side of the rink. The triple Salchow is Charlie's trickiest element. He only started landing it consistently two weeks ago. We could've stuck with easy doubles, but my pride wanted the judges to see what we're capable of, so we've upgraded to the triple.

Approaching the rink's corner, we enter the jump in unison. I land it, but Charlie stumbles. "Keep going," he says through his teeth.

It's a big mistake, but he's right. We need to keep going. I'm the one being judged, not him. His mistake won't really impact whether I pass or not. If I had fallen, it would've been an automatic restart.

At this point, I really just want to get one skate under our belts. Once we have at least a full run-through recorded, I'll be able to relax. Under the virtual test rules, we can record our program as many times as we want and pick the best one to submit.

Halfway through, we perform some slow choreography and catch our breaths. The music changes to "I Could've Danced All Night," my favorite part of the program. We power through our footwork with more speed than normal and go into our last big jump element, a throw triple loop.

Charlie grasps ahold of my waist. I bend my knees and begin to initiate the jump, but just as he's about to throw me, his blade catches an edge, and he falls forward. For a frightening moment, I'm completely lost in the air. It's like trying to drive during a snowstorm in whiteout conditions. One moment I'm upright, and the next, I'm falling, hitting the ice on my right side. All the oxygen leaves my lungs.

Of all the stupid things to fall on. The loop is my favorite jump. It should've been our moneymaker move. Now, because I've bailed, we'll have to start from the beginning again. Slowly, I get up onto my hands and knees. At least it felt like a "normal" fall. I'll be sore and have some colorful bruises later, but no other lingering effects. I can just hear Leslie suggesting I dye my hair to match them.

Turning to my left, I look for Charlie. He took an equally bad spill. I hope he's okay. I guess if something bad was going to happen, at least we could get it out of the way now.

I come to a stand and get my first good look at my partner. His face is ashen. His hands hover as if he's afraid that touching me might break me. "Frankie! I'm so sorry. I didn't mean to . . . I never would . . . I mean to say . . . I'm sorry."

"I'm fine." My voice is slightly hoarse. "I know it was an accident. How are you?"

"I'm sorry. I didn't mean to," he repeats.

"Charlie, look at me." His green eyes are glazed over. He looks right through me as if I'm a ghost. I keep trying to get through to him. "I'm okay. I promise. It. Was. A. Fluke. Fall." I grip his hand and squeeze it hard. "Charlie, I need you to focus on the present, not relive the past."

Leslie rushes over to us, stopping sharply. "Charlie. Frankie. You good?"

"I am, but I don't know about him."

Leslie nods. "Baby bro, I need an answer from you."

He doesn't respond.

"Bro." She claps her hands together. "Chaaaar-lie. Snap out of it. Frankie needs you."

That does the trick. "Frankie?"

"Right here." I wave to him.

Leslie sighs. "Now give me a straight answer. Are you physically okay? From back there, it looked like you hit the ice pretty hard."

"I'm fine," I repeat.

"Okay, then." Leslie's eyebrows knit together. "Charlie, do you think you can run and fetch the first-aid kit from the front desk? I see a few scrapes on you two that need cleaning ASAP."

"First-aid kit?" he says, still dazed.

"Yeah, the one behind the cashier's desk. I'm just going to help Frankie over to the boards."

Charlie finally seems to understand what Leslie needs. "I'll be right back." He jumps to his feet, and I notice a hole in the right knee of his skating trousers.

"Now that he's out of the way, I need a straight answer from you. Are you really okay? Or were you just saying that because my brother was here?"

"It stung, but the fall didn't feel any different from other ones I've taken on jumps before." My butt, hip, and the palm of my hand still ache, but the pain has mostly subsided.

"That's a relief." Leslie exhales. "You did a really impressive karate-style kick out of the loop jump, but when you landed, your feet were still crossed. It looked like you got too far back on your blades."

"Once that happened there was nothing anyone could do to keep from going down. The ice is slippery," I say.

"I'm just glad it wasn't something more serious. Every time I watch Charlie skate, it makes me anxious. But when you start layering in pairs elements, it takes me to the edge of having a nervous breakdown." Leslie and I make our way over to the hockey bench at the edge of the rink. "I have no idea how you can agree to willingly be suspended ten feet in the air over the ice by someone. Or be tossed into a jump like a rag doll."

"I'm an adrenaline junkie?"

We share a soft laugh.

My mind returns to Charlie. "Do you think it would be best if we left it here for today and tried filming the test another time?"

"In the past, I would've said yes, but he's changed. It's something you'll have to discuss with him. After I help you clean up some of the scrapes, I'll give you two some privacy. The one on your chin is pretty gnarly."

My hand goes to the tender spot under my jaw. Checking out my finger, I see a few dots of crimson-red blood. "How did that happen?"

"Welcome to my world. I ask myself that every time I play hockey."

"I've got it!" Charlie exclaims, rejoining us a moment later. "Where did you cut yourself? Does it sting? Let me help." He drops the kit and zealously tries to unzip the rim of the first-aid kit.

"Bro, let me. My hockey kids and the skating students have given me ninja-like first-aid skills."

Charlie relents. Leslie methodically opens the bag and slips a pair of latex gloves onto her hands. "Let's look at your knees first, bro."

"But Frankie—"

"You're worse off than her."

"But—"

"Please." I bat my eyelashes at him.

"Only because you asked me so nicely," he huffs.

"Thank you." I peck him on the cheek, then start stretching. "My muscles are already starting to stiffen. If we decide to skate more today, I'll need a couple extra minutes to warm up again."

His eyes widen. "You're thinking about running the program again?"

"Yeah, I am."

"I think we should postpone it."

"Why?"

"Because."

"That's not a reason."

Leslie clears her throat. "I just remembered, I have to make a quick adjustment to tomorrow's staff schedule." She snaps the gloves off and hands us ice packs. "Ice whatever hurts for ten minutes. I'll be back." She makes herself scarce, giving us some time alone.

"She could've come up with a better excuse." Charlie glares at the ice pack. "It's warm."

"You have to break up the beads inside to activate the ice pack."

"Oh, right." He cracks it and sticks it on top of his kneecap.

We sit silently for a few minutes. The only sound is the crinkling of the ice packs.

"If you want my vote, I'd like for us to get right back out on the ice," I start. "But my vote doesn't matter if you don't agree with it. We're a team. Any decision we make, I want us to both agree on. So, I'll ask you again. What are you thinking? Why would you rather postpone the skate?"

"Because I screwed up."

"Charlie, what happened out there wasn't your fault."

"You're wrong. I was too amped up and lost my footing. I mistimed the release." He frowns.

"Falling is a part of the sport." I crack another ice pack and set it on my hip, sitting with my right leg stretched out on the bench. "Neither of us can be perfect every time we skate."

"I know that. It's just when I tripped and my grip on you slipped, for a few moments, I thought that you might—"

"Have hit my head?"

He nods. "I had a flashback to when Camille and I went down." He rubs his scar. "I don't want you to suffer like I have. You're not just my partner; you're my girlfriend. If I had hurt you—"

My stomach lurches. I scoot closer to him. How can I get through to him that I'm fully aware of the risks of skating?

"You went through the worst possible experience a skater can have. Any other person might have turned their back on the sport and let their injury define who they are. But you didn't." I poke his arm. "You, Charlie, are the man who sought to defy the odds and come back from it. Answer me this—Why do *you* take the risk?"

"At first, it was for purely selfish motives. I saw you as

my way back into the sport. I wanted to prove to the world that I wasn't a broken man; I could still skate." His voice suddenly grows hoarse. "But the more time I spent with you, the more I started to develop feelings for you. I didn't want to skate for myself anymore. I wanted to skate for you."

He grasps my hand. "Not only are you stunningly beautiful, you are driven, passionate, and competitive. But the quality I'm most attracted to is your heart. You have so much more love and kindness to give the world than any person I've ever met."

I hold on to Charlie's every word. It's like he's a flower and I'm a butterfly. I can't look away. The sweet scent of pollen sings to me.

"You've cast your magic spell over me. Because of you, I've rediscovered the joy I had for skating." Charlie presses his leg against mine. His hand brushes against my cheek. I'm breathless. "You asked me why I take the risk to skate pairs. It's because I want to see you achieve your dreams. I want you to have everything you desire because you deserve it and I love you."

"And I love you too."

As I lean toward him for a kiss, I'm reminded of the intensity of an approaching storm. A primordial force that is both powerful and raw. A storm might produce a light mist or a steady stream of sprinkles, but it can also produce downpours, and gale-force winds that rip buildings apart. That's the best way I can describe our relationship and our feelings for one another.

When we break apart, my lips are swollen. "When did you first realize you loved me?" I ask in a whisper.

"The moment you challenged me to do a split twist. You set my heart on fire that day," he says. "I'll ask you the same question. When did you realize you loved me?"

"The night I ran into the woods. Without you, I might still be stumbling around through the darkness."

"You're resourceful. You would've figured out a solution to your problem eventually."

The ice packs have fallen to the ground unnoticed. I rest my head on the bony edge of his shoulder, and my fingers brush against the rough fabric of his costume. "We can postpone the skate. Your mental health always comes first. Skating will always be here."

"Nuh-uh. If you want to skate another program today, we'll make it happen. Hearing you say the three most beautiful words in the English language, I love you, has given me all the mental strength I need to do it. I'll skate with you because I love you."

I rub his knee as he pecks me on the cheek. "As weird as it sounds, the fall kind of scared all the nerves out of me. I feel like it was exactly what I needed to clear my head and get out of my funk. I feel so calm and at peace with my skating."

"That's all I needed to hear."

We kiss a second time. He pulls me in tightly to his body. His arms are the shelter to my storm. My safe haven.

Leslie rejoins us a few minutes later.

"Did you finish the schedule?" Charlie questions.

"Schedule?" She arches an eyebrow. "Oh right, yeah, the schedule. It's done." Her eyes dart from her brother to me. "Is everything cleared up between you two?"

"It is. We're going to skate one more time," I confirm.

In unison, we both stand and cringe. It feels as if I've spent the entire ice session tossing my body around just to see how many falls I could take. I bet Charlie's aches are just as bad as mine. We're probably only going to get one more shot at this today.

"I need to go change my pants. I'll be right back." He

walks off to the locker room while Leslie finishes patching me up.

"Is it weird that I fell hard enough to open the skin, but my tights didn't rip?"

She shrugs. "I wouldn't know. Only figure skaters wear tights."

When Charlie returns, we take the ice to warm up a second time. I can't explain how I know it, but this skate is going to be different.

"Are you ready?" I gaze into my partner's eyes and see love there.

"You bet. Let's do this."

Chapter Twenty-Six

Two weeks later, I hear the front door open and close.

"I'm back." Charlie shrugs off his jacket and hangs it on a peg by the door. "Guess what? Richelle landed a double flip today! That kid really has the potential to go places if her mom would let her focus on skating."

"That's good." My voice is crackly, like a frog's.

"I can't believe how many members of the coaching staff have gone down with the same nasty cold. Funny how I happen to be the only one who seems to have avoided it." Charlie enters the kitchen and pours himself a glass of water. "I finally had to turn my phone off. Les is *still* sending me messages every ten minutes asking me to update her on how the skating academy is running. Sorry if I didn't respond to any messages you might've sent."

"I didn't send anything."

Charlie joins me on the couch and places the back of his hand on my forehead. "Your temperature's down. That's good. You feeling any better?"

"So-so." Picking up my laptop, I open it and tap on the

mouse. I've been waiting all day to share my news with him. "It came."

"The test results? Excellent. About time." He looks over my shoulder. "I bet you passed with honors. How should we celebrate? Do you want to order something for me to run and pick up from Millie's for dinner?"

"Not the results from the skating test." I dry swallow. "The results from the DNA sample I submitted."

"Oh."

"I was too afraid to open it on my own." I bite my lip.

"My Frankie is a world-class figure skater who lets me toss her around the ice doing things that shouldn't humanly be possible. If you can do that, you *can* open the email." Charlie wraps an arm around my shoulder and pulls me close to him. He kisses the top of my head. "Just remember that no matter what, you still have a family and a boyfriend who love you for being you."

"I love you so much." I rest my head against his chest and listen to the sound of his heart beating. "Will you help me?"

He strokes my arm. "If that's what you want."

"I do."

"We'll click on it together."

I reposition myself. With shaky hands, I pull up the email. My hand hovers on the mouse pad. Charlie places his on top of it. It's warm and so much larger than mine. His hands are strong and able to suspend me high in the air. And now, when I'm nervous with anticipation, they bring me comfort.

"On the count of three, we'll click the button," he says.

"Ready? One. Two. Three."

We click the button. The screen reloads. I inhale sharply, skimming the page.

"Well?"

"It says I have a close match. Not a fourth or fifth cousin, but an actual close match!" I sink into the back of the couch and set my computer to the side, taking it all in. A swirl of emotions floods my body. Fear. Excitement. Nervousness.

"Congratulations, Frankie." Charlie hugs me. "You've found her. Now what?"

"I don't know. I guess I have to make a profile, then try sending her a message?" I fumble for the device, skimming the page again. "It doesn't say what to do next." My eyes flutter. "What am I going to say? How much should I tell her?"

I've pictured myself finding my sister for so long, and now I don't know what to do.

"Breathe, Frankie, breathe." Charlie cups my cheeks. "Let's get some food into you while the information sinks in, then you'll figure out what's next. I'm guessing you may even want to call your dad. Does that sound okay?"

"Yeah."

It's times like these I count myself lucky that I have such an amazing man to watch out for me. Although we've only been dating and living together for a short time, it often feels as if we're more like an old married couple. We're truly a pairs team in every sense of the word. On ice and off.

Dear BalletGirl13,

 Well, this is awkward. I'm not even sure what to type. My boyfriend told me to just talk on paper, so here goes.

 Hi. My name is Francesca, but everybody calls me Frankie. I've always known I was adopted, but until recently, I never knew that I had an older sister.

 Since then, I've thought about you constantly. I'd really hoped that we'd be able to meet one day, but I wasn't sure if it would ever happen since our adoptions were both closed. To my shock and excitement, I was wrong. I got the email today confirming we are close relatives.

I know we could be first cousins, but I believe in my heart that you're the sister I've always had and am just learning about.

I have so many questions, but for now, I'll try and keep this short and sweet.

A little about me—I'm twenty-seven, I live in California with my wonderful boyfriend, I'm a figure skater, and I like Hawaiian pizza.

I hope I haven't scared you off, and I also hope that you'll reply soon.

Best,

Frankie aka TripleLoopLover

Dear Frankie,

Oh my goodness, oh my goodness. Hello! I'm sorry it's taken me a full week to respond to you, but I was in shock. I needed some time to process the fact that I have a sister! Like you, I knew from a young age that I was adopted, but nobody ever mentioned a sibling!

I joined the DNA site hoping to find out a little more information about my biological parents, but this is so much better than I ever could have imagined.

You said you're twenty-seven? I just turned thirty-one. So that means I'm the older sibling and we must be about three or four years apart depending on when your birthday falls.

I'm sure you're curious, so here is a little about me—I've been married for just over four years to a witty and dry-humored Brit. We live in London with a spoiled English springer spaniel. I'm rather jealous that you're a figure skater! I can't skate to save *my life, but I did pursue a career that is non-traditional—I'm a ballerina.*

Would you be comfortable speaking over the phone or via video chat with me? I'd love to get to know you better, but there are a few things about my life that I'd rather not share over the internet.

Best,

Clara

*D*ear Clara,

You're a ballerina and live in London? I've hit the sister jackpot!

Please let me know when it would be convenient to talk. I'm available at any time. My number is (559)-555-2300.

Best,

Frankie

*D*ear Frankie,

I think I'm the one who's hit the jackpot. My number is +44 20 5555 5555. How about tomorrow at three your time? I keep late hours because of dance.

Best,

Clara

I hear Charlie puttering around his workshop. He offered to be right by my side when I make the call to my sister, but this is something I need to do on my own.

With trembling fingers, I dial Clara's number. The ring seems to echo the beating of my heart, each tone a reminder of the years we've spent apart.

After what seemed like the longest ten seconds of my life, a gentle melodic voice answers. "Hello?"

"Hi, Clara?" I choke on my words, a mixture of tears and joy. "It's me. Frankie."

She inhales sharply. "I know we planned to have this call and that we've exchanged a few emails, but it's still so surreal to me."

"I know exactly how you feel." A few tears flow freely down my cheeks. "I've spent so much time wondering if I'd ever find you."

"Well, now you have. And I'm not going anywhere." Clara's voice is filled with raw emotion.

I cling to the phone as if it's an extension of my body. "There are so many things I want to ask you. I don't even know where to begin."

"Likewise. I want to know everything about you, about your life, about the years we've missed."

I take a deep breath, and we take turns asking questions about one another and sharing memories of our lives. I learn that, unfortunately, Clara's adoptive parents were in an accident when she was a teenager. Her best friend's parents took her in. I also learn that although she grew up in Seattle, she spent most of her adult life divided between LA and London.

"Clara, I'm dying to know . . . What's your big secret?"

"Are you sitting down?" she asks.

"Yes," I answer slowly.

"Promise you won't freak out or panic on me?"

Now I'm even more curious. What could it be? "Um . . . okay. I'll try."

"Okay. Here it goes." Clara gulps. "When I married David . . . I became a part of a family that isn't exactly normal by any stretch of the imagination."

"Okay . . ."

"David has a title."

I laugh and splay a hand on my chest. A title. That isn't anything to write home about. "Are you trying to tell me that your husband is a lord and you're a lady? Because if you are, that's amazing!"

Clara doesn't laugh. "Not exactly . . . David's a little higher up on the ladder."

"Help me out here. I'm not good with this. What's higher than a lord?"

"David was born a prince, but these days, he's better known as the Duke of Leeds."

"Oh." All the air leaves my body. My brain goes into overdrive trying to process all the information. My sister is married to a prince. My brother-in-law is a royal. Does that make me a royal by extension? Is Clara a princess? Or is she a duchess?

"Frankie? Are you still there?"

"Oh, um, yeah. I am. It's just . . . wow. That's not what I expected to hear from you."

"I know it's a lot of information to take in. I had a hard time at first, too, when I found out." Clara speaks slowly. "On the surface it may seem amazing. People think about the glitz and the glamor that come with the royal lifestyle—the title, the jewelry, the money, and the palaces. But they never realize that everything comes at a hefty price. I've had to pretty much give up on ever having a private life. I can't do anything that I did before I was married, except dance. I'm photographed everywhere I go. People analyze my clothing choices, my hair, my jewelry, even my shoes. I have to be on guard twenty-four-seven."

Hearing Clara share a small glimpse helps me to understand just a little bit about the type of life my sister lives. She's a bird in a gilded cage. A goldfish in a bowl.

"Wow, Clara. I can't even imagine."

She sighs. "There are days I ask myself if it's worth it all. But then . . . I remember that I didn't fall in love with a prince or a duke. I fell in love with David. Even if he were a penniless shoemaker, I'd still love him to bits."

I tilt my head. "A shoemaker?"

"Yes. That's one of David's hobbies. He makes men's dress shoes, although he's branching out a little more these days."

"My boyfriend is into woodworking. I have a feeling if he ever stopped by your husband's workshop, they'd disappear for hours, and we'd have a hard time getting them back."

Clara laughs. "That, I fully believe."

I chat with my sister for three hours before we end the call. We agree that for now, we'll keep the people who know her secret to a minimum.

"Didn't I tell you that life always has a funny way of working out?" Charlie brags a few days later. "You just never know what's around the corner."

"Dad, Suzy, Gemma, and Leslie are the only people we can tell about Clara's secret. We both agreed it would be a nightmare publicly if we were ever to acknowledge that we're siblings at all."

"I'm only teasing." Charlie secures his skate lace, pulls his pant leg over it, and stands. "I hate attention. I like our life just the way it is. Quiet."

I zip up my jacket. "Clara said the constant media attention is something she'll never get used to, but she's happy to pay the price to have a husband like David."

"I can't wrap my head around the fact that we have an open invite to stay in an actual palace."

"Neither can I." We walk out of the pros' room to the rink. "I told her we wouldn't have a date until sometime after regionals."

"You mean nationals," he corrects.

"Chaaaar-lie . . . we've been through this. Don't get too far ahead of yourself. We only *just* found out that I passed my senior test."

Charlie removes his skate guards. "We'll make it to regionals. Trust me. You had like a perfect score on your test. The judges gave you almost all plus-fives out of a possible five on all your skating skills."

"That was different. It was a virtual test. I haven't competed in *years*."

Charlie puffs out his chest. "With me as a partner, you'll be fine."

I resist the urge to toss a skate guard in his direction, although I do admire his fighting spirit and his cheeky grin.

"Come on. Let's get to work. Once you have more practice under your belt and our program feels like second nature, you'll be fine."

We stroke around the rink to warm up.

"I was thinking . . . I don't think we necessarily need a full-time coach, but what would you say about having my friend Fernando from Dreams on Ice step in on a part-time basis? He wouldn't be able to be here all the time at first, but he'd be able to coach us virtually. He's hinted he's thinking about retirement from skating."

Charlie grips my hand. "He was your partner on tour?"

"He was," I confirm. "And before your mind starts

jumping to conclusions, Fernando was only ever a friend. Nothing more. *You're* my boyfriend."

His body relaxes and he clears his throat. "If you think he's a good fit for us, let's give him a try."

I peck him on the cheek. "I love how open you are to new ideas."

"I wasn't always that way, but as you've shown me, sometimes, the rules are meant to be broken."

We share a laugh. "There's something I wanted to ask you," Charlie says.

"Oh?"

"If we're going to give regionals a go, what do you think about us upping our difficulty in the side-by-side jumps to something like triple loops?"

"Why not? Everything we do is a bonus anyway."

We look at one another with wide smiles, knowing that with hard work and a little bit of luck, dreams can come true.

Epilogue

THREE YEARS LATER

The arena is packed to capacity. The sound of cheering for the hometown team from Italy is deafening as they sit in the "Kiss and Cry" area.

Charlie and I hold hands tightly as we skate a few last-minute warm-up laps around the ice. "I still can't believe we're here." My attention travels to my feet as we skate over the Olympic rings in the center of the ice. I shiver in delight. "I never would've imagined we'd make it this far."

Grinning widely, Charlie throws his head back and laughs. "I told you that together, we'd accomplish great things."

"Our big accomplishment was supposed to be making it to nationals, not winning the bronze in our first season together," I tease.

We didn't stop at the bronze. The last two years running, we've upgraded it to gold as two-time national champions. Our experience and commitment to artistry is our secret weapon, according to the judges, and has given us a large advantage over our younger competitors.

"You're forgetting our bronze medal from the World Championships too." Charlie winks. "What can I say? The judges love me." I clear my throat. "Did I say me? What I should've said is us."

"That's more like it."

As the children serving as ice sweepers clear the last of the flowers and stuffed toys, we skate over to the boards, receive some last-minute encouraging words from Fernando, and sip from our water bottles.

The scores for the Italian team are announced. They've moved into the lead ahead of the teams from China and Russia.

"Our next competitors represent the United States of America. Please welcome to the ice Francesca Tomlinson and Charlie Welch."

Nodding to one another, we fist-bump and stroke out to the center of the ice.

"Are you ready to do this one final time?" Charlie asks softly.

"As long as it's with you."

I'll be sad when we retire from competitive skating, but neither of our bodies recovers like they used to. My hip and Charlie's back are going to be happy to have a respite from all the extra practices after this.

Skating the team competition might've been too much, but we have no regrets. We're here representing our country at the Olympic games—and we've already won a silver medal. Tonight is the icing on the cake.

We take our opening poses, oddly at ease. The first strains of melody from the overture of *My Fair Lady* plays out. We decided right before nationals to revive our three-year-old program after being unable to connect to the classical Rachmaninoff program we'd originally planned for the Olympic season.

I let the music consume me. For Charlie and me, the Olympics aren't about skating in a competition. We're here to celebrate the fulfillment of a lifelong dream and being able to finally close out our careers on our terms. The ice is our stage. For the next four minutes, we are one.

Triple twist. Check. Lasso lift. Check. Now for something a little different. "I'm ready, are you?" I whisper into his ear on our combination spin.

"I am."

We exit and set up on a long outside edge. In unison, we tap in for a set of rare side-by-side triple Lutzes. My arms pull in tight, and I know from my air position, we're on. Beside me, Charlie lands the same jump with ease. It's taken me two years to learn the triple Lutz. This may be the one and only time I compete it, but it's the Olympics and our last competition. We're pulling out all the stops.

"Nice one," he mouths to me.

We continue our program, skating with sheer joy. As Charlie lifts me up for one of our final two lifts, I wonder where Leslie, her parents, and Ron might be sitting. Is Leslie even watching right now?

I heard from Ron that during our short program, his wife was so nervous, she covered her eyes and only looked up after it was over. Even at the Olympic games, she can't bring herself to watch us. Go figure.

Charlie sets me down. The crowd has jumped to its feet, and we still have thirty seconds to go. We perform one final set of crossovers and hit our last element, an outside death spiral. As the music comes to an end, I fall into Charlie's arms for our final pose. We breathe deeply, relishing the moment. Stuffed toys rain down on us.

"Thank you. That was more than I ever could've asked for." Charlie sets me upright, then kneels down to kiss the ice.

My attention goes to the stands. In the front row of the upper deck, I see his family and wave. Leslie laughs and points to the ice. As I turn around, I notice Charlie is still down on his knees. Fireworks ignite inside of me as I realize why.

I'm in shock, bursting to the brim with excitement as he pulls out a small black velvet box and mouths, "Will you marry me?"

I fling myself at him and wrap my arms around his back. We fall down onto the ice, laughing wildly and kissing. The ring box slides out of his hands. The crowd's volume increases another decibel.

As we break apart, Charlie looks to me for confirmation. "I take it that's a yes?"

"Yes, it's a yes." I playfully bat his chest.

One of the ice girls slowly approaches us and hands the ring box to Charlie.

"Grazie. Thank you." He winks.

Holding my left hand, he kisses it and slips the ring on. It fits perfectly. On closer inspection, it's made of white and rose gold. The center houses a brilliant-cut solitaire diamond inside of a flower. Tiny diamonds adorn the side of the band.

"This is your own enchanted rose. I was a beast to you when we first met. You saved me, and for that, I will always be eternally grateful to you. I love you."

"I know."

The last team to skate, a duo from Canada, enters the ice.

"We had better clear off," Charlie says.

Standing up, we skate to the door leading off the ice. Fernando gives me a bear hug and high-fives Charlie as he hands us our Team USA jackets, skate guards, and water bottles. "Congratulations. You two were flawless."

"We couldn't have asked for a better skate," I say.

After we sit down in the Kiss and Cry, Fernando passes me

my phone. I tap the screen and call Dad. A moment later, he and Suzy appear, crowded around his screen.

"Hi, Daddy, Suzy! Look! Charlie asked me to marry him! And I said yes!"

Suzy laughs. "We had a front-row seat to it on the TV, dear."

Charlie loops his arm over my shoulders and waves to everyone back home.

Dad beams with pride. "Your young man is a gentleman. He asked my permission right before you left for Milan."

Charlie's cheeks flush. "I wanted to do things right."

Dad chuckles. "Did you know he had that ring custom designed for you? Gemma here recommended the rose as an homage to your time as Belle with Dreams on Ice, and Suzy-kins sketched out the ring's design."

That makes it even more special. I'll never take it off.

Gemma's face appears on the phone. Retired from Dreams on Ice, she's made the move to Sequoia Valley and is now coaching.

"Gemma! I hope you're going to be my bridesmaid," I exclaim.

"And let me know if you have any thoughts on grooms-men. I'll be asking Fernando and my pal Tim, of course." Charlie glances over to our coach.

"Congratulations, you two, but we can chat about it later," Gemma says. "Look up at the scoreboard . . . You two are in first place with one team left."

Charlie's head jerks up.

"We are?" I yelp, dropping the phone. My eyes fly to the scoreboard. Sure enough, our names are at the top of the leaderboard. "We are!" I squeal. I can't believe it! We're guaranteed another medal.

"Wow!" Charlie blinks in disbelief.

We wave to the crowd one final time. I retrieve the phone and promise to call everyone back later. We exit the Kiss and Cry.

"The night keeps getting better and better, but no matter what, I've gotten the best prize of all. *I* get to spend the rest of my life with you!" Charlie picks me up and spins me in a circle. I giggle. A cameraman approaches with a reporter, who clears his throat. He places me back on the ground.

"Charlie, do you have time for a quick word?" He nods. The interviewer holds a microphone up to him.

"This is for everyone back at the Sequoia Valley Ice Sport Center. Make sure you guys are listening to Coach Gemma and following the rules of the rink. I had better not find any wads of chewing gum in the party room when I get back. Or else."

I slap my forehead. "Charlie."

"What? It took me hours after our send-off party to get the tables clean."

"Ignore, Mr. C. Thank you for all your support. We can't wait to see you soon and celebrate with you all."

"Oh . . . is that what I was supposed to say?"

The cameraman and reporter walk away. I shake my head. Sometimes Charlie drives me mad.

We sit in the area for the top couples and wait for the final pair to finish skating. My thoughts, however, center on my relationship with the man beside me. When we first crossed paths, he *was* a beast, but over the last three years, he's become the man I can't live without. My partner. My boyfriend. And now, my fiancé. Humming the tune "Tale as Old as Time" to myself, I reflect on just how much I love this man.

"Charlie, don't ever change."

He gives me a cocky grin. "Don't worry, I won't. You're stuck with me as long as you'll have me."

My heart flutters. "I'm the luckiest woman alive."

We're just kissing again when, suddenly, the volume of the crowd jumps ten decibels. Breaking apart, we lift our eyes back up to the scoreboard.

We're Olympic champions, and all is right in the world.

Dear Reader

Thank you for taking the time to read "The Rules of the Rink."

You can find bonus content for the book by visiting:
   https://tomitabb.com/rules-of-the-rink-bonus-content/

If you enjoyed this book, please take a moment to leave a review on Amazon, Goodreads, Bookbub, or whatever platform you may have discovered this book on. It helps Tomi connect with readers like you!

Love her books? Become a part of her treasured community of readers here.

Stay connected with Tomi by scanning QR code, or by visiting her official website.

Https://TomiTabb.com

Acknowledgments

This book would not be possible without the help of the many people who have helped bring "The Rules of the Rink" to life behind the scenes.

To my editor extraordinaire—Joanne Lui—thank you so much for your thoughtful comments and edits. You are one of the few editors who speak the language of figure skating. I know that I can rely on you to know exactly what I'm talking about when I type words like triple Lutz and triple Salchow. I truly could not have done this without you! You are the reason I had the courage to write a figure skating themed story in the first place.

To Charity, thank you so much for your efficient and thorough proofreading skills. You are my eagle eyes and I can't thank you enough for polishing Frankie and Charlie's story.

To my friend and fellow author Brooke Gilbert, thank you so much for being not only my first ever sensitivity reader, but for also supporting me through the ups and the downs, and the highs and the lows. You keep me going and I am so happy to have met you. I couldn't do this writing journey without you.

To my ARC readers, thank you so much for helping me to bring Frankie and Charlie's story to a wider audience and for becoming an important part of my writing community.

To my longtime skating coach and friends at the rink, thank you so much for answering my questions about being professional show skaters and for providing me with endless stories about your adventures on both sides of the boards.

Lastly, to my family and friends, thank you so much for putting up with my strange sleeping hours and for allowing me to be glued to my computer. I love you.

About the Author

Tomi's publishing journey began in 2020 with the release of her debut novel, *Dancing With a Royal*. Although she's always loved writing fictional stories, Tomi's background is in academic writing. She holds an MA degree in History and is currently pursuing her doctorate degree in the same subject.

In her rare free time, Tomi enjoys figure skating and hunting for new pumpkin flavored foods to try. It's one of the many reasons fall is her favorite season.

Tomi is a California native where she resides with her family and one very spoiled cat.

Website: TomiTabb.com

Also by Tomi Tabb

The Unexpected Royals

-Dancing With a Royal

-Jiving With a Royal

-Designing for a Royal

-More Than a Passing Shot

Friends of the Unexpected Royals

-Designs on Love

-Engineering Love

Novellas Related to the Unexpected Royals Series

-Pointe Shoes and Sugar Plums

-A Game of Small Victories

The Skaters of Sequoia Valley

-The Rules of the Rink

-The Sloth Zone

-Caught in a Loop

The Royals of Isola Nostrum

-The Great Austen Adventure

-For the Love of Dinosaurs

Historical Romance

-The Mysterious Mr. Marcellus